AUNT DIMITY AND THE LOST PRINCE

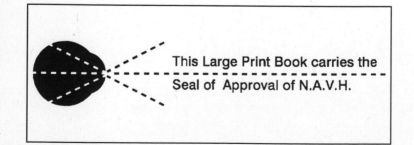

This Large Print Book carries the
Seal of Approval of N.A.V.H.

AUNT DIMITY AND THE LOST PRINCE

NANCY ATHERTON

THORNDIKE PRESS
A part of Gale, Cengage Learning

Detroit • New York • San Francisco • New Haven, Conn • Waterville, Maine • London

GALE
CENGAGE Learning·

LIBRARY OF CONGRESS CATALOGING-IN-PUBLICATION DATA

Atherton, Nancy.
    Aunt Dimity and the lost prince / by Nancy Atherton. — Large Print edition.
        pages cm. — (Thorndike Press Large Print Mystery)
    ISBN 978-1-4104-5696-0 (hardcover) — ISBN 1-4104-5696-X (hardcover)
1. Dimity, Aunt (Fictitious character)—Fiction. 2. Women detectives—England—Cornwall (County)—Fiction. 3. Cornwall (England : County)—Fiction. 4. Large type books. I. Title.
PS3551.T426A9335 2013b
813'.54—dc23   2013008095

Published in 2013 by arrangement with Viking, a member of Penguin Group (USA) Inc.

Printed in Mexico
2 3 4 5 6 7 17 16 15 14 13

For the wildland firefighters of Harvey's Great Basin Team, with my profound thanks

ONE

I've heard it said that when the poet T. S. Eliot was writing *The Wasteland,* he chose February as the cruelest month, then changed it to April in revisions. If you ask me, he got it right the first time. As far as I'm concerned, February's only redeeming feature is its brevity. If it were any longer, I would tear it from my calendar in protest.

Leap years? Don't talk to me about leap years. I suppose they serve a useful purpose, but if we must add an extra day to the calendar every now and again, why not add it to July? Or August? Or September? Why prolong the most miserable month of the year when we have so many pleasant months to choose from? Leap years, I'm convinced, were invented solely to torment me.

January isn't so bad. January offers a pleasant return to routine after the hectic holiday season. The Christmas tree has been mulched or planted or turned into a bird feeder. The twinkly lights and the ornaments have been stored in the attic. The living room is spacious again, the dining room tidy, the kitchen organized. With the cessation of gift shopping, card writing, cookie baking, crèche building, church decorating, and Nativity play rehearsing, time itself is uncluttered. Grown-ups are back at work, children are back in school, and life ticks along with the soothing regularity of a well-oiled grandfather clock.

By the first of February, however, the novelty of normalcy has worn off. Christmas is but a distant memory and spring isn't even a glimmer on the horizon. It seems as though it has always been and will always be winter — bleak, cold, gray, dismal winter — with no respite in sight. If one lived in New Zealand, one might regard the second month of the year as the jewel in summer's crown, but I lived in England and I regarded February as the lump of coal in my Christmas stocking.

It seemed churlish to grumble as yet another February hove into view because my life was in so many ways idyllic. I was married to a wonderful man, we had two beautiful children, and we lived in a honey-colored stone cottage in the Cotswolds, a rural region in England's West Midlands.

The nearest hub of civilization was Finch, a tiny village surrounded by rolling hills, patchwork fields, and not much else. Traffic jams were unknown in Finch, litter was seldom seen, and crime was virtually non-existent. The villagers' lives revolved around local events and a never ending stream of delicious gossip. A better woman might have turned a deaf ear to the tittle-tattle, but I wasn't a better woman. I believed quite strongly that inquisitive neighbors were preferable to indifferent ones and I behaved accordingly.

Though my husband and I were American, we'd called England home for almost a decade and our nearly eight-year-old sons had never lived anywhere else. Bill ran the European branch of his family's venerable law firm from a building overlooking Finch's village green, Will and Rob attended Morningside School in the nearby market town of Upper Deeping, and I scrambled to keep up with the myriad roles of wife, mother, community volunteer, busybody-in-training, and chairwoman of the Westwood Trust, a nonprofit organization that funded worthy projects.

Stanley, who lived with us in the cottage, did little but eat, sleep, frolic, and strike elegant poses, but since he had four paws and a tail, nothing more was expected of him. Stanley was a gleaming black cat with dandelion-yellow eyes and a dog-like devotion to Bill.

The rest of us were devoted to Bill's father, William Arthur Willis, Sr., a white-haired widower with a fondness for orchids, antiquarian books, and long walks in the countryside. Willis, Sr., was as wise as he was kind, an old-fashioned gentleman, and a doting grandfather. When he retired from his position as head of the family firm and moved into Fairworth House, a splendid Georgian mansion not far from the cottage, our family circle was complete.

With so many blessings raining down on my head, I had no right to whine about February, but when my husband was called away on the first of the month to attend to a client in Majorca, I couldn't help feeling hard done by.

I was, of course, accustomed to Bill's frequent business trips. He was an estate attorney with an international clientele and I couldn't blame him for doing his job. I could, however, blame him — severely — for basking in the sun on a flower-strewn Mediterranean island while I was cooped up in the cottage with a pair of bored and irritable little boys.

To be fair, Will and Rob were rarely bored or irritable. As identical twins, each had a built-in playmate, and as my offspring, they weren't lacking in imagination. Under normal circumstances, my sons were cheerful, energetic, and eminently capable of entertaining themselves. In winter, I could rely on them to spend their after-school hours in the meadow behind our back garden, sledding, throwing snowballs, and constructing everything from snow forts to snow dragons.

On Saturdays, I would drop them off next door at Anscombe Manor, where they would be free to pursue their primary passion: horseback riding. Nothing on earth, including my oatmeal cookies and Bill's imitation of a *Tyrannosaurus rex,* pleased them more than a day spent galloping over hill and dale on their gray ponies, Thunder and Storm.

Sundays were spent first at church, then at Fairworth House, where Will and Rob had free rein to play hide-and-seek, explore the attics, and hone their shot-making skills at their grandfather's billiards table. If the spirit moved us, we'd go on a family outing to a local attraction. All in all, my sons had little reason to complain that their lives were dull, dreary, and confined.

February's curse was upon us, however, and I could do nothing but stand by and watch as our pleasant routine disintegrated. Bill's departure coincided with a cold front that swept in from the North Sea, plunging our region into a deep freeze that proved to be too much for Morningside School's high-tech heating system. The school's head-mistress telephoned me on Sunday evening to inform me that classes would be suspended for at least a week because the parts needed to repair the complex furnace were buried somewhere in a snow-covered warehouse in Helsinki.

Will and Rob liked school very much, but they were quick to see the advantages of an unscheduled vacation. Since dangerous wind chills prevented them from playing outdoors, they found new and creative ways to blow off steam. Overnight, every chair in the cottage became a trampoline, every table a launching pad, and every inch of floor space an obstacle course of train tracks, model cars, building blocks, dinosaurs, stuffed animals, and whatever else they could drag from their toy boxes and scatter underfoot. In self-defense, Stanley retreated to the guest room and hid under the bed, emerging only at night, when the boys were fast asleep and the coast was clear.

Unlike Stanley, I had nowhere to hide. On Wednesday, I imposed martial law, threatening my sons with dire consequences if they continued to behave like barbarians. They dutifully cleared the decks and settled down to more civilized pursuits, but drawing, reading, writing, and other forms of quiet play were poor substitutes for racing around the back meadow like a pair of untamed colts.

Unable to rid themselves of their pent-up energy, the twins' tempers became frayed and their imaginations ran dry. When they weren't quarreling over crayons, books, board games, and toys, they were sitting morosely on the window seat in the living room, their identical noses pressed to the frigid panes, longing to be released from bondage. I was run ragged, trying to calm them down one minute and cheer them up the next.

I called Willis, Sr., for backup, but he'd contracted a nasty head cold, and his housekeeper, a caring and capable young woman named Deirdre Donovan, had barred the door to visitors. When I heard his hoarse voice, I agreed that peace and quiet would be his best medicines and put away all thoughts of setting my sons loose at Fairworth House.

The germ afflicting Willis, Sr., had evidently spread far and wide because all of the boys' school friends were sick as well. Though a few beleaguered mothers offered to offload their runny-nosed darlings on me, I was understandably reluctant to expose Will and Rob to such a virulent virus and gently refused to set up playdates.

As our options for escape narrowed, the cottage seemed to close in around us, becoming smaller and smaller with the passing of each spat-filled hour. During a brief moment of calm, I considered building a recreation center in the back meadow, equipped with a swimming pool, a cricket pitch, a riding ring, and miles of monkey bars. It seemed like a perfectly rational plan to me, but it also seemed likely that Bill would wish to have a say in it, so I shelved it for the moment and returned to the living room to keep peace among the pirates storming the sofa.

By Friday morning, the only weapon left in my maternal arsenal was the promise of spending Saturday at the stables. I unsheathed it during breakfast, reminding the boys that in less than twenty-four hours we would be on our way to the Anscombe

Riding Center for a full day of horsey fun. Even if the cold snap prevented them from riding their ponies, I told them, they could spend the day cleaning tack, climbing hay bales, talking horse with their fellow equestrians, and grooming Thunder and Storm.

My pep talk worked like magic. Will and Rob bounced upstairs to play checkers in their room and I spent much of the morning singing, smiling, and baking cookies for them to share with their stable mates. I blithely disregarded February's malevolent influence until the telephone rang and I stiffened, gripped by a chilling sense of impending doom.

"Lori?" The voice on the other end of the line belonged to my best friend, Emma Harris, owner of the Anscombe Riding Center. "I hate to say it —"

I groaned inwardly and braced myself for bad news.

"— but the stables will be closed for the foreseeable future," Emma continued.

"Stables?" I echoed weakly. "Closed?" I cast a haunted glance at the wall calendar, sank onto a kitchen chair, and put a weary hand to my forehead. "How could you do this to me, Emma? Will and Rob have been bouncing off the walls *all week.* They *need* to see their ponies. Do you have the slightest inkling of what will happen when I tell them they *can't*?" I covered my eyes and heaved a dolorous sigh. "You have condemned me to a foreseeable future filled with terminal crankiness."

"I'm sorry to inconvenience you, Lori," Emma said tartly, "but we're suffering a few inconveniences ourselves. The water pipes leading to the stables are frozen solid and one has burst. Derek and his crew are working on it, but at the moment, the stable yard is a skating rink."

Derek Harris was Emma's husband. Since he restored old buildings for a living, he had the tools, the skills, and the manpower needed to deal with just about any household emergency. If Derek couldn't repair or replace the damaged pipes quickly, no one could.

"It's the curse," I muttered.

"Oh, Lori," Emma said impatiently. "You're not going on about February again, are you?"

"What month is it, my friend?" I retorted. "And what has happened to your pipes?"

"Pure coincidence," Emma replied. "Cold spells happen in winter and pipes sometimes freeze during cold spells. It has nothing to do with a curse."

"What about the school's broken furnace

and the universal head cold?" I demanded.

"Coincidence," Emma said airily.

"So you say," I grumbled, but even as I spoke it occurred to me that I might not be responding as a best friend should in a crisis. With a heroic effort, I thrust my own troubles aside and focused on Emma's. "You poor thing. How can I help? Hot soup? Warm beds? A truckload of blowtorches? Name it and it shall be yours."

Emma chuckled. "Thanks, Lori, but we're managing. It's a big job, though, and it'll take time to put everything back together again. The stables are high and dry, thank heavens, so we won't have to move the horses."

"Are the horses okay?" I asked.

"They're jittery because of the noise and the commotion," Emma replied, "but they'll settle down once they get used to it. Tell Will and Rob not to worry about their ponies. We'll look after them."

"I know you will, and so do the boys," I said. "You must be up to your eyebrows in emergency management, Emma, so I'll let you go. If you need anything, day or night, you know who to call."

"I have your number on speed dial," Emma assured me, and hung up.

I returned the receiver to its cradle and

searched my mind for an alternate activity that would placate a pair of profoundly disappointed seven-year-olds, but for once my imagination failed me. I could think of absolutely nothing that would compensate Will and Rob for a Saturday devoid of horsiness. With my brain running on empty, I sat paralyzed at the kitchen table, unable to bring myself to break the disastrous news to my unsuspecting sons. I was still in a state of suspended animation when the doorbell rang.

I flew up the hallway to answer it, hoping to find a magician or an acrobat or a troupe of juggling chimpanzees on my doorstep, but what I found there was even more astonishing than a passing circus.

When I flung the front door open, I saw flames.

TWO

I didn't shriek, grab the fire extinguisher, or race upstairs to rescue Will and Rob because a second glance told me that the flames in question weren't flames at all, but the short, spiky locks of my nineteen-year-old neighbor, Bree Pym. It was an easy mistake to make because Bree had, for reasons beyond my understanding, dyed her lovely, lustrous dark-brown tresses a vivid, almost fluorescent, shade of red.

"Good grief," I said. "What have you done to your hair?"

"Like it?" said Bree, turning her head to one side to show off her eye-popping new look.

"It looks like your head is on fire," I said.

"Brilliant," she said happily. "Just the effect I was aiming for. I call it my portable hearth. There's nothing like red hair to take the edge off a cold snap."

I laughed. I couldn't help laughing when

Bree was around. She was the breath of fresh air that kept the rest of us from turning into stale windbags.

Aubrey Aroha Pym, more commonly known as Bree, was from New Zealand, but she'd inherited a lovely old house as well as a bucket of money from her great-grandaunts, the late and much-lamented Ruth and Louise Pym, who'd lived on the outskirts of Finch. Although Bree had lived in her great-grandaunts' house for nearly a year, a handful of villagers still found her faintly alarming. They weren't accustomed to sharing a church pew with a vibrant young foreigner who sported multiple tattoos as well as a gleaming ring in one nostril. They would, I thought, faint dead away when Bree strode into St. George's with flaming red hair.

"It's . . . stunning," I said sincerely. I tore my eyes away from her head long enough to notice that she was carrying a suitcase. "Going somewhere?"

"Yes," she said. "Here, I hope. I've come to throw myself on your mercy."

"You want to stay here?" I said, my pulse quickening.

"If you'll have me," she replied diffidently.

"If I'll have you?" I stepped forward and threw my arms around her, crying, "Of

course I'll have you! You're the answer to my prayers!"

Bree allowed herself to be dragged across the threshold, looking thoroughly bemused. She placed her suitcase on the floor, hung her puffy black jacket on the coatrack, and stepped out of her pink polka-dotted snow boots to reveal a pair of bright purple wool socks.

"Am I to understand that I've chosen a good moment to impose on you?" she asked, brushing snow from the legs of her jeans.

"Your timing couldn't be more perfect," I told her. "Come into the kitchen. I'll explain everything over a pot of tea and a plateful of freshly baked cookies."

Bree followed me up the hallway, took a seat at the kitchen table, and helped herself to a cookie while we waited for the kettle to whistle.

"Nummy," she declared, licking the crumbs from her fingers. "What was it?"

"They go by many names," I replied, setting out the tea things, "but my mother called them pecan balls. Here." I tossed a napkin to her. "You've got powdered sugar on your chin."

"A small price to pay," Bree said, wiping

her chin while reaching for a second pecan ball.

I finished making the tea, sat across the table from Bree, folded my hands, and said gravely, "You've arrived in the nick of time to save me and my children from a toxic case of cabin fever."

"Cottage fever, surely," she said, glancing around the kitchen. "What about Bill? Is he immune?"

"Bill's in *Majorca,*" I said bitterly, and went on to describe the preceding week in excruciating detail. "With the stables closed," I concluded, "I didn't know how the boys and I would survive the weekend, but you've put an end to my worries."

"How?" said Bree, looking genuinely per-plexed.

"Are you kidding?" I said. "You're more interesting than a magician, an acrobat, and a troupe of juggling chimpanzees all rolled into one. Will and Rob will go googly when they find out you're here."

"I don't know," Bree said doubtfully. "I'm a pretty poor substitute for Thunder and Storm."

"Don't sell yourself short," I said. "The boys think you're the best thing since baled hay."

"I think they're very nice, too," said Bree,

her eyes twinkling. She popped a third pecan ball into her mouth and chewed thoughtfully before saying, "I guess it was meant to be. I considered throwing myself on Peggy Taxman's mercy, but since she doesn't have any, I came here instead."

"Why throw yourself on anyone's mercy?" I asked.

"Because I'm an idiot," she replied matter-of-factly. "I decided to give my bedroom walls a fresh lick of paint this morning." She shook her head. "Bad idea. Fresh paint requires ventilation, but if I open my windows, my pipes will go the same way as Emma's. I'll have to wait for the weather to warm up a tad before I can give the place a proper airing. In the meantime —"

"In the meantime," I interrupted, "you're staying here."

"Thanks," she said.

"The thanks are all mine." I pushed the plate of cookies toward her and stood. "Have another pecan ball. I'll fetch the boys."

"Don't build me up too much," Bree called as I left the kitchen. "I can't compete with juggling chimpanzees!"

Will and Rob wilted visibly when I told them about the stables, but they revived instantly when they saw who was waiting for them at the bottom of the stairs.

"Breeeeeee!" they chorused, thundering downstairs and all but tackling Bree with simultaneous bear hugs.

"Can we dye our hair, Mummy?" Will asked, standing back to take in Bree's new look.

"I want blue," Rob declared.

"No, you may not dye your hair," I said firmly, "but you may take Bree's luggage up to the guest room."

"Guest room?" said Will.

"Are you staying with us?" Rob asked, gazing wide-eyed at Bree. "Overnight?"

"Over the next few nights, I expect," she replied. "If it's all right with you."

"It's all right," Will assured her fervently.

"It's better than all right," said Rob, reaching for Bree's suit-case.

The rest of the day passed in a happy blur. Bree was, as it turned out, a magician, an acrobat, and a juggler, all rolled into one. While I prepared lunch, she drilled the boys on a disappearing-coin trick until they could perform it like seasoned pros. After lunch, she taught them to stand on their heads with their legs folded, yoga-style. While dinner was cooking, she began juggling lessons, using stuffed animals instead of balls to keep furniture damage to a minimum. I played the part of an appreciative audience and saw, to my relief, that my guest was having as much fun as Will and Rob.

During dinner, Bree proposed a cure for our claustrophobia.

"Let's get out of the cottage and go somewhere really interesting," she said. "I have a place in mind. I've been meaning to go there on my own, but now we can go there together."

"What sort of place is it?" asked Will, looking up from his mashed potatoes.

"I thought we might visit Skeaping Manor," Bree told him. "I'm sure you've been to Skeaping Manor a thousand times, Will, but I've never been there. I think you and Rob might enjoy showing it to me."

"As a matter of fact," I piped up, "we've never been to Skeaping Manor, either. I've heard of it, but our expeditions always seem to end up at the Cotswold Farm Park or the Cotswold Wildlife Park or the Cotswold Falconry Center or the Bibury Trout Farm or the Prinknash Bird and Deer Park or . . ." I shrugged. "You get the general idea. The boys like animals."

"I like animals, too," said Bree, "but if you want an indoor adventure on a cold winter's day, Skeaping Manor is the place to go."

"It's near Upper Deeping, isn't it?" I asked.

"It's on the edge of Skeaping village," Bree replied, "about three miles south of Upper Deeping. According to a brochure I found at the tourist office, Skeaping Manor is" — she tilted her head back and recited as if from memory — "a Jacobean treasure house featuring a collection of curiosities assembled by Sir Waverly Jephcott, noted Edwardian physician, naturalist, archaeologist, anthropologist, historian, and philanthropist."

"What's Skeaping Manor?" Rob asked, looking bewildered. Bree's description of the place had evidently sailed over his head.

"It's a museum," Bree told him, and before his face could fall too far she added, "But it's not a boring old dusty museum. It has all sorts of cool stuff in it."

"Does it have dinosaurs?" Rob asked hopefully.

"The brochure didn't mention dinosaurs," Bree conceded, "but it did mention a display of shrunken heads."

"Shrunken heads?" Will echoed, his face brightening.

"And skeletons," Bree went on. "And mummies. And bugs. And an axe." She paused, then finished in a thrilling whisper,

"A *bloodstained* axe."

"May we go to Skeaping Manor, please, Mummy?" the boys clamored, turning their dark-brown eyes on me.

If my children had been emotionally fragile or prone to nightmares, I would have nipped the idea in the bud. Bree knew, however, that my sons weren't easily cowed. They, unlike their mother, found grotesque objects fascinating rather than frightening. They might draw pictures of skeletons and shrunken heads for weeks to come, but they wouldn't be haunted by them.

"May we, Mummy?" said Rob.

"Please?" said Will.

"It's open only three days a week during the winter," Bree put in. "Thursdays, Fridays, and Saturdays. If we don't go tomorrow, I may not be around long enough to go with you."

"Please?" the boys chorused imploringly.

"Yes, we'll go," I said, to avoid being badgered to death. "If —"

"We clear the table," said Will.

"And load the dishwasher," said Rob.

"And play nicely until bedtime," said Will.

"And go to bed without arguing," said Rob.

"And promise to behave ourselves in the car," Will concluded.

"How quickly they learn," I said, laughing.

The boys made polite but pressing attempts to wrangle more information about Skeaping Manor from Bree, but she refused to be drawn.

"If I tell you too much, I'll spoil too many surprises," she said. "And Skeaping Manor is full of surprises."

Bree must have been thinking of my sons' unquenchable thirst for all things gruesome when she uttered those fateful words. She could not have known that a delicate object of great beauty would deliver the biggest surprise of all.

THREE

The temperature soared to just below freezing on Saturday morning and the brutal wind became a slightly less brutal breeze. Bree, declaring it balmy, dressed lightly in a black turtleneck, a pair of jeans, and her polka-dotted boots. She donned her puffy black jacket, but refused to wear a hat or gloves.

She was made of tougher stuff than I. While I was willing to concede that the weather had taken a turn for the better, I refused to describe it as *balmy*. After making a substantial breakfast for the troops, I bundled the boys and myself up to the eyeballs, making sure mittens, hats, scarves, and winter boots were securely in place before we left the cottage. As a result, we waddled out to my canary-yellow Range Rover like three overstuffed teddy bears while Bree strode nimbly ahead of us, as sure-footed as an arctic hare.

It was a beautiful day for a drive through the countryside. The sun shone brightly in a crisp blue sky, snowflakes clung to the hedgerows in twinkling clusters, and the snow-covered fields looked as tidy as freshly made beds. Will and Rob played word games with Bree as we passed the Anscombe Riding Center's curving drive, Bree's mellow redbrick house, and the wrought-iron gates that guarded the entrance to the Fairworth estate.

I stopped the car briefly at the top of the humpbacked bridge to savor the sight of Finch in its winter finery. Freed from its heavy burden of Christmas regalia, Finch looked like a gingerbread village come to life, with smoke curling from each snow-capped chimney and curtains twitching behind each frosty pane.

Upper Deeping, with its whirl of traffic, was grimier than Finch, but it was also much livelier and its businesses, buildings, and residents were a great deal more varied. I took a slight detour to allow the boys the pleasure of showing Bree their school before heading south on the main road to find the turnoff for Skeaping village.

Bree spotted the sign heralding our destination, and a ten-minute drive down a winding lane ended at a second sign directing us to the parking lot at Skeaping Manor. As Bree's brochure had foretold, the building was a classic Jacobean edifice, three stories tall, half-timbered, and bristling with porches, bays, gables, dormers, and a trailing cluster of additions. It sprawled haphazardly across a low prominence overlooking the village, which appeared to be larger than Finch, but equally sleepy.

The manor had many windows, but they all seemed to be covered in heavy drapes or blocked by large pieces of furniture. The darkened windows made the place seem a bit unwelcoming, like a fortress under siege. An overhanging bay supported by massive oak beams sheltered an iron-banded door, which was conveniently labeled MAIN ENTRANCE.

"We beat the crowds," Bree observed as I parked the Rover between a dented old blue Ford Fiesta and a gleaming red Fiat. "Only four cars in the lot and they probably belong to the staff."

"Maybe we'll get a private tour," I said.

"The brochure didn't mention tours," Bree informed me. "Besides, tours are for ninnies. I'd rather explore the place on my own."

"Me, too," Will and Rob asserted emphatically.

I caught the scent of heroine-worship in the air and resigned myself to spending the next few hours wandering aimlessly from one repulsive exhibit to the next.

"I'd hate to pay the museum's heating bills," Bree commented as we clambered out of the Rover and crunched across icy snow to the oak door. "And it would cost a fortune to replace the roof."

"You're too practical for your own good," I said. "Think of how wonderful it would be to have so many rooms all to yourself."

"But you wouldn't have them all to yourself," Bree countered. "You'd need an army of servants to keep them clean."

"An army of servants," I murmured dreamily, recalling the baskets of laundry awaiting me at the cottage. "Sounds good to me."

Bree gave me an amused but doubtful glance, opened the oak door, and strode into the manor. The boys darted in after her and I followed close upon their heels, but we all came to a stumbling halt a few steps beyond the threshold. After the dazzling brightness of the sunlit, snowy parking lot, the museum's entrance hall seemed as dark as a cave. I felt as if I'd gone blind.

I grabbed the boys to keep them from blundering into Bree and tightened my grip when the oak door closed behind us with a thud.

"Welcome to Skeaping Manor," said a sepulchral voice.

I shut my eyes briefly to allow them to adjust to the gloom. When I opened them again, I could see that we were in a window-less, low-ceilinged foyer lined with carved oak panels so blackened with age that they looked as though they'd been charred. An old-fashioned wooden swivel chair sat behind a large wooden desk to my left, next to a wall rack filled with colorful brochures advertising local attractions. An elaborately carved oak door straight ahead of us appeared to be the primary point of access to the rest of the museum, but since it was shut, I couldn't see what lay beyond it.

The foyer was dimly but adequately lit by a green-shaded banker's lamp on the desk and a stained glass chandelier on the ceiling. The ceiling fixture cast an eerie glow over the room's most remarkable feature: a tall, thin, clean-shaven gentleman dressed in formal Edwardian garb.

"By jove!" Bree exclaimed. "It's the ghost of Sir Waverly Jephcott!"

"Cool," chorused the boys.

"Very droll, madam," said the man, smoothing his embroidered waistcoat. "I

33

fear I must disappoint you, however, for I am no ghost. My attire is intended to entertain and to educate those interested in Sir Waverly's era." He bowed gracefully. "I am Miles Craven, curator and caretaker of Skeaping Manor, and I am at your service. May I place your outerwear in our cloakroom?"

"Yes, thank you," I said, glad to be relieved of parental coat-lugging duties.

We handed our jackets, hats, scarves, and mittens to the curator, who disappeared with them through a door hidden in the paneling behind the desk, then reappeared, holding a numbered slip of paper.

"Your cloakroom ticket, madam," he said, handing the slip of paper to me. "You may not need it, as I do not expect many visitors today, but one never knows. Is this your first visit to Skeaping Manor?"

"It is," I replied.

"We want to see the bloodstained axe," Rob declared.

"And the mummies," Will put in.

"And the bugs," said Bree. "And the skeletons."

"I can, for a nominal sum, provide you with a guidebook," Mr. Craven offered.

"No, thanks," Bree said firmly. "We're on a voyage of discovery."

"You will not be disappointed," Mr. Craven assured her. "There is much to discover at Skeaping Manor."

He began to walk toward the carved oak door, but stopped in midstride when I cleared my throat.

"We haven't paid the admission fee," I reminded him.

"Admission is free during the winter months," he informed me. "Donations are, however, gratefully accepted throughout the year."

"Go ahead," I told Bree as Will and Rob began to fidget. "I'll take care of the donation and catch up with you."

"Onward, explorers!" said Bree.

"Onward!" the twins echoed.

"Bon voyage," Mr. Craven said genially.

He opened the door and the three adventurers sailed through it as eagerly as racehorses released from a starting gate. It warmed my heart to see Will and Rob looking so bright-eyed and bushy-tailed, and as I dug through my shoulder bag for my wallet I thanked Bree silently for proposing such a splendid expedition.

"Is Skeaping Manor affiliated with the National Trust?" I asked Mr. Craven, referring to the conservation group that owned hundreds of historic houses throughout England.

"It is not," he replied. "Skeaping Manor is a private institution funded by the Jephcott Endowment and by the munificence of our patrons."

I handed him what I hoped was a munificent donation, turned to face the open door, and hesitated.

"Do I detect in you a certain reluctance to enter the museum?" Mr. Craven inquired.

"I'm afraid you do," I admitted sheepishly. "To be perfectly honest, Mr. Craven, I'm not a big fan of bloodstained axes and shrunken heads. If you ever repeat it to my sons, I'll deny it, but the truth is: I'm pathetically squeamish."

"Fear not, madam," he said. "Your secret is safe with me. And you need not spend your entire visit wishing you were elsewhere. Our brochure may paint a lurid picture of Skeaping Manor, but it does not tell the whole story. Though Sir Waverly Jephcott was a connoisseur of oddities, he also amassed fine collections of porcelain, silver, and jade as well as woodcuts and musical instruments. Indeed, it is possible to spend many hours in the museum concentrating on those collections alone." He studied me in silence, then ventured, "May I deduce from your accent that you are an American?"

"Yes," I said. "Why? Is it important?"

"Possibly," he said. "If you were English, I would direct you to the first floor —"

"Which, in America, is considered the second floor," I broke in, nodding. "I've lived in England for nearly ten years, Mr. Craven. I understand that we're on the ground floor, and that the first floor" — I pointed to the ceiling — "is upstairs."

"Excellent." He withdrew a gold pen from the inner recesses of his frock coat and a booklet from the wall rack. "I shall mark a route for you in the guidebook that will take you as directly as possible to the first-floor exhibits. I'm certain you will enjoy them."

"You're very kind," I said, and reached into my shoulder bag again. "How much do I owe you for the guidebook?"

"It shall be my gift to you," he said, placing the annotated booklet in my hands. "Please accept it as a small token of my gratitude."

"Gratitude?" I said, puzzled.

"The vast majority of our visitors focus on the museum's grislier aspects," he explained, smiling. "It's refreshing to meet one who appreciates the finer things in life."

■ ■ ■ ■

I'm sure Miles Craven did his best, but there was no avoiding the grisly in Skeaping Manor. The dark, labyrinthine corridors opened without warning into rooms lined with dimly lit glass cases displaying barbaric surgical instruments or deformed human skulls or the mounted corpses of long-deceased beasts whose unblinking eyes seemed to follow me reproachfully as I swept past them to touch base with Bree.

I didn't see another living soul as I scurried along, which was just as well. A random visitor might have been annoyed by the boys' — and Bree's — unrestrained chatter, but I used the noise as a tracking device and quickly found the explorers clustered around a particularly distressing display of spiny, long-legged insects skewered on pins. I had no idea what kind of insects they were, but they were bigger and nastier looking than any I'd ever encountered.

"Giant weta," said Bree, pointing proudly to the display. "They're New Zealand natives, like me. Never thought I'd see weta here in England."

"Some weta get to be as big as sparrows," Rob informed me importantly.

"They can bite and hiss and scratch," said Will with relish.

"Only when threatened," Bree interjected. "Weta are harmless vegetarians who like the dark. They'd rather hide than fight."

"Charming," I said, averting my gaze from the loathsome bugs. "Would you mind looking after Will and Rob while I run upstairs?" I asked Bree. "I'd like to take a peek at the porcelain."

Bree smiled knowingly, as though she could sense my skin crawling, but assured me that she and the boys would survive without me.

"Thanks," I said. "I'll check in with you in an hour."

"No hurry," said Bree. "We haven't even gotten to the best bits yet."

The mere thought of "the best bits" made me shudder, so I planted hasty kisses on the twins' heads and retraced my steps to a stone staircase Miles Craven had flagged in the guidebook. If my sons had been present, I would have walked upstairs at a sedate pace, but since they were too far away to be influenced by my bad behavior, I took the stairs two at a time and heaved a sigh of relief when I reached the first floor.

The lighting upstairs was just as murky as it had been downstairs, but to my delight the glass cases held objects that stimulated my sense of beauty rather than my gag reflex. The jade room was a joy, the porcelain room a pleasure, the woodcuts were wonderful, and the musical instruments were nothing short of magnificent.

I drifted blissfully from one collection to the next, enjoying the brief respite from a week of high-octane mothering, and feeling a powerful sense of gratitude to Sir Waverly Jephcott for planting an oasis of loveliness above his little shop of horrors. I was convinced that I had the oasis to myself until I stepped into the silver room and saw that someone else had gotten there before me.

A girl not much older than Will and Rob stood motionless in the center of the room. Her hair was the color of burnished copper, her eyes were emerald green, and her fine-featured face was as pale as a porcelain doll's. She was an exceptionally beautiful child, but compared to my robust boys, she seemed painfully thin.

Though her hair was neatly styled in a sweet, face-framing bob, she appeared to be wearing secondhand clothes — droopy black woolen tights, scruffy brown ankle boots, a too-short purple skirt, and a pale pink winter parka that was far too big for her. The parka was a sad little jacket, worn and faded, its pink hood trimmed with a matted strip of gray polyester fur, but I was glad she had it on; she looked like a child who would always feel cold.

She seemed unaware of my presence. Her expression was somber, as if she were lost in thought, and though the room contained a gleaming hoard of platters, centerpieces, goblets, vases, and jewel boxes, her gaze was fixed unwaveringly on one small but beautiful object: a horse-drawn sleigh made entirely of silver.

I crept a step closer and saw for myself why the sleigh held the child's attention. Although it was no more than four inches long, its creator had endowed it with a marvelous wealth of details.

The sleigh was drawn by three high-stepping horses arrayed in an elaborate harness hung with bells and ornamented with rosettes. The horses were exquisitely wrought and superbly dynamic — their nostrils flared, their manes flew as if tossed by the wind, and their tiny hooves seemed to dance along an unseen road.

The sleigh was unoccupied, but it was a tour de force of decorative invention. Every inch of its exterior was embellished with minute tassels, rosettes, pinwheels, birds, and stars. It had a high, scrolled back and its interior appeared to be upholstered in the finest, most deeply cushioned leather. The exuberant patterns made the sleigh glitter like a multifaceted jewel in the dim light. I could only imagine how brightly it would sparkle in the sun.

I'd seldom seen a more enchanting example of the silversmith's art. I gazed at it, entranced, for many minutes, but when I chanced to look again at the girl, I was struck by the contrast between her apparent poverty and the richness of the object that fascinated her. I recalled the dented Ford Fiesta in the parking lot, wondered where her parents were, and wished they hadn't left her alone to peer longingly at a treasure that was so far beyond her reach.

The girl must have felt my gaze, because she slowly turned her head to look up at me.

"Hello," I said. "I'm sorry if I disturbed you."

"You didn't," she said gravely.

"Good," I said, though I was slightly disconcerted by her directness. "I don't mean to be nosy, but . . . where's the rest of your family? I'm sure you didn't come here all by yourself."

"Mummy brought me with her today," she

said, resuming her contemplation of the sleigh. "It's just me and Mummy now. Daddy left."

Her simple answer seemed to explain a lot. *Daddy left,* I thought angrily, leaving Mummy to scrimp and save and struggle to make ends meet. Was that why the girl was so thin, so ragged, so joyless? I wanted to scoop her up and whisk her away to Upper Deeping for a hearty meal and a shopping spree, but instead I just stood there, feeling useless.

"It's a saltcellar," she said softly.

"What is?" I asked.

She raised a slender finger and pointed at the sleigh.

"It's a saltcellar," she repeated, "a container for salt. It sat on a long polished table draped in unblemished white linen. There were silver vases, too, filled with white roses and trailing vines, and there were white candles in silver candelabra. The ladies wore their hair piled high and their dresses cut low to display necklaces worth a king's ransom. The gentlemen wore diamond studs in their stiff collars and gold links in their cuffs. They ate and drank late into the night while the world outside grew darker and colder."

The girl fell silent. I realized that my

mouth was agape and closed it, but I continued to stare at the child in amazement. It seemed impossible to me that the words she'd uttered and the images she'd conjured were her own, yet she'd described the elegant supper party with the quiet conviction of someone who'd witnessed it first-hand.

"Did Mr. Craven tell you about the . . . the saltcellar?" I stammered.

"No," she replied with a dreamy smile. "Mr. Craven just pretends. The dinners were real."

A woman's anxious voice sounded suddenly from the doorway.

"Daisy? What are you doing here? How many times have I told you not to wander off while I'm working?"

A young woman strode into the room, looking flustered. She wore a beige coverall, faded jeans, and down-at-the-heel loafers, and she carried a plastic bucket filled with dust cloths. I thought she might be in her late twenties and I assumed she was a cleaning woman, but one look at her green eyes and her copper-colored hair was enough to convince me that she was Daisy's mother.

"I'm sorry," the young woman said to me. "My daughter is supposed to stay with me while I work, but —"

"There's no need to apologize," I interrupted. "I have two children of my own. I know how hard it is to keep track of them. Besides, I've been enjoying Daisy's company. I'm Lori Shepherd, by the way. I live in Finch."

"I'm Amanda Pickering," said the young woman, "and I'm afraid I have to get on with my work. Daisy?" She extended her free hand to the girl. "Come along, love. I'll make a nice cup of cocoa for you and you can drink it in Mr. Craven's office while I finish up."

"Nice to meet you, Daisy," I called as the pair left the room hand in hand. "You, too, Amanda."

"Nice to meet you, Lori," Amanda called from the corridor.

I listened to their footsteps fade into the distance, then turned to gaze once more at the silver sleigh, wishing I'd been able to spend more time with Amanda Pickering's remarkable daughter.

FOUR

We left Skeaping Manor at noon and treated ourselves to lunch at a café in Upper Deeping. Bree, Will, and Rob spent much of the meal discussing the museum's gruesome highlights, but their conversation didn't dampen my appetite as it might have some other time. While they chatted cheerfully about blood, bones, bugs, and shriveled flesh, my mind was far away, dwelling on Daisy Pickering.

I couldn't stop thinking about the girl and her queer utterances, but since my lunch companions wouldn't let me get a word in edgewise, I was obliged to keep my reflections to myself. I wasn't sure what I would have said to them, even if they'd given me the chance. An incidental conversation with an unusual child would have seemed like very small potatoes to someone who'd had a face-to-face encounter with a giant weta.

By the time we returned to the cottage,

the sun had warmed the air considerably and the wind had ceased altogether, so I gave in to the boys' demands and sent them outside to play. Bree, of course, went with them. I elected to remain indoors not only because I needed to toss a basket of laundry into the washing machine, but because I was bursting to speak with someone who would take an interest in my encounter with Daisy Pickering.

Fortunately, there was someone in the cottage who valued little girls above blood-stained axes. Unfortunately, she wasn't someone I could easily introduce to Bree. After peering through the kitchen window to make sure the boys and their idol were fully engaged in their snowy pursuits, I went to the study to speak with a friend Bree would never meet.

The friend's name was Dimity Westwood and she wasn't, in the technical sense, alive. She had, in fact, died a year before I'd first set foot in England, but though her body reposed in the churchyard in Finch, her spirit remained in the cottage. It wasn't the sort of thing I could explain to myself, much less to a houseguest, though the story behind it was easy to understand.

Dimity Westwood, an Englishwoman, had been my late mother's closest friend. The

47

two women met in London while serving their respective countries during the Second World War and the bond of affection they forged in wartime lasted a lifetime.

After peace was declared in Europe and my mother sailed back to the States, she and Dimity maintained their friendship by sending hundreds of letters back and forth across the Atlantic. When my father died unexpectedly, the letters became my mother's refuge, a tranquil sanctuary that renewed and refreshed her after long days spent working full-time as a teacher while raising a rambunctious daughter on her own.

My mother was very protective of her sanctuary. She told no one about it, including me. I knew Dimity Westwood only as Aunt Dimity, the redoubtable heroine of a series of bedtime stories my mother invented. I was unaware of the real Dimity Westwood's existence until both she and my mother were dead.

It was then that Dimity bequeathed to me a comfortable fortune, the honey-colored cottage in which she'd grown up, the precious correspondence she'd shared with my mother, and a curious blue-leather-bound book filled with blank pages.

It was through the blue journal that I

finally met my benefactress. When I gazed at the journal's blank pages, Aunt Dimity's handwriting would appear, a graceful copperplate taught at the village school at a time when airplanes were still a rare and wondrous sight. I nearly had kittens the first time it happened, but I quickly came to realize that Aunt Dimity had nothing but my best interests at heart.

I didn't understand how Aunt Dimity managed to bridge the gap between the living and the not-quite-living, and she wasn't too clear about it herself, but the *how* didn't matter to me. The one thing I knew for certain was that Dimity Westwood was as good a friend to me as she'd been to my mother. And that was enough.

The study was crisscrossed with shadows thrown by the desiccated strands of ivy that clung to the diamond-paned windows above the old oak desk. I turned on the mantel lamps, lit a fire in the hearth, and paused to greet another dear friend.

"Hi, Reg," I said. "You're the only kind of stuffed animal I ever want to see again."

Reginald was a small, powder-pink flannel rabbit with hand-stitched whiskers, black-button eyes, and a pale purple stain on his snout — a souvenir of the time I'd let him taste my grape juice. Reginald had been my confidant and my companion in adventure for as long as I could remember and though I no longer carried him with me everywhere I went, I felt no need to consign him to the scrap heap of memory simply because I'd grown up. Instead, he sat in a special niche on the bookshelves beside the fireplace, where I could give him the love and attention an old friend deserves.

I reached out to touch Reginald's snout, then took the blue journal from its place on the bookshelves and sat with it in one of the tall leather armchairs before the hearth. I glanced over my shoulder to make doubly sure I'd closed the study door, then opened the journal.

"Dimity?" I said. "The strangest thing happened this morning."

I smiled fondly as the familiar lines of royal-blue ink began to curl and loop gracefully across the page.

Oh, goody. I love it when strange things happen. What sort of strange thing was it?

"It concerns a young girl who seems to be channeling a much older soul," I said.

You have my undivided attention. Carry on.

I gave Aunt Dimity a succinct account of my encounter with Daisy Pickering, then leaned back in my chair to await her reply. It came almost instantly.

Skeaping Manor? Ugh! I visited the ghastly place once, on a school trip, and had horrible nightmares for weeks afterward. I'm afraid I share your aversion to the grotesque, Lori. I'm glad Bree was there to spare you the worst of it.

"Me, too," I said. "But what do you think of Daisy?"

I probably think what you think. The girl and her mother have had a rough time of it since Mr. Pickering abandoned them, but Daisy seems to find solace in contemplating beautiful objects.

"Yes, but what about the way she spoke?" I asked.

What about it?

"Don't you think it was . . . peculiar?" I ventured.

Not especially peculiar, no.

I decided that my succinct account had failed to convey the full effect of Daisy Pickering's haunting monologue, and tried again.

"Her tone of voice was melancholy," I said, "almost nostalgic, as if she were remembering a scene she couldn't possibly have seen. I mean, she knew that the silver sleigh was a saltcellar. How many children her age know what a saltcellar is? *I* didn't know what a saltcellar was until she told me." I frowned in concentration and tried to recall Daisy's words exactly. "She said the gentlemen at the dinner party wore diamond studs in their stiff collars, but I'm willing to bet she's never seen a diamond stud or a stiff collar in her life. She talked about white roses and trailing vines and ladies wearing necklaces worth a king's ransom and she described the linen tablecloth as 'unblemished.' What kind of kid uses words like 'unblemished'?"

An intelligent kid with a retentive memory? Let's at least try to be rational about this, Lori. If Amanda Pickering takes Daisy to work with her on a regular basis, then Daisy will have spent a lot of time at Skeaping Manor. She's probably heard dozens if not hundreds of visitors discuss the silver sleigh. I suspect she was parroting words she'd heard others utter and adding some imaginative embroidery of her own.

"I doubt she's heard more than a handful of people comment on the silver sleigh," I retorted. "The curator told me that hardly anyone goes upstairs to look at the pretty exhibits. According to him, most visitors concentrate on the icky stuff."

Most, perhaps, but not all. You and I are living proof — more or less — that some people prefer the pretty to the icky. It's possible that a single, vivid discussion of the silver sleigh made a strong impression on Daisy, one that stayed with her long after she'd overheard it. And what makes you think she's never seen a diamond stud or a stiff collar? You told me yourself that the curator dresses in Edwardian clothes. It seems likely to me that such a man would be perfectly happy to explain his attire to a bright and inquisitive child.

"I think he would have explained it to me, if I'd shown the smallest sign of interest," I said with a wry smile. "He's an enthusiast."

There you are, then. You have a little girl who prowls the museum on her own, asking the curator questions, listening in on other people's conversations, and repeating what she's heard.

"Without supernatural intervention," I said, shaking my head at my own foolishness.

Soul channeling isn't as common an activity as so-called mediums would have you believe, my dear. It is, in fact, an extremely rare occurrence, one which you yourself experienced a few years ago. As I'm sure you'll recall, the soul in question changed your entire aspect. It altered your behavior as well as your voice. Daisy may have employed an unusual vocabulary, but her voice and her manner didn't change radically from one moment to the next,

53

did they?

"No," I admitted.

In that case, I think we can safely rule out supernatural intervention.

"I'm sure you're right," I said. "But honestly, Dimity, the way Daisy looked at the silver sleigh and the way she talked about it . . . It just seemed very . . . odd . . . at the time."

You were under the influence of dim lighting and bizarre surroundings, Lori. Your encounter with Daisy was bound to seem odd.

"I suppose so," I conceded. "And I may have let my emotions get the best of me. I felt so sorry for her, with her skinny legs and her ratty old parka. I wanted to reach through the glass and give the silver sleigh to her. I wish . . ." My voice trailed off into a forlorn, frustrated sigh, but Aunt Dimity seemed to read my mind.

You wish you could rescue her. The thing is, Lori, she doesn't seem to need rescuing. Her father may have failed her, but she has a hardworking mother who appears to care very much for her. Daisy may not be as well fed or as well dressed as Will and Rob, but she seems to be well loved. And love, as you know, can make up for deficiencies in diet and dress.

"Even so —" I broke off as the sound of

raucous voices came to me from the kitchen. "Sorry, Dimity. Gotta run. The arctic adventurers are back and they're howling for hot chocolates."

Go, my dear. And try not to worry about Daisy. I seem to remember another bright and inquisitive little girl who was raised by a hardworking mother — and she turned out quite well.

I smiled ruefully, closed the journal, returned it to its shelf, and gave Reginald's pink flannel ears a fond twiddle before heading for the kitchen. I tried to put all thoughts of Daisy Pickering behind me as I left the study, but when I saw my rosy-cheeked sons I couldn't help remembering the girl's pale face and the burning look in her eyes as she gazed at the silver sleigh.

FIVE

The boys' headmistress telephoned on Sunday afternoon to inform me that Morningside School's ailing heating system had been restored to good health and that classes would resume on Monday morning. The news didn't sit well with Will or Rob, who'd hoped to spend the rest of their lives building snow yurts with Bree in the back meadow, but they cheered up when I reminded them that their friend intended to stick around for a few more days.

"I'm glad I didn't ask Peggy Taxman for shelter," Bree said. "The look she gave me at church this morning would have curdled milk. I don't think she approves of my hair."

It was early evening. We'd finished dinner and repaired to the living room to lounge lazily on the couch. Stanley had emerged from his self-imposed exile in the guest room to take possession of Bill's favorite armchair and the boys knelt at the coffee table, drawing pictures of deformed skulls to take to school for show-and-tell.

"I like your hair," Will said loyally.

"Me, too," said Rob. "It's cheerful. Like a clown's."

"Thanks, Rob," said Bree, grinning. "What's on your agenda for tomorrow, Lori? You'll let me know if I'm in the way, won't you? I can always make myself scarce."

"You can make yourself at home," I said. "I'll be in Upper Deeping for most of the day, helping out at the charity shop."

"Charity shops are known as op shops in New Zealand," Bree informed me. "Short for opportunity shop."

"I know," I said. "Op shops are called thrift stores in America, but in England they're known as charity shops."

"An English op shop," said Bree. "Sounds thrilling. May I tag along?"

"Of course," I said. "We can always use an extra pair of hands."

Will and Rob, who'd caught every word of our conversation, glanced up from their artwork.

"The charity shop in Upper Deeping is called Aunt Dimity's Attic," said Rob, bending to blacken a hollow eye socket.

"And it's Mummy's shop," Will chimed

in, putting a jagged edge on a broken tooth.

"Is it?" Bree asked interestedly, turning to me.

"It was my brainchild," I replied, "but it doesn't belong to me. It's one of a chain of six shops owned by the Westwood Trust, a charitable organization founded in the 1950s by the woman who left me this cottage."

"Dimity Westwood," said Bree, nodding. "The vicar's mentioned her a few times and I've seen her headstone in the churchyard."

"Dimity was the sort of person who'd appreciate a good thrift store," I said, "and since I happen to be the Westwood Trust's current chairwoman, I named our shop after her — Aunt Dimity's Attic."

"Who gets the money?" Bree asked.

"It's all about locals helping locals," I said. "The trust owns the property, but local people manage the shop, donate the goods, and buy the goods. The money they raise goes to local schools — publicly funded schools, that is. Places like Morningside don't get a penny."

"Places like Morningside don't need a penny," Bree observed.

"Exactly," I said. "Aunt Dimity's Attic helps to pay for cultural programs — art, music, drama, the sort of thing that's all but disappeared from state-funded education because of budget cuts."

"I'm impressed," said Bree.

"You're also optimistic," I said. "Monday mornings at Aunt Dimity's Attic aren't so much about treasure hunting as they are about trash collecting. You'd be surprised at some of the garbage people dump on our doorstep on Sundays. We're closed on Sundays," I explained, "so donors who wish to remain anonymous leave their so-called donations in our doorway when no one's there to stop them. Some thoughtful soul once left a sack filled with dirty diapers."

"One woman's trash is another woman's treasure," Bree said confidently. "I intend to find something astounding."

"Like a skull with three eyeholes," Rob said proudly, holding up his drawing.

"Or a skull with *fangs*," said Will, putting the finishing touch on his masterpiece of the macabre.

The conversation went downhill from there, with Bree, Will, and Rob vying with one another to come up with the most outlandish item a bargain hunter might find at a thrift store. I'm sorry to say it, but their suggestions made a sackful of used diapers seem deeply desirable.

■ ■ ■ ■

Bree and I delivered Will and Rob to Morningside School on Monday morning, then drove to Upper Deeping's main square, where Aunt Dimity's Attic was located, nestled comfortably between a bank and a bookstore. I left the Rover in the parking lot behind the shop, unlocked the back door, and ushered Bree into the storage and sorting room, where we found Florence Cheeseman, the shop manager, already hard at work.

Florence was a petite, gray-haired dynamo with an eye for bargains, an ear for gossip, and an old-fashioned work ethic. She was always the first to arrive at the shop and the last to leave and she made the most of the time in between. Even so, she refused to accept a paycheck, grumbling irritably: "If I needed the money, I wouldn't work as a volunteer in a charity shop, would I?" Florence had dressed for the day in a bulky black turtleneck, a pair of designer jeans, and gigantic hoop earrings that glinted in the overhead light.

"I've brought reinforcements, Florence," I said. "My friend Bree Pym is from New Zealand, but she lives near Finch."

"What in heaven's name have you done to your hair, girl?" Florence exclaimed, staring at Bree. "You look like a fireworks display."

"Just thought I'd brighten things up a bit," said Bree, unfazed.

"You're obviously mad," Florence declared, shaking Bree's proffered hand, "but you're welcome all the same. Our neighbors have been busy over the weekend, Lori."

She gestured to four cardboard boxes and five trash bags piled on the large oblong table that occupied the middle of the room. "I found these in the doorway when I arrived. Heaven knows what horrors await us." She pulled a box toward her. "At least nothing's squirming. You may find it hard to believe, Bree, but someone once left us a snake."

"We found a good home for it," I put in.

"You didn't take it back to the cottage with you?" Bree asked mischievously.

"Certainly not," I said, adding loftily, "Dimity the snake is now living in Cheltenham with an eminent herpetologist."

"Sounds ideal," said Bree. "I'll bet Will and Rob would love to visit the happy couple." Before I could threaten her with grievous bodily harm should she ever so much as mention the herpetologist to my sons, Bree stepped up to the table. "Enough

61

small talk, ladies. I'm here to work. What's the drill?"

I pointed to my right. "Stand at the end of the table. Open a bag or a box and sort through the contents. Put the unspeakably filthy, the hopelessly irreparable, and the utterly useless items in the appropriate recycling bins and leave the rest on the table. Florence or I will take it from there."

"If you have any questions, ask," Florence added, examining a chipped china cow. "And try not to dawdle. We open at ten o'clock, which leaves us just over an hour to get through this mess."

"Yes, ma'am." Bree snapped off a salute, grabbed a cardboard box, and marched with it to the end of the table.

I moved to the opposite end, dragged a trash bag toward me, opened it, and saw that it was filled with children's clothing.

"Have a nice weekend?" Florence asked, turning her attention to a dented brass candlestick.

"Very nice," I replied. "Bree and I took the boys to Skeaping Manor on Saturday."

"Skeaping Manor isn't my idea of *nice,*" Florence said, grimacing. "I'll take out-of-town guests there if they insist on going, but I always try to talk them out of it. The exhibits there are even creepier than our

Monday morning haul." She eyed a head-less wooden monk with disfavor and tossed it into a recycling bin.

"Some of the exhibits are quite beautiful," I said.

"Beautiful exhibits? At Skeaping Manor? Don't make me laugh," Florence scoffed. "The displays are nothing but creepy. The curator is creepy, too. Miles Craven — did you meet him? Just as twisty as his exhibits."

"He didn't seem twisty to me," I pro-tested. "A little theatrical, maybe, but not twisty."

"He's creepy," Florence said firmly. "How could he not be? He *lives* there, for pity's sake. How could anyone live in Skeaping Manor and *not* be creepy?"

"He lives in the museum?" I said, sur-prised.

"In a flat round the back," Florence confirmed. "Myrna Felton saw him in the garden one day, dressed like an Edwardian undertaker and declaiming poetry. *She* thinks he's balmy. So does Barbara Halstow. *She* saw him . . ."

While Florence cataloged Miles Craven's many eccentricities, I made my way through the layers of clothing in my trash bag, plac-ing sweaters, wool skirts, corduroy trousers, and winter-weight tights in separate piles on the table. It looked as though a child had outgrown her wardrobe, and though the clothes were far from new, they were clean and in acceptable condition. Nothing caught my attention until I reached the last item at the very bottom of the bag.

A pale pink winter parka lay there. It was a sad little jacket, worn and faded, its pink hood trimmed with a matted strip of gray polyester fur. The moment I saw it my mind spun back to Skeaping Manor's silver room, and Florence's rattling rant gave way to a young girl's dreamy soliloquy.

. . . The gentlemen wore diamond studs in their stiff collars and gold links in their cuffs. They ate and drank late into the night while the world outside grew darker and colder. . . .

I glanced at the clothes I'd already placed on the table, saw a purple skirt and a pair of black woolen tights, looked again at the pink parka, and knew beyond doubt that the child who'd outgrown her wardrobe was Daisy Pickering.

Dazed by the unsettling coincidence of finding Daisy's jacket at the shop so soon after seeing it on her, I reached into the bag to confirm by touch what my eyes had already told me. A pang of pity shot through me when I felt a lump in one pocket and realized that she'd left something in it — a small, cherished toy, perhaps, something that meant as much to her as Reginald did to me.

I slipped my fingers into the pocket and withdrew the forgotten object. The thought of returning it to Daisy was foremost in my mind when what in my wandering hand should appear but a miniature sleigh pulled by three tiny horses. Three *silver* horses. Pulling a *silver* sleigh. A glittering, exquisitely wrought silver sleigh — a masterpiece of the silversmith's art. However much I blinked and stared, there was no mistaking it. The forgotten object I'd retrieved from the pink parka was the silver sleigh I'd last seen at Skeaping Manor.

I was thunderstruck. I didn't gasp or squeak or cry out in surprise because my entire head had gone numb. Though the silver sleigh rested firmly in the palm of my hand, I half expected it to vanish in a puff of fairy dust. When it didn't, I was forced to ask myself a painfully obvious question: How had the priceless artifact ended up in Daisy Pickering's pocket?

"Found a snake?"

"What?" I said, startled out of my ruminations.

"Have you found another snake?" Bree asked. "You've been looking into that bag for the last five minutes. What's in it? A Cotswold cobra?"

"A jacket," I said. I pulled the pink parka out of the bag with my free hand, gave it a shake, and held it up for Bree to see.

"Sorry," said Bree, shaking her head. "It wouldn't suit Rob *or* Will."

"Good one," I said, forcing a smile.

I glanced at Florence, saw that she and Bree were exchanging grins, and quickly slipped the silver sleigh into my shoulder bag. I wasn't sure what I would do with it, but I needed time to think things through before I revealed my astounding find to anyone.

Six

I placed the parka on the table, opened a cardboard box, and sorted through its ragtag contents while my mind raced toward an unpleasant conclusion.

Daisy Pickering had stolen the silver sleigh. It was the only explanation that made sense. Miles Craven might be eccentric, but I couldn't envision him giving the museum's treasures away to his employees' children. Amanda Pickering looked as though she could use some extra cash, but if she'd taken the sleigh, she would have kept it in a safe place until she could sell it. She wouldn't have stuffed it carelessly into a jacket she intended to donate to a charity shop.

If I put my mind to it, I could construct a scenario in which a random thief dropped his loot into Daisy's pocket to avoid being caught with it, but to blame the theft on a faceless criminal was to ignore the fact that

Daisy was a far more likely suspect. She'd had the motive, the opportunity, and, I strongly suspected, the intent to commit a crime that might not have seemed like a crime to her.

No, I thought unhappily. Daisy was the thief. Daisy Pickering had stolen the silver sleigh. She'd gazed at it, longed for it, dreamed of it until she could no longer resist the temptation to have it for herself. She'd taken the display case key from Miles Craven's office after she'd finished the hot cocoa her mother had made for her. She'd slipped back to the silver room unseen, unlocked the case, and pocketed the sleigh. She couldn't have known what her mother planned to do with the pink parka. If she had, she would have hidden the silver sleigh somewhere else.

"Florence," I said, "have you heard anything about a theft at Skeaping Manor?"

"A theft at Skeaping Manor?" Florence repeated incredulously. "What self-respecting burglar would waste his time on that awful place? The market for shrunken heads isn't what it used to be."

"Maybe not," I said, "but what about the market for jade or porcelain or, um, silver?" I felt myself blush guiltily and hurried on. "As I told you before, there are beautiful things there, too, and I think they're pretty valuable."

"Then Miles Craven should take better care of them," Florence retorted. "The museum's security system is a joke."

"Is it?" said Bree. "I spotted security cameras around the outside of the building and in every room."

"They don't work," Florence stated flatly. "Never have. They're dummies, meant to deter theft, but they don't record anything. As for the guards —"

"What guards?" Bree interrupted.

"You might well ask," said Florence with a disparaging sniff. "The museum's crack team of security specialists consists of Les and Al, a pair of doddering old codgers who spend most of their work hours guzzling tea in the staff room. They're as useless as the cameras. The display cases are locked, I'll grant you, but the locks are a thousand years old. It would be child's play to pry them open."

"Child's play," I echoed, wincing inwardly. "If something was stolen, Miles Craven would report it to the police, wouldn't he?"

"If something was stolen from Skeaping Manor," Florence declared, "Miles Craven would climb up on the roof, fire a blunder-buss, and announce it to the world."

"Which means that you would have heard about it," I said.

"The blunderbuss would probably catch my attention," Florence said dryly. She gave me a sidelong look. "Why are you going on about thefts at Skeaping Manor, Lori? Are you planning a break-in?"

"Yes," I said, smiling. "I've always wanted a collection of giant weta."

"That's as may be," Florence said sternly, "but the shop doesn't want a collection of nasty old beer mats." She pointed at the table space in front of me. "Please feel free to toss that lot, Lori."

I looked down at the assortment of sticky, stained beer mats I'd stacked neatly beside the pink parka, and grinned sheepishly at Florence.

"Sorry," I said. "I was daydreaming about giant weta."

Florence and Bree laughed. I dropped the beer mats into the recycling bin and tried to focus on my work.

The shop was unusually busy all day. Florence blamed it on the cold spell, saying that people were eager to get out and about after being trapped indoors for a week. Whatever the reason, I was glad to have Bree on hand to help because my mind wasn't on the job.

When I wasn't gazing distractedly into the middle distance, I was asking customers if they'd heard rumors about a burglary at Skeaping Manor. The responses were uniformly negative, and since Upper Deeping's gossip grapevine was almost as efficient as Finch's, I concluded with some confidence that Miles Craven hadn't yet noticed the theft.

The thought of his ignorance filled me with hope because I knew what I wanted to do with the silver sleigh. And what I wanted to do was a tiny bit illegal.

"Dimity?"

Four hours had passed since dinnertime. Bree, Will, and Rob were asleep in their respective beds, Stanley was asleep in mine, and I was seated in one of the tall leather armchairs in the study, with a fire burning merrily in the hearth and the blue journal open in my lap. I'd decided that it might be a good idea to explain my plan of action to Aunt Dimity before I followed through on it.

"Dimity?" I repeated. "Something really strange happened today."

Aunt Dimity's handwriting appeared, curling lazily across the page, as if she couldn't quite work herself into a froth of excitement over my announcement.

I hope today's strange event was stranger than yesterday's because, frankly, yesterday's wasn't very strange at all.

"Today's will knock your socks off," I promised. "Remember the silver sleigh I told you about, the one I saw at Skeaping Manor?"

The twinkling trinket that entranced young Daisy Pickering? How could I forget it?

"What would you say if I told you it was in my shoulder bag?" I asked.

I'd say: Bravo! You've piqued my curiosity! Have you embarked on a life of crime, my dear?

"No, but I'm about to," I said. I took a deep breath and launched into a highly detailed account of my day at the charity shop. I told Aunt Dimity about my discovery of the silver sleigh, my belief in Daisy's guilt, and my conviction that Miles Craven was unaware of the crime. I was about to reveal my slightly illegal scheme to her when she asked a question that hadn't even occurred to me.

Why would Amanda Pickering donate her child's winter coat to the charity shop? The pink parka didn't appear to be too small for Daisy when you saw her wearing it, did it?

"No," I said. "If anything, it seemed to

72

swallow her up. As I said, she's a little wisp of a thing."

Why, then, would a woman in Amanda's precarious financial position give away a perfectly good winter coat?

"Because it isn't perfectly good?" I ventured. "The parka is miles too big for Daisy and it's too tatty to sell at the charity shop. Amanda must have found a nicer jacket for her daughter."

I hope so, for Daisy's sake. I don't yet see how your life of crime comes into the picture, my dear, but I'm sure you'll make it clear to me before dawn.

"I will," I said, eager to move on from a digression that held no interest for me. "It could be argued that I broke the law when I put the silver sleigh into my shoulder bag. I should have reported the theft to the police immediately, but I didn't, and I don't intend to."

You intend to return the sleigh to the museum before anyone notices it's missing because you wish to keep Daisy from getting into trouble and because you're afraid Amanda Pickering will lose her job if her daughter's misdeed comes to light.

"I . . . uh . . . yes," I faltered. It was disconcerting to have Aunt Dimity describe my plan to me before I'd described it to

73

her. "That's what I intend to do. How did you know?"

I know you, my dear, and it's just the sort of noble, selfless, and completely wrongheaded thing you would do.

"How is it wrongheaded?" I demanded.

The answer is perfectly obvious, my dear. Daisy can't be allowed to wander through life taking things that don't belong to her. She must learn the difference between right and wrong and she must learn to take responsibility for her actions. You must, therefore, give her the opportunity to return the sleigh herself.

"I can't do that," I protested. "What if Miles Craven blames Amanda Pickering for the theft? What if he fires her? Daisy's father has already walked out on her, Dimity. What will happen to her if her mother can't find another job?"

If you insist on playing the "what if" game, why not take a more positive approach? What if Miles Craven isn't the ogre you imagine him to be? What if he knows Daisy better than you do? What if he's aware of her fascination with the sleigh and forgives her for taking it? What if he accepts some responsibility for the incident and guards his domain more securely from now on?

I began to sputter, but Aunt Dimity's

handwriting continued as if I hadn't made a sound.

You don't know how Miles Craven will react, Lori. You do know, however, that the sleigh must go back to the museum. After a moment's calm reflection, I'm sure you'll agree that Daisy must be the one to bring it back.

I stopped sputtering, clamped my lips together, and with great reluctance began to reconsider my position. Though I hated to admit it, Aunt Dimity had a point. If I'd found a mummified hand in Will's or Rob's pocket on Saturday afternoon, I would have marched the offender back to Skeaping Manor to make a confession, an apology, and an offer of restitution to Miles Craven. Why would I bend the rules for Daisy Pickering?

"She's a waif," I said helplessly. "She's a scrawny little waif dressed in cast-off clothing, yet she sees the world as a magical place filled with glittering people. I know she shouldn't have taken the sleigh, Dimity, but I can understand why she did."

Poverty is no excuse for crime, Lori. Your pity won't help Daisy to learn the lessons all children must learn if they are to become honest and trustworthy adults.

"All right," I said with a heavy sigh. "I'll find out where Daisy lives, go to her, and persuade her to make a clean breast of things."

If Amanda Pickering loses her job at the museum because of her daughter's mistake, you can always offer her a position at the charity shop.

"What a good idea," I said, feeling as though a weight had been lifted from my shoulders. "You're a genius, Dimity. I'll give Amanda a job if she needs one and I'll invite Daisy over to meet the boys. With her imagination, she'll fit right in."

And you'll have a chance to fatten her up.

"I'll do my best," I said.

You always do.

"I'll have to tell Bree what's going on," I continued. "I can't leave her to twiddle her thumbs while I deal with Daisy."

She may not wish to be involved.

"I'll leave the choice to her," I said, "but she doesn't strike me as much of a thumb-twiddler."

I agree.

"I won't tell her until after we take the boys to school," I said.

Very wise. Will and Rob have highly developed eavesdropping skills. Heaven knows what tales they'd tell their teacher if they overheard you. The handwriting paused for a moment before recommencing at a slower than usual pace. *Lori? I hope you don't think I'm being too hard on Daisy.*

"I don't," I said gently. "I think you have her best interests at heart. And I think I needed a refresher course in Parenting 101."

It would have come back to you eventually. But I'm always happy to help!

"I know you are," I said, smiling. "Good night, Dimity."

Good night, my dear. And good luck with Daisy.

I waited until the graceful lines of royal-blue ink had faded from the page, then closed the journal and returned it to its shelf. Reginald's black button eyes gleamed encouragingly as I curled up in the tall leather armchair and revised my scheme for the silver sleigh's return.

SEVEN

The cold snap snapped in the wee hours of Tuesday morning, when a warm front swept across the Midlands and sent Old Father Winter packing. Bree and I drove the boys to school through streams of rapidly melting snow and dropped them off in a playground flooded with puddles.

"Remind me to throw a few towels in the car when we get back to the cottage," I said resignedly as I pulled away from the curb. "And maybe a mop."

"Will do," said Bree. She hesitated, then said, "Uh, Lori? Where are we going?" She hooked a thumb over her shoulder. "Finch is that way."

"We're not going back to the cottage," I said. "We're going to Skeaping Manor. I would have told you sooner, but if the twins had caught wind of my plans, they would have wanted to skip school and come along with us."

"We're returning to the house of horrors?" said Bree, her eyebrows rising. "You astonish me for two reasons. One: You can't stand the place. And two: It's not open on Tuesdays."

"You're right on both counts, but neither one matters," I said. "I don't have to enter the museum to speak with Miles Craven —"

"Because he lives in a flat at the rear of the building," Bree finished for me. "Curiouser and curiouser. Am I allowed to know why you wish to speak with the creepy curator?"

"I'm afraid so," I said. I pulled into a convenient parking space, switched off the engine, and brought Bree into the circle of knowledge that surrounded the silver sleigh.

"So *that's* the big mystery," she said when I'd finished. "I wondered what it could be. You were so preoccupied yesterday and you asked so many strange questions at the charity shop . . ." She began to chuckle. "I thought one of the *twins* had pinched something from Skeaping Manor."

"I almost wish one of them had," I said. "I can discipline my own children, but when it comes to someone else's . . ."

"Not so easy," said Bree. "Do you have the trinket with you?"

I opened my shoulder bag and lifted the silver sleigh into the sunlight, where it glittered and gleamed as though it were studded with stars. Bree gazed at it in rapt silence for a long time before she finally found her voice.

"Daisy Pickering has good taste," she said. "It's a saltcellar, isn't it?"

"Trust you to know what a saltcellar is," I grumbled.

"Amazing," Bree murmured. "A troika saltcellar."

"A *what* saltcellar?" I asked.

"A troika," she said. "Your saltcellar is a troika."

"I believe you," I said, "but I don't know what a troika is."

"It's a Russian sleigh," Bree explained. "Troikas have been around for centuries. They're light, streamlined, and packed with horsepower." She pointed to the three prancing horses. "Just the ticket for racing along the rough, snow-packed roads of the old Russian Empire. Plain old workaday troikas were used to deliver express mail, but fancy ones were the playthings of aristocrats. Think sports car, not family sedan. People who owned fancy troikas, like people who own fancy sports cars, tended to be very well off. The saltcellar's original owner must have been stinking rich."

"Where did you learn about troikas?" I asked as I returned the silver sleigh to my bag.

"Takapuna Grammar," said Bree, referring to the school she'd attended in New Zealand. "Some of my classmates were from Russia. They liked to talk about their country and I liked to listen." She frowned slightly. "Are you sure Creepy Craven is still in the dark about the theft?"

"It wasn't mentioned in this morning's paper," I said, "and I read every line in every section, including the classifieds. Besides, the sleigh is one tiny artifact in the midst of ten thousand. Unless Miles Craven carries out a thorough inventory every day —"

"A shrunken-head count?" Bree put in. "Doubtful. If Florence Cheeseman is right about Craven, he's not the most conscientious curator in the world."

"Even if he were," I said, "the museum is so dark and over-crowded that it might take him years to notice one small empty space in one display case. Which means that we still have time to make an honest girl of Daisy. The trouble is, I don't know where she lives. Amanda Pickering isn't listed in the phone book, but Miles Craven should have her contact information on file."

"Have you tried ringing him?" Bree asked

"Yes," I said, "but I couldn't get through. His phone must be on the blink."

"Which explains our return to Skeaping Manor." Bree nodded. "Let's hope he's at home."

I gave her a sidelong look. "Are you sure you want to get mixed up in this? If not, I'll take you straight back to the cottage."

"Don't be silly," she said. "I'd much rather help a weird little kid than sit on my bum all day. Drive on!"

I heaved a sigh of relief when I pulled into the parking area at Skeaping Manor and spotted the same shiny red Fiat I'd noticed there on Saturday morning.

"It has to be Miles Craven's car," I said. "It was here the other day and it's the only car parked here now."

"We've struck lucky," said Bree. "Unless our curator likes to trudge through slush, he must be at home. Do you have a cover story, by the way? A good reason to ask for Amanda Pickering's address?"

"Of course I do," I said confidently. "Cover stories are my specialty."

"Then let's do this and get out of here," said Bree, climbing out of the Rover. "I want to meet Daisy."

We followed a slush-covered brick path to a door at the rear of the manor house, where an elegantly engraved brass plaque confirmed Florence Cheeseman's claim regarding the curious location of Miles Craven's residence. I rang the doorbell and stood back to survey the curator as he opened the door.

He was a sight to behold, swathed in a red velvet smoking jacket and a paisley cravat that billowed like a silken cloud from between his embroidered lapels. His brown trousers were immaculately creased and cuffed, his socks matched his smoking jacket, and his tasseled loafers were polished to a beautifully muted shine.

"My American friend," he said, smiling down at me. "What a pleasant surprise."

"I tried to call," I began.

"But you couldn't get through," he said with a sympathetic nod. "It's my fault, my fault entirely. While the rest of the human race accepts mobile phones as the norm, I cling stubbornly to my landline. I regret to say that our local service was disrupted this morning by a plague of icicles. Repairs are under way as we speak, but until they're completed, I must depend on my computer to connect me to the outside world." He shrugged. "One must make some concessions to modernity. Won't you come in?"

I didn't dare meet Bree's eyes as he ushered us through the doorway because one sidelong look from her would have sent me into a prolonged and embarrassing giggle fit. I hadn't met someone as entertaining as Miles Craven in years and I was delighted to see that his apartment was as flamboyant as he was.

The living room was a cheerful Edwardian mishmash of styles. The walls were hung with vintage art nouveau advertising posters featuring sinuous and scantily clad women, and the furniture ranged from a hefty Victorian armchair to a lighter-than-air neoclassical divan. In one corner, a wicker chair with a broad back and curled arms sat before a bamboo occasional table. The laptop computer on the bamboo table was the only visible concession to modernity.

Our host motioned for us to be seated on the divan, but he remained standing.

"I hope you'll overlook my louche garb," he said, bending to close the laptop. "I permit myself to dress informally when I work from home."

"So do I," I said, though my idea of informal attire — sweat pants and T-shirts — was a lot less formal than his. "My name is Lori Shepherd, by the way, and this is my friend, Bree Pym."

"A pleasure," he said, bowing to each of us in turn. "May I offer you a spot of tea?"

"No, thank you," I said. "We don't want to take up too much of your time. The fact of the matter is, I've come to ask a favor of you."

"How intriguing," he said. He smiled winsomely, sat in the wicker armchair, crossed his legs, and tented his long fingers over his smoking jacket. "Ask away, dear lady, ask away."

"I wonder if you might give me Amanda Pickering's address?" I said.

Miles Craven's smile vanished and his eyes flickered down to his fingertips before shifting between my face and Bree's.

"An unusual request," he observed.

An uncomfortable silence ensued. I took it as my cue to trot out my cover story.

"I have two young and very lively sons," I explained hastily, "so I don't have much time to spare for housekeeping. When I ran into Amanda on Saturday, she seemed like an ideal candidate: a hardworking young woman who —"

"Ah," he interrupted. "You need a char."

"It would only be for a few hours a week," I assured him. "I wouldn't dream of luring her away from the museum, but I thought, if she needed a little extra cash in the kitty, she might be willing to work for me on a part-time basis. I'd like to discuss the idea with her in person, but I couldn't find a listing for her in the telephone book." I peered at him entreatingly. "So I came to you."

"I wish I could oblige you, Mrs. Shepherd," he said, smoothing his cravat.

"Lori, please," I said, resisting the temptation to explain that, since I'd kept my own last name when I married Bill, I was Ms., not Mrs., Shepherd. "Everyone calls me Lori."

"I wish I could oblige you, Lori," he began again, plucking at his sleeve, "but the one thing you ask of me is the one thing I am unable to provide. My staff's personal information is private and confidential. I cannot in good conscience —" He broke off as the doorbell rang. "Dear me, I am popular today. Pray excuse me . . ." He rose from the wicker chair and left the room.

Bree promptly jumped to her feet, darted over to the bamboo table, opened the laptop, and began tapping away at the keys.

"What are you doing?" I whispered.

"Finding Amanda's address," she muttered.

"And I was worried about involving you in a slightly illegal scheme," I said, rolling my eyes. "You've taken lawbreaking to a whole new level."

"All in a good cause," Bree murmured. "Here it is. Payroll records. There's Les and Al, the useless security guards, and . . . here's Amanda." She scanned the screen, tapped a few more keys, closed the laptop, and flung herself onto the divan mere seconds before Miles Craven reentered the room.

"The telephone repairman requires access to the museum," he informed us. "Is there anything else I can help you with?"

"No," I said, getting to my feet. "I guess I'll just have to find another cleaner. Thank you very much for your time, Mr. Craven."

"Not at all," he said. "I'll show you out."

Our exit from the apartment was considerably more hurried than our entrance had been, but neither Bree nor I commented on it until we were seated in the Rover.

"Is it my imagination or did he seem eager to get rid of us?" I asked.

"It's not your imagination," Bree replied. "If you ask me, he's been up to no good with Amanda Pickering."

"He did react a bit oddly when I mentioned her," I agreed.

"A bit oddly?" Bree scoffed. "He was Mr. Charming Chatterbox until her name came up. Then he went all quiet and twitchy." She did a passable imitation of Miles Craven looking shifty-eyed while he smoothed his cravat and plucked at his sleeve.

"Okay," I conceded, "his reaction was more than a bit odd. He doesn't strike me as a womanizer, though. Quite the contrary."

"You can't judge a book by its cover," Bree reminded me.

"You can judge some things," I countered. "His clothes didn't come off a department store rack and his furniture must be worth a fortune. I judge, therefore, that he has expensive tastes, which means that the Jephcott Endowment must pay him a generous salary. Either that, or . . ." I gave Bree a meaningful glance.

"Or," she said, catching on, "he pays himself a generous salary without the endowment's knowledge." She peered at the dummy camera facing the parking lot. "It would explain why he hasn't installed a proper security system in the museum. He doesn't spend a lot on guards, either. Les and Al earn a pittance."

"Security systems and competent guards cost money," I said, "money a refined gentleman might prefer to spend on smoking jackets and period furniture." I gazed thoughtfully at the museum's main entrance. "I wonder if my donation went into the endowment's coffers or into Miles Craven's bank account?"

"Maybe Amanda knows where the donations go," Bree said. "Maybe that's why he wouldn't give us her address. He doesn't want us to talk to her because he's afraid she'll expose his little racket."

I looked at Bree and started to laugh.

"What's so funny?" she asked.

"If jumping to conclusions were an Olympic sport," I said, "we'd both be gold medalists. We've classified Miles Craven as a womanizing embezzler in under a minute. Must be a world record."

"I'm having second thoughts about his womanizing," said Bree, "but he must be up to something shady. Why else would your interest in Amanda make him nervous? Why else would he refuse to give us her address?"

"Maybe he just doesn't want me to poach his cleaning woman," I said reasonably. "Dependable cleaning women are rarer than troika saltcellars these days. If Amanda worked for me, I wouldn't want to share her." I put the key into the ignition. "All I know for sure is that Miles Craven didn't look, sound, or act like a worried curator. If you ask me, he still doesn't know that the silver sleigh is missing."

"No blunderbuss," said Bree, nodding.

"Not one shot fired over the parapet," I agreed. "I say we stop speculating about Miles Craven's theoretical foibles and start solving Daisy Pickering's very real dilemma."

"I concur," said Bree. "Next stop, 53 Addington Terrace."

"Oh, dear," I said, grimacing.

"Something wrong?"

"Let's put it this way," I said, starting the engine. "Upper Deeping has many lovely streets, but Addington Terrace isn't one of them."

EIGHT

When travelers dream of seeing the "real" England, they seldom have places like Addington Terrace in mind. The street was located in an enclave of low-rent housing that had been built in the 1950s and quickly forgotten. Everywhere Bree and I looked we saw signs of neglect and poverty: peeling paint, broken windows, overflowing trash cans, and multiple layers of graffiti. It hurt my heart to imagine Daisy living in such squalor, but it helped me to understand why Amanda took her daughter to work with her instead of leaving her at home.

The neighborhood's run-down row houses were set back from the street, behind small grassless gardens separated by waist-high cinder block walls. Fifty-three Addington Terrace looked every bit as decrepit as its neighbors.

"Reminds me of Takapuna," Bree said as we pulled up to the curb. "My hometown."

Her remark would have puzzled a native New Zealander, but I was familiar with Bree's background and knew exactly what she meant. Though Takapuna was an affluent community, Bree had been raised by a father who drank too much and worked too little. Their shabby apartment building had been a blot on an otherwise pristine landscape.

"Not all of Takapuna," she went on. "Just my part of it. I'm glad Daisy has a lively imagination. You need a good imagination when you live in a place like this. You need to believe that one day things will be better."

"They got better for you," I said encouragingly.

"Not everyone has a pair of great-grandaunts to see them right," said Bree. "I doubt *they* do."

She nodded at three ill-clad children playing in the garden next door. The dark-haired girl appeared to be the same age as Daisy, but the two boys looked a bit younger. The boys paid more attention to their soccer ball than they did to us, but the girl stood at the cinder block wall to watch us open Number 53's rickety gate and approach the front door.

"Hi," Bree said, lagging behind me to

speak to the girl. "I'm Bree Pym. What's your name?"

"Coral," said the girl. "Coral Bell." She tilted her head toward the boys. "Those are my brothers, Tom and Ben. Did you color your hair yourself?"

"I did," said Bree. "Like it?"

"Daisy has ginger hair, too," Coral said thoughtfully, "but hers is quiet. Yours is like a . . . like a shout."

"Just what I had in mind," said Bree. "Thanks."

"You're welcome," said Coral.

"I don't mean to pry," said Bree, "but shouldn't you and your brothers be in school?"

"The school nurse sent us home," Coral explained. "We're infectious. Mum had to take the day off work to look after us, but she couldn't stand the noise, so she sent us outside to play. She says the fresh air will do us good."

"What do you say?" Bree asked.

"I'm glad it's warmer today than it was yesterday," said Coral.

"Me, too," said Bree, smiling. She waved good-bye to the girl, then hastened to join me on the doorstep.

I'd already tried the doorbell several times without success, but three sharp raps on the door brought a harassed call of "I'm coming! I'm coming!" from within. A short time later the door was opened by a tall, angular woman in late middle age. She had short, wiry, gray hair, a long bony face, and a pair of brown eyes that held not one hint of softness. She was dressed in a buttoned-up gray cardigan, black trousers, and fluffy blue bedroom slippers. A half-smoked cigarette dangled from the corner of her mouth.

"Yes?" she said coldly.

"Good morning," I said. "My name is Lori Shepherd."

"And I'm Bree Pym," Bree piped up. She put out her hand. "How do you do, Mrs. . . . ?"

"MacTavish," the woman said in a clipped Scottish accent. Her eyes lingered on Bree's hair for a long moment before she deigned to shake Bree's hand. "Mrs. Eileen MacTavish. If you've come about the flat —"

"You rent apartments?" I said.

"I let one flat at the rear of the house, complete with kitchenette and en suite facilities," Mrs. MacTavish informed me haughtily. "Have done ever since Mr. MacTavish passed. Would you care to see it?"

"I'm sorry," said Bree, "but we haven't come about the flat."

"I didn't think you had." Mrs. MacTavish

looked past us to survey the Range Rover. "People who drive posh cars don't look for accommodations in Addington Terrace." She took a long drag on her cigarette and blew a stream of smoke into the air. "Why have you come, then? Is it your day to do charity work? Or are you writing a sensitive article about the deserving poor?"

"Neither," I said, ignoring the woman's sarcastic tone. "We'd like to speak with Amanda Pickering."

"Visiting nurses, are you?" asked Mrs. MacTavish. "Come to see little Daisy?"

"No," I said, faintly alarmed. "Why would Daisy need to see a nurse? She's not sick, is she?"

"She's always sick," Mrs. MacTavish replied. "Weak chest. Spends more time out of school than in it."

"Would you please tell Mrs. Pickering we're here?" Bree said, with ill-concealed impatience.

"You're too late," said Mrs. MacTavish. "She's gone, her and that queer little girl of hers. No warning, no two-weeks' notice, not even a note. Just packed their bags and left."

"When?" I said, taken aback. "When did they leave?"

"Yesterday," Mrs. MacTavish replied. "And don't ask me where they went because

95

I don't know." She eyed me s[...]
Mrs. Pickering work for you?"

"No," I said. "I do my own [...]
"How do you know her, the[...]
"I don't really know her," I [...]
met her at Skeaping Manor
morning and we had a brief
—"

"Did you?" Mrs. MacTavish[...]
surprised to hear it. Mrs. Pic[...]
one for conversation." She took[...]
on her cigarette and exhale[...]
cloud of smoke that engulfe[...]
head. "The woman lived here[...]
year, but I still don't know wh[...]
from or what happened to the [...]

"He walked out on them," I t[...]
ing that one tidbit of gossip w[...]
another.

"I thought so," said Mrs. Ma[...]
a satisfied nod. "But Mrs. Pic [...]
said. Too busy for idle chatter[...]
She worked all the hours God[...]
on Sundays, when she took [...]
Daisy on outings."

"She worked six days a week[...]
Manor?" Bree said. "No wo[...]
knows the place so well."

"Did I say she worked six da[...]
Skeaping Manor?" Mrs. Mact[...]

door brought a harassed call of "I'm coming! I'm coming!" from within. A short time later the door was opened by a tall, angular woman in late middle age. She had short, wiry, gray hair, a long bony face, and a pair of brown eyes that held not one hint of softness. She was dressed in a buttoned-up gray cardigan, black trousers, and fluffy blue bedroom slippers. A half-smoked cigarette dangled from the corner of her mouth.

"Yes?" she said coldly.

"Good morning," I said. "My name is Lori Shepherd."

"And I'm Bree Pym," Bree piped up. She put out her hand. "How do you do, Mrs. . . . ?"

"MacTavish," the woman said in a clipped Scottish accent. Her eyes lingered on Bree's hair for a long moment before she deigned to shake Bree's hand. "Mrs. Eileen Mac-Tavish. If you've come about the flat —"

"You rent apartments?" I said.

"I let one flat at the rear of the house, complete with kitchenette and en suite facilities," Mrs. MacTavish informed me haughtily. "Have done ever since Mr. Mac-Tavish passed. Would you care to see it?"

"I'm sorry," said Bree, "but we haven't come about the flat."

"I didn't think you had." Mrs. MacTavish

speak to the girl. "I'm Bree Pym. What's your name?"

"Coral," said the girl. "Coral Bell." She tilted her head toward the boys. "Those are my brothers, Tom and Ben. Did you color your hair yourself?"

"I did," said Bree. "Like it?"

"Daisy has ginger hair, too," Coral said thoughtfully, "but hers is quiet. Yours is like a . . . like a shout."

"Just what I had in mind," said Bree. "Thanks."

"You're welcome," said Coral.

"I don't mean to pry," said Bree, "but shouldn't you and your brothers be in school?"

"The school nurse sent us home," Coral explained. "We're infectious. Mum had to take the day off work to look after us, but she couldn't stand the noise, so she sent us outside to play. She says the fresh air will do us good."

"What do you say?" Bree asked.

"I'm glad it's warmer today than it was yesterday," said Coral.

"Me, too," said Bree, smiling. She waved good-bye to the girl, then hastened to join me on the doorstep.

I'd already tried the doorbell several times without success, but three sharp raps on the looked past us to survey the Range Rover. "People who drive posh cars don't look for accommodations in Addington Terrace." She took a long drag on her cigarette and blew a stream of smoke into the air. "Why have you come, then? Is it your day to do charity work? Or are you writing a sensitive article about the deserving poor?"

"Neither," I said, ignoring the woman's sarcastic tone. "We'd like to speak with Amanda Pickering."

"Visiting nurses, are you?" asked Mrs. MacTavish. "Come to see little Daisy?"

"No," I said, faintly alarmed. "Why would Daisy need to see a nurse? She's not sick, is she?"

"She's always sick," Mrs. MacTavish replied. "Weak chest. Spends more time out of school than in it."

"Would you please tell Mrs. Pickering we're here?" Bree said, with ill-concealed impatience.

"You're too late," said Mrs. MacTavish. "She's gone, her and that queer little girl of hers. No warning, no two-weeks' notice, not even a note. Just packed their bags and left."

"When?" I said, taken aback. "When did they leave?"

"Yesterday," Mrs. MacTavish replied. "And don't ask me where they went because

I don't know." She eyed me shrewdly. "Did Mrs. Pickering work for you?"

"No," I said. "I do my own housework."

"How do you know her, then?" she asked.

"I don't really know her," I admitted. "I met her at Skeaping Manor on Saturday morning and we had a brief conversation —"

"Did you?" Mrs. MacTavish cut in. "I'm surprised to hear it. Mrs. Pickering wasn't one for conversation." She took another pull on her cigarette and exhaled a noxious cloud of smoke that engulfed her whole head. "The woman lived here for nearly a year, but I still don't know where she came from or what happened to the girl's father."

"He walked out on them," I told her, hoping that one tidbit of gossip would lead to another.

"I thought so," said Mrs. MacTavish, with a satisfied nod. "But Mrs. Pickering never said. Too busy for idle chatter, I suppose. She worked all the hours God sent, except on Sundays, when she took her precious Daisy on outings."

"She worked six days a week at Skeaping Manor?" Bree said. "No wonder Daisy knows the place so well."

"Did I say she worked six days a week at Skeaping Manor?" Mrs. Mactavish asked tartly. "She worked there on Saturdays." She took a last pull on her cigarette and used it to light another before tossing the glowing butt into a slush puddle. "I know where she worked and when because she left contact numbers with me in case of emergencies." The landlady peered skyward as she recited, "Hayewood House — with an *e* in the middle, mind, to make it *extra* posh — Risingholme, Shangri-la, Tappan Hall, Mirfield, and Skeaping Manor. A different place each day of the week and nothing but the best for our Mrs. Pickering. She claimed to have a knack for polishing silver."

"Silver?" I said weakly.

"I didn't doubt her," Mrs. MacTavish went on, with a careless shrug. "She kept her rooms as neat as a pin, and as far as I know, she never lied to me. She didn't say very much at all. I had an earful from the women at Hayewood House and Risingholme today, though."

"About Mrs. Pickering?" I said.

"Who else?" Mrs. MacTavish snapped. "Apparently, Mrs. Pickering failed to show up for work yesterday and today. Didn't call in sick or give notice or anything. Simply didn't put in an appearance." The landlady sucked on her cigarette and let the smoke trickle through her nostrils. "I expect to hear from the rest of her employers once they realize she's left them in the lurch. They won't be too happy with her. All that lovely silver, tarnishing away." She looked down her bony nose at me. "I suppose you have a fine collection of silver."

"Too much work," I said. "I don't have Amanda's passion for polishing."

Mrs. MacTavish allowed herself a grudging chuckle.

"Is there anything else you can tell us about Mrs. Pickering?" Bree asked.

"How could there be?" she asked in return. "She never told me anything about herself."

"Thank you, Mrs. MacTavish," I said. "You've been very patient with us. We won't take up any more of your valuable time."

"Leaving already?" she said, raising an eyebrow. "I don't blame you. If I could afford to live somewhere else, I'd leave, too." Mrs. MacTavish hollered at Tom and Ben to keep the noise down, then retreated into her house and closed the door.

"Good grief," I said, turning to Bree. "Amanda's on the lam."

"For all we know she could still be in Upper Deeping," Bree protested. "She could have found a nicer flat with a nicer landlady in a nicer neighborhood."

"I doubt it," I said. "If Amanda is still in Upper Deeping, she would have gone to work as usual this week. At the very least, she would have telephoned her employers to request a day off. She wouldn't have taken an unannounced leave of absence, not if she expected to go on working for them."

"Maybe she found a better job," Bree suggested.

"Without a reference? Not in this day and age." I shook my head. "Amanda didn't move to another flat in Upper Deeping. She grabbed Daisy and vamoosed. And I think I know why." I walked a few steps away from the door, then stopped short, frowning in concentration as a fresh scenario took shape in my mind. "What if *Amanda*'s the thief? What if she's been pilfering silver from her multitudinous employers for nearly a year in order to get her and her child away from Addington Terrace?"

"If she has, she'll get no quarrel from me," said Bree. "Living in a place like that would make any child sick. Look at Coral. Look at Tom and Ben. Home from school because they're —"

"What if Daisy found out what her mother was up to?" I interrupted. "What if she saw Amanda take the silver sleigh from the display case on Saturday?" I wheeled around to face Bree. "What if Daisy decided to *take it back*?"

"Let me see if I have this straight," Bree said slowly. She held up one finger. "First, Amanda takes the sleigh from Skeaping Manor." She raised a second finger. "Then Daisy takes the sleigh from Amanda and tucks it into her pocket, intending to return it to Skeaping Manor, where it belongs."

"But the sleigh never reaches Skeaping Manor," I said excitedly, "because Amanda accidentally donates it, via the pink parka, to Aunt Dimity's Attic." I clapped a hand to my forehead. "Amanda must have been lightening her load for the great escape. That's why she took Daisy's old clothes to the charity shop."

"No," said a small urgent voice. "You've got it wrong. You've got it all wrong!"

We turned to see Coral Bell peering at us over the cinder block wall.

NINE

Bree and I exchanged bemused glances, then strode over to stand before Coral, who was clutching the cinder block wall as if her life depended on it.

"What have we gotten wrong?" Bree asked.

The girl bit her lip and ducked her head, as if overcome by shyness. Since Bree's direct approach seemed to intimidate her, I decided to take the long way round with my questions.

"Are you and Daisy Pickering good friends?" I asked.

"Best friends," Coral said in a voice so low it was barely audible. "She came to my house to get her hair cut. My mum works at the New You salon, but she did Daisy's hair for free."

"That was a very nice thing to do," I said, "and your mother is very good at her job. Daisy's hairstyle frames her face beautifully.

Did you and Daisy chat when she came to your house?"

Coral nodded, but said nothing.

"When I chat with my best friend," I said, "I like to share secrets. Did you and Daisy share secrets?"

Coral slowly raised her head. She scanned our faces anxiously, then said, "You're foreign. I can tell by the way you talk."

"You have a good ear for accents," I told her. "And you're right, neither Bree nor I are English. I'm from America."

"And I'm from New Zealand," said Bree.

"Not Russia?" said Coral.

I blinked and promptly lost my train of thought. Thankfully, Bree kept her cool and carried on as if it were perfectly natural for a little girl living in Addington Terrace to bring up the subject of Russia shortly after a priceless Russian artifact had been found in her best friend's pocket.

"No," said Bree, "we're not from Russia. Are you interested in Russia?"

"Yes," said Coral.

"It's an interesting place," said Bree. "What made you think we were from Russia?"

"Because you know about the silver sleigh and it's Mikhail's and he's from Russia, so I thought you might be, too," Coral said in a rush. "Honestly, Daisy didn't take the sleigh for herself. She meant to bring it to Mikhail. It's all he has left."

"Who's Mikhail?" I asked, bewildered.

"He's the lost prince," Coral answered.

"The lost prince?" I said uncertainly.

"The lost prince," Coral repeated, and the repetition seemed to free her tongue because she plunged on frantically. "He was driven from his kingdom by a band of wicked men who stole his castle and his horses and nearly everything he owned, but a faithful servant warned him of the brigands' swift approach and he had time to pack a few things in a bag before he fled. And he crossed the frozen rivers and he crept through frozen woods and he sailed over the ocean to a safe place far away, but an evil man betrayed him, threw him in a deep, dark dungeon, and took all his precious things and he's still there in the dungeon, without the least hope of escape." She gulped air, then raced on. "Daisy tried to rescue him, but he's too old to move fast, so she tried to fetch the sleigh for him instead." Coral took a long, shuddering breath and her dark eyes filled with tears. "And now it's all gone wrong. Daisy had to go away too soon. Mikhail will never see his silver sleigh again. And the lost prince will never be found."

The girl was gripping the edge of the cinder block wall so tightly I thought her hands would bleed. I didn't know what to make of her extraordinary recital, but I knew I had to calm her down before she injured herself.

"Did Daisy tell you about Mikhail and the silver sleigh?" I asked.

Coral nodded forlornly. "She told me over and over until I had it by heart. It was our biggest secret. But I don't know what to do, now she's gone."

"Do you know where she went?" Bree asked.

Coral shook her head and a trickle of tears spattered the wall.

"Don't worry, Coral," I said. "You don't have to do a thing. Bree and I will take the sleigh to Mikhail."

"We will?" said Bree, looking startled.

"Yes, we will," I muttered, stepping on her foot.

"Right," she said, wincing. "Leave it to us, Coral. Lori and I will make sure the sleigh gets to the prince."

Coral peered at us questioningly.

"Did Daisy give the sleigh to you?" she asked.

"I met Daisy at Skeaping Manor on Satur-

104

day," I told her, "and I found the sleigh in her pink parka yesterday. I work at Aunt Dimity's Attic — the charity shop on the square. Daisy's mother left the parka there without checking the pockets first."

"Oh," said Coral. It was the drawn-out "oh" of comprehension dawning.

I reached over to pry her hands gently from the wall. To my relief, they were frigid, but unscathed. Bree took a pair of green mittens from her jacket pocket and passed them to Coral. The girl looked at them in confusion, but when Bree nodded, she put them on.

"Keep them," said Bree. "I have lots more at home."

"I left mine at school," said Coral. "Thanks."

"No worries," said Bree nonchalantly.

"Will you really take the sleigh to Mikhail?" Coral asked, drying her damp face on her new mittens.

"We'd like to," I said, "but we don't know where Mikhail lives."

"He's in one of the big houses," Coral said eagerly. "One of the houses where Daisy's mum worked. Daisy never told me which one." She paused, bent closer to us, and murmured, "She said it would be dangerous for me to know."

"That's okay," I assured her. "Bree and I are pretty clever. We'll figure it out."

"And we're not afraid of anything," Bree chimed in.

Coral's entire body relaxed, as if she'd shed a terrible weight, but she stiffened again when her brothers ran up to the wall to stare at us.

"I'm Tom," the taller boy said. He elbowed his brother in the ribs and added, "He's Ben. Can we have a ride in your car?"

"Not without your mother's permission," I replied.

"Mum won't let us get in a car with strangers," Tom grumbled. "We're not supposed to talk to strangers, either. Has Coral been telling you stories?"

"We've been having a pleasant conversation with your sister," I replied.

"She's always making up stories," Tom scoffed. "Just like Crazy Daisy. None of it's real."

Tom punched Coral in the shoulder, clipped Ben behind the ear, and took off, with Ben hot on his heels, howling for revenge. A wrestling match was already under way when a young woman with bleached blond hair put her head out of an upstairs window and called for the children to come in.

The boys obeyed instantly, but Coral lingered long enough to defend her honor.

"It's *not* a story," she whispered fiercely. "The lost prince is *real.*"

"I wonder where Daisy is?" I mused aloud.

"Somewhere warm, I hope," said Bree.

Bree and I had stopped for lunch at the same café we'd patronized after our first visit to Skeaping Manor, but our conversation bore little resemblance to the one she'd had with Will and Rob that day. Instead of discussing bugs, bones, and blood, we spoke of two young girls and one fantastic tale.

"I'm glad you gave Coral your mittens," I said. "Her hands were like ice."

"I wanted to give her a new life," said Bree, "but I didn't have one in my pocket."

"I wouldn't worry too much about her," I advised. "If imagination is what you need to survive in a place like Addington Terrace, then Coral won't merely survive, she'll flourish."

"You don't believe her story?" said Bree.

"Do you?" I asked in return.

"I asked first," Bree rejoined.

"Well . . ." I took a long sip of tea before continuing, "I can understand why Coral would believe it. Daisy Pickering is . . . mesmerizing. I hardly breathed while she was spinning her tale at the museum. She would have no trouble casting a spell over Coral."

"So you think Daisy invented the story of the lost prince to entertain her friend?" said Bree.

"No," I said. "I think Daisy believes in the lost prince, too. The last thing Coral said to us reminded me of something Daisy said to me at Skeaping Manor. When I asked her if she'd learned about the saltcellar from Miles Craven, Daisy said, 'Mr. Craven just pretends. The dinners were *real*.' "

"What if they were?" Bree said boldly. "The sleigh was probably made to order for a family wealthy enough to hold extravagant dinner parties."

"Parties where ladies wore necklaces worth a king's ransom," I said as more of Daisy's monologue came back to me, "and gentlemen wore diamond studs in their stiff collars."

"That kind of thing, yes," said Bree. "You wouldn't find a silver troika saltcellar in a peasant's cottage. It's a quality piece made for quality people. It could even have been made for a Russian prince."

"How did Prince Mikhail get to England?" I asked.

"Like Coral said, he sailed over the

ocean." Bree paused to flutter her eyelashes at an elderly woman who was staring unabashedly at her from the next table.

"Love the color, dear," the woman said with a rueful smile. "But you have to be young to wear it."

"You're only as young as you feel," Bree responded. She winked at the woman and returned to the subject at hand. "My classmates at Takapuna Grammar told me hair-raising stories about Russian aristocrats who came to England after the Russian Revolution. Most of them were running for their lives. The Bolsheviks took a dim view of fat cats."

"The Bolshevik uprising took place in 1917," I pointed out. "If Mikhail was there when it happened, he'd be a hundred years old by now. It's not the sort of age you'd expect a man to attain while imprisoned in a dungeon."

"I'm not saying Coral's story is one hundred percent accurate," Bree temporized. "But it's not beyond the realms of possibility, is it?"

"Not quite," I said. I pushed my half-eaten quiche aside and rested my folded arms on the table. "That's the trouble. I can barely . . . sort of . . . almost . . . believe that Daisy met an old man in one of the houses Amanda Pickering cleaned, that the old man told her a sad tale about a stolen heirloom, and that she tried to retrieve it for him."

"I nominate Miles Craven as the thief," Bree said without a moment's hesitation. "We've already decided he's working some sort of fiddle at Skeaping Manor. He could be financing his expensive lifestyle by raiding the cupboards of defenseless old men."

"So we're adding elder abuse and cat burglary to his rap sheet," I said skeptically, "to go along with the embezzlement and the womanizing?"

"I'm willing to acquit him of the womanizing," Bree conceded.

"But he didn't use the silver sleigh to finance anything," I argued. "He didn't sell it on the black market or trade it in for a new smoking jacket. He displayed it in a public place. Even if Miles Craven is receiving stolen goods, he'd have to. be totally bonkers to exhibit them in his own museum. If they were recognized, his whole scam would unravel and he'd more than likely end up in jail."

"He is a bit eccentric," Bree offered feebly.

"Eccentric isn't the same as totally bonkers," I declared. "Sorry, Bree, but I don't think we can pin the theft of Mikhail's sleigh on Miles Craven."

"Mikhail's sleigh?" Bree gave me a sly, sidelong look. "It sounds as though you're beginning to fall for Coral's story."

"Maybe I am." I smiled sheepishly, but my smile faded quickly. "No matter how hard I try, I can't shake the image of a frail old man asking for a young girl's help. Call me gullible if you like, but I don't think I'll be able to rest until I find out for certain if the image is . . . *real.*"

"I must be gullible, too," said Bree, "because I'm as curious as you are to find out if Mikhail exists."

She pulled a pen from her pocket and began to scribble on her napkin.

"What are you doing?" I asked.

"I'm making a list of the houses Mrs. MacTavish mentioned," she replied. "Amanda Pickering's workplaces. We may have to visit them all."

"I can't believe you remember them all," I said, trying to read the list upside down. "The only one I remember is Skeaping Manor."

"I'm good at remembering things," said Bree. "I had to be, to get through Takapuna Grammar on a full scholarship." She finished writing and held the napkin out to me. "There you are."

111

I took the napkin from her and read the list of workplaces aloud, " 'Hayewood House, Risingholme, Shangri-la, Tappan Hall, Mirfield, Skeaping Manor.' Well done," I said, reaching across the table to pat her arm. "A house for every day of the week, except Sunday."

"How will we get inside to search for Mikhail?" Bree asked. "We can't very well knock on the front door and say, 'Good morning. Do you by any chance have a Russian prince locked in your cellar?' "

I turned the problem over in my mind, then slapped the table and laughed out loud as a solution came to me from an unexpected source.

"We'll take a leaf from dear old Mrs. MacTavish's book," I said, recalling the landlady's sneering comments about our reason for visiting Addington Terrace. "We'll be journalists writing a sensitive story about the rich."

"Brilliant," Bree exclaimed. "Rich people can't resist seeing their names in print. You really are good at coming up with cover stories."

"I've had a lot of practice," I admitted.

"So I've heard." Bree grinned, raised her teacup, and said, "To Daisy and her lost prince."

I tapped my cup against hers, but even as I repeated the toast I couldn't help wondering whether the scheme Bree and I were about to hatch was eccentric or just plain nuts.

TEN

I knew what Bill would say if I told him that Bree and I planned to disguise ourselves as journalists and scour the English countryside for a dungeon containing a Russian prince who'd been driven into exile by a marauding band of Bolsheviks.

So I didn't tell him.

I did, however, tell Aunt Dimity. Her reaction was much more sympathetic than Bill's would have been.

Well. You and Bree have had quite a day.

Stanley, the twins, and our house guest were asleep upstairs. I was in the study and the silver sleigh was sitting in Reginald's special niche on the bookshelves, where I'd placed it after everyone else had gone to bed. Reginald sat beside it, a soft silver gleam in his black button eyes.

I had no intention of leaving the tiny masterpiece in such a highly visible spot, but I needed to see it plainly while I spoke with Aunt Dimity. The sleigh was the only tangible evidence I had to tie what seemed like a fabulous fairy tale to something approximating the truth. I regarded it speculatively while the flames crackled in the hearth, the mantel clock chimed the midnight hour, and Aunt Dimity's elegant copperplate unfurled silently across the blue journal's blank pages.

It sounds as though you've set yourselves quite a tall task as well, but first things first: Is William feeling better?

"Sorry?" I said, dragging my gaze away from the sleigh and peering distractedly at the journal.

When last we spoke, your father-in-law was suffering from a severe head cold. Has his condition improved?

"He's over the worst of it," I said, "but Deirdre won't let him leave the house or receive visitors until Dr. Finisterre gives him the all-clear. If he's a good boy and does what he's told, she may allow him to attend church on Sunday." I chuckled. "I don't think William knew what he was getting into when he hired Deirdre as his housekeeper."

Deirdre may be a tyrant, but she's a sensible and good-hearted tyrant. William would be wise to heed her advice.

"I doubt he has much choice," I said.

"Deirdre's a lot stronger than he is, even when he isn't recuperating from an illness."

Any word on when Bill will return from Majorca?

"None," I replied. "He claims to have a dithering client, but I think he's just waiting to see if our warm spell will last until spring."

I'm sure he misses the boys and you as much as you and the boys miss him.

I snorted derisively.

What's happening at Emma's riding school? Has Derek repaired the damaged pipes?

"He decided to replace them," I said. "He and his crew finished digging up the old pipes yesterday and plan to connect the new ones tomorrow. The stables should be open for business by Friday."

Have you delivered the happy news to Will and Rob?

"Not yet," I said. "I don't want them to get their hopes up too soon. If the repairs are finished on time, I'll take them to the stables at the crack of dawn on Friday, so they can spend a couple of hours communing with Thunder and Storm before school."

They'll be tickled pink.

"They'll be over the moon," I agreed, "though having Bree around has *almost* made them forget how much they miss their

116

ponies."

Have the fumes in Bree's house dissipated?

"Not completely," I said. "She went home to crack a few windows after we got back from Upper Deeping, but she had to close them again before nightfall to keep her pipes from freezing. According to her, the place is still uninhabitable. I can't say I'm disappointed. She did me a huge favor when she threw herself on my mercy."

I suspect you are doing her an even bigger favor.

"What do you mean?" I asked.

Has it not occurred to you that Bree might get lonely, living in Ruth and Louise's big house all by herself?

I stared at Aunt Dimity's words, nonplussed.

"It never crossed my mind," I admitted. "She's so independent, so upbeat . . ."

She's also a teen-ager and she's a long way from home. It wouldn't surprise me in the least to learn that her house is perfectly habitable, but that she prefers to stay with you regardless. I imagine she finds the bustle of family life both refreshing and stimulating after the silence and the solitude of her own home.

"She's fantastic with Will and Rob," I acknowledged. "And they're crazy about her."

I'd venture to say that she values your company as much if not more than she values the boys'. You're the only person in the Northern Hemisphere who saw firsthand what her life was like in New Zealand. You may be the only person in the world with whom she can discuss the bad old days.

"She alluded to her old life several times today," I said thoughtfully. "Fifty-three Addington Terrace seemed to remind her of the dump her father rented in Takapuna. I don't think she's mentioned it since we left New Zealand."

If she does so again, be a good listener. Even the freest spirits need to lean on a friendly shoulder from time to time.

"She can lean on mine for as long as she likes," I said. "Anyone who talks back to Peggy Taxman is aces in my book."

Mine, too. Now, about your remarkable day . . . I find it astonishing that neither Mrs. MacTavish nor Coral Bell know where Amanda and Daisy Pickering went. I would have expected Amanda to leave a forwarding address with her landlady, and Daisy to confide in her best friend.

"It's strange, all right," I said, nodding. "They took off without a word to anyone. I'd like to know why they left so abruptly."

I'm not convinced that Amanda's departure

118

was as precipitous as Mrs. MacTavish seems to think it was. Some planning must have gone into it. If it had been a spur-of-the moment decision, Amanda wouldn't have taken Daisy's old clothes to the charity shop. She would have dropped them into a handy rubbish bin on her way out of town.

"If Amanda knew in advance that she'd be leaving Upper Deeping," I countered, "why didn't she notify her employers?"

I don't know. Aunt Dimity's handwriting paused briefly, then continued. There's quite a lot we don't know about Amanda Pickering. We don't know where she came from, for example, and we don't know where she went. She appears to be a woman of mystery.

"A trait she passed on to her daughter," I said, with a wry smile. "I hope Daisy isn't tying herself into knots over the silver sleigh. She must have been seriously rattled when she realized that it had gone astray. If I knew how to contact her, I'd tell her not to fret. As it is, there's not much I can do to ease her mind."

It seems I may have been mistaken about Daisy's motivation for removing the sleigh from Skeaping Manor. If it was stolen in the first place, she can hardly be blamed for making an effort to restore it to its rightful owner.

"Do you believe Mikhail is the rightful

owner?" I asked.

As Bree observed, it's not beyond the realm of possibility. Her comments regarding Russian émigrés are, by and large, correct. A number of dispossessed landowners sought sanctuary in England during and after the Bolshevik revolution. Some came with nothing but the clothes on their backs. Others managed to salvage a few mementos. A handful arrived in style and continued to live much as they had in the old country, minus the serfs, of course. I would, by the way, hesitate to characterize the Bolsheviks simply as "wicked men." Their methods may have been deplorable and their goals debatable, but they were attempting to restore balance to a society that had become distressingly top-heavy.

"It was a turbulent time," I said. "But even if Mikhail survived the 1917 revolution and somehow made it to England, he'd be dead by now, wouldn't he?"

A second wave of Russian immigrants arrived in England during the Second World War, before the Iron Curtain was raised. Many were Russian nationalists who'd fought a losing battle to restore their country's prerevolutionary way of life. If Mikhail came to England at that time he could still be alive, though he would be a very old man indeed.

"Did you know many Russian émigrés?" I

asked. "Did any of them live near Upper Deeping?"

Members of the Russian émigré community tended to keep themselves to themselves, Lori. A number of them were involved in plots to overthrow the Soviet government. Naturally, secrecy was their byword. Even those who avoided such entanglements were bound together by ties of language, religion, and culture. The few I met at social functions lived exclusively in London. If a Russian family lived near Upper Deeping in my lifetime, I was unaware of it.

"Daisy hasn't left us an easy puzzle to solve," I said with a heavy sigh.

Easy problems are hardly worth solving. Where does your investigation stand at the moment?

"Bree used Bill's desktop to find out everything she could about Amanda's employers," I said.

Clever girl. What did she discover?

"Mrs. MacTavish was telling the truth when she said 'nothing but the best' would do for Amanda," I replied. "Daisy's mother polished silver in some pretty impressive country houses."

There are some fine estates not far from Upper Deeping.

"The owners like their privacy," I said,

"because Bree couldn't find out much about them apart from their names and addresses. The addresses helped her map out the route we'll take tomorrow and the names helped her choose which house we'll visit first."

Which house would that be?

"Hayewood House," I said triumphantly, "because Hayewood House just happens to be owned by a couple named Madeleine and Sergei Sturgess."

Sergei is a Russian name, I'll grant you, but Sturgess couldn't possibly be more English.

"It's the closest thing we have to a lead," I grumbled. "Don't spoil it."

Sorry.

"Sergei is the only Russian name Bree came across," I went on. "The rest don't even come close. And she didn't find a single Mikhail."

Mikhail might be a former employee rather than a homeowner. As I explained earlier, some Russian émigrés came to England with few possessions. They would not have had the wherewithal to purchase small houses, let alone large estates. Mikhail might have become a cook or a gardener or an odd-job man for a well-to-do family. His employers might have allowed him to continue to live on the property after his retirement. If so, his name wouldn't necessarily be listed with the home-owners'.

"I hadn't thought of that," I said, "but now that you mention it, it makes all kinds of sense. As a charwoman's daughter, Daisy would be much more likely to meet up with a retired gardener than with the head of the house."

Which means that you and Bree mustn't limit your search to the big houses. If there are smaller dwellings on the grounds, you'll have to search them as well.

A smile crept over my face as I recalled Bree's unsanctioned use of Miles Craven's laptop. If she deemed it necessary to poke around in a cottage or two during our quest for the lost prince, I was fairly sure she'd do so, with or without the landowner's permission.

"We'll manage," I said breezily. "Bree and I are nothing if not resourceful." I gazed into the fire for a moment, then shook my head. "Imagine a prince reduced to living in a cottage on someone else's property. A cottage might very well seem like a dungeon to a prince."

I confess that I find Mikhail's title perplexing. There were no princes in the Russian Empire. The heir apparent to the throne was known as the tsarevitch.

"Mikhail probably thought 'tsarevitch' was too much of a mouthful for a little girl," I said. "You have to admit that Prince Mikhail is easier to say than Tsarevitch Mikhail."

But that's my point. There was no tsarevitch named Mikhail. The last tsarevitch was Alexei Nikolayevich, the only son of Czar Nicholas II. Sadly, young Alexei was summarily and brutally executed with the rest of the Russian imperial family in 1918.

"Turbulent times," I murmured, shuddering.

I suppose Mikhail could have invented his royal title to impress Daisy. Either that, or he belongs to a lesser dynasty. The Russian Empire was a patchwork of minor principalities. Mikhail might be a prince in name if not in power.

"If I find him, I'll ask him," I said. "In the meantime, I'd better get some shut-eye. Bree and I plan to tackle Hayewood House right after the school run tomorrow."

I like the thought of you and Bree riding to Mikhail's rescue.

"In a canary-yellow Range Rover," I said, smiling. "It does make for a memorable image."

What I mean to say is: I'd like nothing better than to be proven wrong about Daisy Picker-

ing. Find the lost prince, Lori. Prove me wrong.

As the curving lines of royal-blue ink faded from the page, I lifted my gaze to the silver sleigh and tried to imagine the kind of life the lost prince had left behind.

"If you exist, Mikhail, I'll find you," I said under my breath. "I can't let Daisy *or* Aunt Dimity down."

Eleven

While Will and Rob were getting dressed for school on Wednesday morning, Bree burst into the kitchen bearing a shoe box filled with what she called our "journalist essentials." These included two mini tape recorders, two digital cameras, two small spiral notebooks, and an assortment of ballpoint pens. I didn't recognize a single item.

"Where did you find this stuff?" I asked as she tipped the box's contents onto the kitchen table.

"I brought it from home after I closed my windows last night." She struck a pose, hand on hip, head thrown back dramatically. "Please note that I'm wearing professional attire as well: posh blouse and trousers instead of jumper and jeans." She gave my sweater and jeans a haughty glance and wagged a finger at me. "I recommend that you smarten yourself up before we leave, madam. First impressions, you know."

I wondered what impression her flaming red hair and her nose ring would make on Madeleine and Sergei Sturgess, but kept my thoughts to myself.

"One more thing," said Bree. She reached into the neat black purse she'd tucked under her arm and produced a business card. "While I was at home, I ran up a few of these on my computer. If anyone wants to know where we work, we pull one out and say —"

"Country House Monthly," I broke in, reading aloud the words printed in bold type on the fake business card. "We work for *Country House Monthly* magazine? Never heard of it."

"That's because I made it up," she said. "I settled on *Country House Monthly* because it's generic enough to be believable. It sounds like all of those slick, dull magazines designed to make the landed gentry feel good about themselves."

"But you put your real name and address on the card," I said in dismay. "Is that wise?"

"I may be a fraud," said Bree, "but I'm an honest fraud." She swept her share of journalist essentials into the black purse and snapped it shut. "Who knows? I may write an article based on our experiences and submit it to a real magazine one day. For now, though, let's use the cards only if we have to."

"Agreed." I heard the thunder of little feet on the stairs, stuffed the rest of the journalist essentials into my pockets, and pointed imperiously toward the pot of porridge bubbling on the stove. "You're in charge of breakfast, ace reporter. I have to smarten myself up."

Before we left the cottage, Bree refined her disguise by donning a crisply tailored black trench coat. I followed her example and slipped into my old beige trench coat, wishing I had a fedora to complete the look. Instead, I pulled on a rather fetching brown velvet beret I'd picked up for a song at a church jumble sale. Though the sun smiled down on us as we herded the boys into the Rover, it wasn't quite warm enough yet to go outside bareheaded.

"Why are you dressed as spies?" Will asked as he climbed into the backseat.

"Because it's fun," said Bree, which was a much better answer than any I had in mind.

"Can we play spies after school?" Rob asked.

"Absolutely," said Bree. "I'll show you how to write in invisible ink."

"Cool," the boys chorused.

It took us twenty minutes to drive to Morningside School and another forty to drive from there to Hayewood House. Thanks to Bree's route map and her peerless navigational skills, we didn't take a single wrong turn, despite the fact that we were traveling in unfamiliar territory.

Hayewood House sat at the end of a long, graveled drive lined with cypress trees that effectively blocked our view of the grounds. The house was nearly twice as big as my father-in-law's Georgian residence, but it was built in the same style and of the same material — a golden-hued limestone commonly found in our part of the Cotswolds.

The gardens flanking the house looked as soggy and unkempt as gardens usually do in February, but the building itself appeared to be in excellent repair. The tall windows sparkled in the morning sun and there wasn't a chipped balustrade or a cracked roof tile in sight.

I parked the Rover at the bottom of a short flight of steps that led to the front door, clambered out of the driver's seat, and took a deep breath of fresh country air.

"It's lovely, isn't it?" I said, surveying the house with an approving eye.

"Nothing but the best for our Mrs. Pickering," Bree said, mimicking Mrs. MacTavish's Scottish brogue. "It makes a nice change from Addington Terrace. I'd give Hayewood two *e*'s in the middle, for being extra, extra posh."

"So would I," I said. "Ready?"

"For anything," she replied with the brashness of youth. "Let's go!"

As we climbed the stairs, I prepared an introductory speech that would, I hoped, gain us access to Hayewood House, but I needn't have bothered. Our shoes had barely skimmed the top step when a woman flung open the front door and stood beaming at us as if we were her oldest, dearest friends.

"Welcome to Hayewood," she said. "I'm so glad you're here. Won't you come in?"

I was too taken aback to move, but Bree seized my wrist and dragged me with her as she surged past the woman into a light and airy entrance hall.

"I'm Madeleine Sturgess," said the woman, following us inside, "and I'm delighted to meet you at last. I hope you'll treat my home as yours during your stay."

Madeleine Sturgess was a classic English beauty, tall, slender, and blue-eyed, with a peaches and cream complexion and silky blond hair wound into an exquisitely coifed French roll. She wore an attractive full-skirted dress, low-heeled pumps, and the merest hint of makeup. I thought she might be in her early forties.

"You've arrived a tiny bit earlier than I expected," she continued, closing the door, "but never mind. Your rooms are as ready as they'll ever be." She paused with her hand on the doorknob and an almost comical look of consternation on her face. "I should fetch your bags, shouldn't I? Shall I go now or would you prefer to see your rooms first?"

"I'm afraid there's been a small misunderstanding, Mrs. Sturgess," said Bree, taking command of the situation. "My name is Bree Pym, my colleague is Lori Shepherd, and we're not guests. We're journalists."

"Have you come to do a story about Hayewood House? How thrilling!" Madeleine released the doorknob and her beaming smile returned. "Bunny Fordyce-Triggs said you might turn up without warning. Give me your coats and come through to the drawing room. I'll ring for tea. And please do call me Maddie. 'Mrs. Sturgess' is far too formal for a cozy tête-à-tête."

In what seemed like the blink of an eye, Bree and I found ourselves seated side by side on a high-backed mahogany settee across from Madeleine, who sat on the very edge of a Hepplewhite armchair, talking a mile a minute, while we pulled out our pens and notebooks and tried to act as though we knew what we were doing.

"I should have guessed that you weren't the Graham sisters from Dundee," she said. "The Graham sisters aren't due to arrive until supper time, but Bunny says guests tend to show up when you least expect them, so I thought you might be they. Have you interviewed Bunny?"

"No," I said, feeling a bit shell-shocked.

"Oh, you should," she said earnestly. "She's been in the business for years and she'd love the publicity."

"How would you describe your business, Maddie?" Bree asked, her pen poised over her notebook.

"Hayewood House is an exclusive, high-end guesthouse," Madeleine informed us. "Bunny's was so successful that my husband and I decided to take the plunge ourselves. Well, it was my idea more than his, really. My husband works in London during the week, you see, and comes home only on weekends. With him gone and the children grown and flown, I have rather too much time on my hands, so I thought I'd try running my own business."

"How enterprising of you," I said.

"I'm not doing it just to fill time," Madeleine said earnestly. "Hayewood House costs the earth to maintain, so we could do with the extra income." She waved a hand in the air to indicate the room in general. "Nothing's ready-made, you see. Everything has to be handcrafted — doors, window-panes, floorboards, absolutely everything. As you can imagine, it adds up."

"So you decided to take in paying guests," I ventured, "to help pay for the house's upkeep?"

"It was a secondary consideration," said Madeleine, "but a consideration nonetheless. The place seemed rather empty with the children gone, so I thought, why not put it to good use? We have seven bedrooms and nearly as many bathrooms and my husband and I can hardly use them all."

"Have you been in the B and B business for very long, Maddie?" Bree asked.

A rosy blush tinted Madeleine's cheeks.

"To tell you the absolute truth," she said, "we haven't started yet. If you'd been the Graham sisters, you would have been our first paying guests. We rather hoped word of mouth would bring the right sort of people to our door, but so far it hasn't brought anyone but the Grahams. Bunny told them about us when she was visiting friends in

Dundee last August."

"Have you considered creating a website?" Bree asked delicately, as if she wished to give our hostess a hint about how to run a business.

"A website would be a great help, of course," Madeleine acknowledged, "but my husband has been terribly busy at work lately and I'm no good at all with computers, so we haven't got round to setting one up."

"How long has your family lived at Haye-wood?" I asked.

"Let's see . . ." Madeleine tapped an index finger against her pursed lips, then said in an amazed tone, "Gosh! It'll be twenty-five years next December. How time flies when one's raising a family!"

A gray-haired woman in a maid's uniform entered the drawing room and deposited a heavily laden tea tray on the satinwood table at Madeleine's elbow.

"Will there be anything else, Mad— er, madam?" the maid asked.

"No, thank you, Ernestine," said Maddie.

"Look, Lori," said Bree, pointing to the plate of dainties Ernestine had brought with the tea. "Pecan balls."

"I beg your pardon?" said Madeleine.

Bree looked at Ernestine.

"Those round biscuits covered with icing sugar," she said. "They're pecan balls, aren't they?"

"No, ma'am," the maid answered. "No pecans in them. They're made with hazelnuts and Cook calls them Russian tea cakes."

"Russian tea cakes?" I said. "Is your cook Russian?"

Ernestine and Madeleine exchanged amused glances.

"Goodness, no, ma'am," said Ernestine. "Cook was born and raised not ten miles from here. She got the recipe for the Russian tea cakes from the receipt book."

"What's a receipt book?" Bree asked.

"It's a book cooks keep," Ernestine told her. "They write recipes in it and hand it on to the next cook."

"Who wrote the Russian tea cake recipe in Cook's receipt book?" I asked.

"No idea, ma'am," said Ernestine. "Our book goes a long way back, you see. Some of the recipes in it are more than a hundred years old." She turned to Madeleine. "Will that be all, madam? Only, I promised Cook I'd help her prep for supper."

"Yes, that will be all, thank you," said Madeleine.

The maid curtseyed and left the room.

"Ernestine is a treasure," said Madeleine, turning to gaze soulfully at the door through which the maid had exited. "I don't know what I'd do without her."

"As a matter of interest," I said, "did a Russian family ever own Hayewood House?"

"No," Madeleine replied. "Hayewood House was the country seat of the Haye-wood family for three hundred years until Sergei and I bought it."

"Sergei," I said, taking the bull by the horns. "It's an interesting name. Is your husband Russian?"

"We do seem to have a theme going, don't we?" Madeleine said, nodding at the tea cakes. "But, no, my husband isn't Russian. His mother was mad for the Russian ballet, so she named her three sons Sergei, Vaslav, and Rudolf, after Sergei Diaghilev, Vaslav Nijinsky, and Rudolf Nureyev." She rolled her eyes. "You can imagine how well that went over with their schoolmates."

Bree and I chuckled politely, and though I felt a tiny stab of disappointment, I pressed on.

"Do you have a full indoor and outdoor staff?" I asked. "Any retired retainers on the premises?"

"Retired retainers?" Madeleine exclaimed,

smiling. "No one has retired retainers anymore. Ernestine is our only full-time employee, and she has an apartment here in the house. The dailies come in from the surrounding villages or from Upper Deeping. I can't think of anyone who has a full complement of live-in staff, apart from the royal family, of course. For the rest of us, the world of *Upstairs, Downstairs* is long gone. People are happier in their own homes nowadays than they would be in servants' quarters." She placed her empty teacup on the tray. "When you've finished, I'll be happy to show you the guest rooms."

"We'd like to see the cellars," Bree said firmly.

"The cellars?" Madeleine's brow wrinkled briefly, then smoothed. "Looking for signs of vermin. I understand. I can assure you that Hayewood House is completely pest-free, but of course you can't take my word for it. The cellars shall be our first port of call."

Bree and I finished our tea as quickly as we could without actually slurping it and jumped up to trail behind Madeleine as she gave us the grand tour. The cellars were both immaculate and devoid of captives, as were the attics, the guest rooms, the reception rooms, and the rest of the rooms Bree decided to "inspect." While I took random photographs, Bree took full and shameless advantage of Madeleine's eagerness to please by peering into every wardrobe, cupboard, trunk, and storage space we passed, but she didn't discover a bound and gagged Russian prince in any of them.

Still Bree soldiered on, invading the kitchen for a peek at the receipt book. If she hoped to find Cyrillic writing in it, she was disappointed. The Russian tea cake recipe was unsigned, undated, and written in plain English.

By the time we returned to our seats in the drawing room it was midday. I was hungry, tired, footsore, and ready to leave, but Bree was still fresh as a daisy.

"Do you offer your customers guest cottages as well as guest rooms, Maddie?" she inquired craftily.

Madeleine's face fell. "We don't have guest cottages, I'm afraid. There was a row of workmen's cottages on the property, but according to our tenant, one was hit by a stray bomb during the war and the others were demolished after the war. Will it count against us, do you think? I realize that people enjoy staying in cottages, of course, but I rather thought staying in the main house would have its own special appeal.

Bunny says it gives common folk a chance to live like Lord and Lady Muck." She began to laugh, caught herself, and blushed charmingly. "I hope you won't quote Bunny in your story. She meant it as a joke, but it might come across as . . . condescending. She'd be furious with me for talking out of turn."

"We'll pretend we didn't hear it," Bree assured her. "We would like to hear more about your tenant, though."

"To be exact, we have two tenants," said Madeleine, clearly welcoming the change of subject, "a married couple, but they live in a converted barn a half mile east of the main house, so neither they nor our guests will be inconvenienced."

"How long have they lived in your barn?" asked Bree.

"Goodness knows," Madeleine replied. "They've been here longer than we have. They came along with the house, so to speak, but they're so quiet and retiring we sometimes forget they're around."

"They sound like the perfect tenants," I said, and made a mental note to "inspect" the converted barn before we left.

"Do you mind if I ask how you heard about Hayewood House?" said Madeleine.

"Not at all," I answered. "My colleague

and I were inspired to come here by a conversation I had with a woman named Amanda Pickering."

My just-about-truthful reply seemed to strike Madeleine like a thunderbolt.

"When did you speak with Amanda?" she asked, wide-eyed.

"On Saturday," I said.

"Astonishing," said Madeleine, shaking her head. "I don't know if you're aware of it, but Amanda Pickering and her daughter have disappeared without a trace. She was supposed to work here on Monday, but she didn't show up. When I rang her landlady — a thoroughly disagreeable woman, by the way, with a voice like a cheese grater . . ." Madeleine frowned at the recollection, then went on. "At any rate, the landlady told me that Mrs. Pickering had cleared out her flat on Sunday and left for parts unknown. Do you know where she's gone?"

"I'm sorry, but I don't," I said. "She's not a close friend. I met her only once, at Skeaping Manor."

"That horrible place." Madeleine wrinkled her nose in distaste. "I'll never understand how Amanda could take her daughter there. It seems like an unhealthy environment for a girl Daisy's age."

"Did Amanda bring her daughter to Hayewood House as well?" Bree asked.

"Yes," Madeleine replied. "Daisy has respiratory problems that keep her away from school fairly often and Amanda doesn't like to leave her at home with no one but the appalling landlady to look after her. Daisy's such a well-behaved little thing that I didn't mind having her around. To tell you the truth, I didn't see much of her. She spent most of her time in the converted barn, visiting our tenants."

I felt Bree twitch beside me, like a hound scenting a hare, and decided it was time to move on. We'd plumbed Hayewood House's depths and come up empty, but the converted barn seemed to offer us a fresh line of inquiry, so I dropped my camera into my shoulder bag and got to my feet.

"Thank you for your cooperation, Maddie," I said. "You've been a delightful hostess and an incredibly patient guide. I believe we have all the material we need."

"We'll let you know when the story comes out," Bree added, rising.

"Where will it be published?" Madeleine inquired as she escorted us to the entrance hall. "I meant to ask earlier, but it completely slipped my mind."

"We're freelancers," I said before Bree could open her mouth. "We're not sure where our story will appear, but I can tell you right now that you deserve a rave review. Hayewood House has everything anyone could desire in an exclusive, high-end B and B."

"You're too kind," said Madeleine, beaming.

She retrieved our coats and walked with us to the front door.

"Would it be all right with you if we took a turn around the grounds, Maddie?" Bree asked. "We'd like to take pictures of the house from different angles."

"I'll come with you, if you like," Madeleine offered.

"We wouldn't dream of taking up any more of your valuable time," I said. "Thanks again, Maddie. I'm sure the Graham sisters from Dundee will love every minute of their stay here."

"If you run into Amanda again," Madeleine said as she opened the door, "would you please ask her to send me a forwarding address? I don't know what to do with her last paycheck."

"If I run into her, I'll tell her," I said. "Good-bye, Maddie. I wish you the best of luck with your new venture."

Bree and I shook hands with Madeleine and trotted down the stairs. She paused on the threshold to wave to us before closing the door.

"What a twit!" Bree exploded as we strode away from the house in an easterly direction. "She didn't even ask to see our business cards. Can you imagine letting two reporters — reporters with *foreign accents,* no less — snoop around your house without asking them for some form of identification?"

"I wouldn't let a reporter snoop around my house, period," I said, "but I wouldn't call Madeleine Sturgess a twit. She was a little overexcited, that's all. It was her first day on the job and there she was, faced with a golden opportunity to get some free publicity."

"It's better than no publicity," Bree scoffed. "How could she even consider breaking into the hospitality industry without a website?"

"She's new to the game," I said. "She'll figure it out."

"Why did you tell her we were freelancers?" Bree demanded. "We work for *Country House Monthly,* don't we?"

I came to a halt and gave Bree a look that stopped her in her tracks.

"Madeleine Sturgess is a nice woman," I said sternly. "She may not be the canniest businesswoman on the planet, but she's the sort of woman who worries about sending a paycheck to an employee who left her in the lurch. I won't have her wasting her time searching the local newsstands for a magazine you invented."

"Right," said Bree, looking chastened. "Sorry."

"No worries," I said and walked on.

"So much for our Russian connection, eh?" Bree said as she caught up with me. "The Russian tea cakes weren't made for a Russian family because a Russian family never owned Haywood House. And Sergei Sturgess is as Russian as I am."

"I'm holding out hopes for the tenants," I told her.

"Me, too," she said. "If Daisy spent time with them, she might have told them about Mikhail."

"Or they might be hiding him." With those words I forgot about my fatigue, my sore feet, and my grumbling tummy and hurried forward, muttering, "C'mon, Bree. Let's find the converted barn."

TWELVE

Bree and I soon stumbled upon a dirt road leading east from Hayewood House. Snow-melt had turned much of the dirt into mud and the mud bore the imprint of fresh tire tracks.

"I hope Maddie's tenants haven't gone out for the day," I said as we picked our way along the road's less muddy margins.

"If they have," said Bree, "you can keep a lookout while I slip inside for a shufti."

"How will you get inside?" I asked. "Did you bring a set of picklocks with you?"

"People who live in the country don't lock their doors," she said authoritatively.

I couldn't argue with her — my doors were never locked — but it seemed like an opportune moment to remind my young friend of the difference between resourcefulness and criminality.

"Even if you enter a house through an

unlocked door," I said, "it's still trespassing."

"With the best of intentions," Bree retorted. "You're the one who came up with the haunting image of a frail old man begging for help. Do you want to help Mikhail or not?"

"Let's see what we find when we get there," I counseled.

What we found when we got there was a building lofty enough to hold a winter's worth of grain, though signs of its conversion were everywhere. Six skylights had been set into its slate roof, a dozen or more windows inserted in its rough stone walls, and the square gap through which farm carts had once rolled had been filled with a sliding door made of galvanized steel.

Smoke rising from the chimney suggested that someone was at home.

"Disappointed?" I said, nodding at the smoke.

"A little," Bree admitted. "I've always wanted to risk arrest for a worthy cause. Can we at least scope out the place before we announce our presence?"

"Lead the way," I said. Circumnavigating the converted barn might be less daring than breaking and entering, but it was also less likely to land us in jail.

We looked through each window we passed as we crept stealthily around the side of the building, but since the windows we passed were curtained, we couldn't see very much. We could, however, see into the large solarium protruding from the barn's rear wall. A tall, rawboned woman stood before an easel in the glass-enclosed room, paint-brush in hand. She was older than Madeleine Sturgess. Her short, dark hair was shot through with gray and her face was beautifully lined. She wore an oversized white shirt, liberally spattered with paint, and a pair of khaki trousers.

Since we were silent, motionless, and half hidden by a leafless shrub, Bree's red hair must have caught the woman's eye because she looked up from her canvas suddenly, squinted in our direction, and signaled for us to meet her at the solarium's back door.

"Have you lost yourselves?" she asked when we arrived. She had soft gray eyes and an extremely pleasant voice.

"No," said Bree. "We're journalists. We were up at the big house, interviewing Madeleine Sturgess, and we thought we might have a word with you as well."

"About what?" she asked.

"About living in a converted barn," I said on the spur of the moment. "We're sure our readers would love to hear about your home, Mrs . . . um . . ."

"Wylton," she said. "Frances Wylton, but Frances will do."

"Lori Shepherd," I said in turn and when Bree remained unaccountably mute I added, "and Bree Pym."

"Come in," said Frances.

She led us through the solarium and into an open-plan great room with a kitchen at one end, a sitting room at the other, and a dining area in between. An intricate web of elm beams supported the roof, a thick layer of whitewashed plaster concealed the stone walls, and a spiral staircase beside the front door led to a high-ceilinged loft that might once have been used to store hay bales.

The furniture was old, solid, and comfortable looking. Overstuffed chairs and sofas clustered companionably around a wood-burning stove at the far end of the great room and a large wooden desk piled high with papers sat beneath a window overlooking a sodden meadow. The polished flagstone floor was strewn with an assortment of vintage rugs ranging in style from Turkish to French and the air was redolent with a savory aroma that made my mouth water.

"Toss your coats anywhere," Frances said. "I was about to break for lunch. Will you join me?"

"If it's not too much trouble," I said as my stomach gave an embarrassing rumble.

"I made the bread first thing this morning and the soup is simmering on the cooker," said Frances. "It couldn't be much less trouble."

"Thanks," I said. "We'd love to join you." I dropped my coat on an armchair and asked, "How long have you lived here, Frances?"

"Almost forty years," she replied, throwing cloth napkins onto the oak dining table. "My husband and I moved in a year after we were married. We've never wanted to live anywhere else."

"I can see why," I said, peering up at the elm beams. "Your home is charming."

"The location suits us," said Frances. "We're not the most sociable of creatures. We prefer living in splendid isolation."

Bree hadn't said a single word since we'd entered the barn, nor had she removed her trench coat. She stood midway between the desk and Frances, looking from one to the other with an intensely perplexed expression on her face.

"Are you *the* Frances Wylton?" she blurted suddenly. "The romance writer?"

"Yes and no," said Frances. The crow's

feet at the corners of her eyes crinkled into a thousand splintery wrinkles as she smiled. "Take off your coat and have a seat, Bree. I'll explain while we eat."

I didn't know what Bree was talking about or what explanation Frances had in store for her and I was too hungry to care. The soup Frances ladled into three earthenware bowls was a pottage rich and thick enough to serve as a complete meal, but she buttered thick slices of her homemade bread for us as well. While she and Bree conversed, I ate like a ravening beast.

"I am Frances Wylton," Frances began, "but I'm not the romance writer. That would be my husband, Felix."

"Felix?" Bree echoed blankly, ignoring her food.

"Felix Chesterton," said Frances. "Felix borrowed my name when he wrote his first novel because he was convinced that a romance written by a woman would sell better than one written by a man. I don't know if he was right or not, but the book was such a hit he went on using my name."

"You *husband* wrote *Lark Landing*?" Bree said, looking staggered.

"I'm afraid so," Frances said gently.

"And *Sundown Mountain*?" said Bree.

"He wrote each and every one of them,"

Frances said. "Have a bite to eat, Bree. You'll feel better."

Bree reached for a slice of bread, as though she didn't trust herself to handle a soup spoon.

"I'm sorry it's come as such a shock to you," Frances continued. "I thought all of my husband's fans were in on his secret."

"I don't pry into my favorite authors' private lives," Bree told her seriously. "Knowing too much about them might change the way I feel about their books."

"I wish more readers were like you," said Frances. "Unfortunately, they're not. Felix was outed several years ago by a prying, spying fan. He thought it spelled the end of his career, but it had the opposite effect: His sales numbers soared. Which simply proves what I've said all along: Predicting what book buyers will like or dislike is as pointless as throwing darts at jelly. I'm glad to know that Felix is one of your favorite authors."

"He's right up there with Tolkien," Bree said passionately. "If it weren't for their stories, I don't think I'd be alive today."

Frances's eyes flickered toward mine and I gave a small nod. It was true. Immersing herself in her favorite books had helped Bree to survive a childhood blighted by her

151

father's dissolute habits.

"I don't know how many times I've read *Lark Landing,*" Bree went on, as if she hadn't noticed the looks that had passed between Frances and me. "People who knock romances have never read your husband's books."

"I'll tell him," Frances said softly. "You have no idea how much it will mean to him." She gazed down at her bowl for a moment, as if to collect herself, then continued lightly, "I wish you could tell him yourself, but he's gone down to London to meet with his editor and he won't be back until tomorrow."

"No worries," said Bree. "I don't really want to meet him."

"Because meeting him might change the way you feel about his books?" said Frances, her eyes twinkling.

Bree nodded. "Best to keep the two separate, I think."

"So do I," said Frances. "Now. What would you like me to tell you about my home?"

"We didn't come here to ask you about your home," Bree said. "And we're not journalists."

I choked, and clapped a napkin to my mouth to avoid spraying the table with soup.

Frances, by contrast, heard Bree's announcement without betraying the faintest hint of alarm.

"I see," she said calmly, resting her chin in her cupped hand.

"Maddie Sturgess swallowed our cover story whole," Bree continued, "but it wouldn't be right to tell a lie here" — she gazed reverently at the paper-strewn desk — "in the place where *Lark Landing* was written."

"Those are bills," Frances informed her, following her gaze. "I was attempting to file them when I was overcome by an irresistible urge to paint. Paperwork has that effect on me." She pointed toward a door to the left of the refrigerator. "My husband's office is through there, so please feel free to tell as many lies as you like."

"No, I, uh . . ." Bree faltered, blushing to her roots.

I mopped the last vestiges of soup from my chin and smiled ruefully at Frances, who raised an interrogative eyebrow.

"I apologize for the subterfuge," I said. "It seemed like a good idea at the time, but the time has clearly passed so we'll give honesty a whirl and see where it takes us." I pushed my bowl aside and folded my hands on the table. "Bree and I are trying to find out if a story a young girl told us recently is true. The girl's name is Coral Bell and she heard the story from her best friend —"

"Daisy Pickering," Frances interrupted. "Does the story concern a Russian prince named Mikhail?"

"Yes it does," I said, taken off guard. "Did Daisy tell you the same story?"

"Daisy tells us lots of stories," said Frances. "She visits us whenever her mother brings her to work and every visit is an adventure. Felix says she's a creative genius and I must say I agree with him." Frances got up to refill my bowl, but continued to talk as she ladled soup from the pot on the stove. "It's what comes of being sick so often, I suppose — that, and being an only child. She has to rely on her imagination more than most children. For a long time she entertained us with thrilling tales about her best friend — Coral Bell — battling mummies, skeletons, and gigantic insects, but about a month ago we began to hear about Mikhail."

"What did she say about Mikhail?" I asked.

"It's a tale that grew in the telling." Frances placed my bowl before me and returned to her chair at the table. "Mikhail started out as an interesting new acquaintance, but he evolved into a deposed Russian prince who fled his kingdom only to be kidnapped and held hostage by an evil man who took his treasures and cast him into a dungeon." Frances paused. "Sound familiar?"

"Very," I said firmly.

"Daisy hoped Felix and I would help her to free Mikhail," Frances explained, "but we put her off as kindly as we could. Making up stories is one thing. Believing them is another. Since I'm not a creative genius, I can't imagine what Daisy did to convince you that such an incredible tale might be" — she smiled wryly — "credible."

Bree gave a sharp gasp and swung around to face me, crying, "Daisy meant to bring it *here.*"

"She meant to bring what where?" Frances inquired.

Bree planted her forearms on the table and leaned toward Frances.

"Daisy was desperate to free Mikhail, but she couldn't do it on her own," she said rapidly. "She asked you and your husband for help, but you wouldn't help her because you didn't believe in Mikhail."

"How could we believe in him?" Frances said reasonably. "He's a fantasy figure."

"If Daisy managed to get her hands on

155

one of Mikhail's stolen treasures," said Bree, "would you still regard him as a fantasy figure?"

"I might reconsider my position," Frances allowed.

"Lori?" said Bree. "Exhibit A, please."

I reached into my shoulder bag and produced the silver sleigh. Frances stared at it as if she couldn't believe her eyes, then took it from me and examined it from every angle.

"It's a troika saltcellar," said Bree. "It's Russian, it's portable, and it's worth a lot of money. It could have been smuggled out of Russia during or after the Revolution by a fleeing nobleman."

"And the nobleman's name could be Mikhail," murmured Frances. She placed the sleigh on the table, where it glinted and gleamed and splashed the room with shards of reflected light. "How did Daisy come by it?"

"I'd rather not say," I answered. If Bree and I were ever accused of concealing a crime and withholding evidence from the police, it would give me some small measure of comfort to know that I hadn't drawn Frances into our web of naughtiness. "It's for your own protection. The less you know, the better off you'll be."

"In other words," said Frances, "Daisy stole it from the evil man who stole it from Mikhail."

"My lips are sealed," I said.

"In that case, I won't bother asking how it ended up in your bag." Frances ran a fingertip along the sleigh's delicate runners. "Perhaps Daisy was telling us the truth after all. When she comes here again, I'll ask her to tell me more about Mikhail."

"You're too late," I said. "Daisy and her mother have disappeared."

"Disappeared?" Frances said, frowning. "When? How?"

I recounted everything Mrs. MacTavish and Madeleine Sturgess had told us about the Pickerings' abrupt departure, but I said nothing about Skeaping Manor or the charity shop.

"We think the move took Daisy by surprise," Bree added. "She was swept away before she could show the sleigh to you."

"Or return it to Mikhail," I interjected.

Frances sighed deeply. "Felix will be sorry to hear about Daisy. I have to confess that I'm sorry as well, not only because she's an enchanting child, but because we failed her. I would have liked to apologize to her for doubting her."

"You don't doubt her anymore?" asked Bree.

"I can't argue with hard evidence." Frances leaned back in her chair, clasped her hands behind her head, and regarded us with an air of amused speculation. "You must think Daisy met Mikhail in a house her mother cleaned. And you must have come here today to find out if Felix and I were the culprits who robbed and imprisoned him."

"Something like that," I mumbled, blushing.

"If we'd known who you are," Bree said earnestly, "we never would have suspected you."

"Think nothing of it," Frances said easily. "Once one accepts the basic premise, everyone becomes a suspect."

"Not quite everyone," I said. "Amanda worked for six different employers. We're hoping to find one with a Russian connection. We tackled Hayewood House first because Madeleine Sturgess's husband is named Sergei, but he's as English as a pint of ale. Are you aware of a family or an individual of Russian descent living in the vicinity of Upper Deeping?"

"No," said Frances. "I believe I mentioned earlier that Felix and I aren't particularly sociable. As a result, I'm not as familiar with my neighbors as I should be." Frances pursed her lips for a moment, then asked, "Did Daisy's mother work at Risingholme by any chance?"

"Yes," Bree and I chorused.

"If I were you, I'd make Risingholme my next stop," Frances advised.

"Why?" asked Bree. "According to my research, Risingholme is owned by Lord and Lady Boghwell. Boghwell doesn't sound like a Russian name."

"It's pronounced 'buffel,' " Frances informed her gently, "and it isn't a Russian name. I'm not suggesting that Lord and Lady Boghwell had anything to do with Mikhail's alleged kidnapping, but I think they might prove helpful nonetheless." Frances grinned. "I've met them only once, but they've lived in Risingholme forever and Madeleine Sturgess tells me they're the most frightful old gossips she's ever met. If a Russian invaded the neighborhood within the past hundred years, I expect they'll know about it."

"Brilliant." I plucked the silver sleigh from the table and dropped it into my shoulder bag. "We'll attempt to wangle our way into Risingholme next."

"If I might offer a word of advice?" said

Frances, looking directly at Bree. "You may want to tone down your appearance before you approach the Boghwells. They're an old-fashioned couple."

"How old-fashioned?" Bree inquired.

"Your hair would scare them," Frances stated flatly. "And you won't be received at Risingholme with a ring in your nostril."

"Right," said Bree. "Thanks for the tip."

"Thanks for everything, Frances," I said. "The meal, the conversation, your forbearance . . ."

"Each was given with great pleasure," Frances assured me. "I don't often say it, but you're welcome to stay for tea."

"I wish we could," I said, glancing at my watch, "but if we don't leave right now, my little boys will have to hitchhike home from school, which would give them a thrill and me a stroke."

"I understand," said Frances. "Bring your boys with you next time. Children seem to like it here."

We all got up from the table. While Bree and I donned our coats, Frances excused herself and went into her husband's office. She reappeared a moment later holding a hardcover book, which she handed to Bree.

"It's a signed first edition of *Lark Landing*," she explained. "Felix would want you to have it."

Bree tried to speak, but the stifled croak she emitted expressed her gratitude more eloquently than words.

"I've tucked one of Felix's business cards into the book," Frances said as she opened the galvanized steel door. "If you do find Mikhail, please let us know."

"We will," I promised. "Good-bye for now, Frances."

"Good-bye, Lori," she said. "Be well, Bree." Bree could do nothing but nod, and as we strode into the late afternoon sunlight, she turned her head away from me, as though she hoped to hide the tears tumbling down her face.

THIRTEEN

Bree's eyes were dry when we reached the Rover, but it took her awhile to find her voice. We were more than halfway to Upper Deeping before she emerged from her cocoon of introspection and shared her thoughts with me.

"I wasn't joking when I told Frances that her husband's books saved my life," she said.

"I didn't think you were," I said.

"They're not . . . silly," she went on. "You know right from the start that each story will have a happy ending, but you can't imagine how the characters will ever get there." She caressed the copy of *Lark Landing* Frances Wylton had given her. "When Dad would go on a bender, I'd shut myself up in my room and disappear into a world where everything came right at the end. I didn't believe deep down I would find my own happy ending, but the books made it seem . . . possible. So I held on." She glanced shyly at me, looking much younger than her nineteen years. "Then you turned up."

"Sent by your great-grandaunts," I reminded her.

"They were my fairy godmothers, and you were their wand," Bree said, with a watery smile. "Sometimes, just sometimes, life is even better than books."

She clutched the first edition to her chest and said nothing more until Will and Rob were bouncing impatiently in the backseat. Their high spirits couldn't help but lift hers.

"Spies!" Rob shouted.

"Invisible ink!" bellowed Will.

"I'm on it!" Bree exclaimed. "Unless your mum is out of lemon juice . . ."

Fortunately, I had sufficient quantities of lemon juice on hand at the cottage to keep Bree and the boys entertained for hours. While I fielded telephone calls from Emma, Bill, and Willis, Sr., my spies-in-training dipped toothpicks in the juice, wrote their names carefully on a sheet of paper, and watched in amazement as the juice dried and the writing vanished. They waited on tenterhooks while Bree held the sheet of paper over a warm lightbulb and they went bananas when their names "magically" reappeared.

Once they got the hang of it, Rob and Will were off and running. They drew invisible pictures of their ponies, made an invisible sign for their bedroom door, wrote an invisible letter to their father, and scribbled invisible notes, which they passed to me and to Bree covertly during supper. By bedtime their fingers were as puckered as prunes.

Bree seemed indisposed to talk when we finally had the living room to ourselves, so I settled on the couch with a basket of clean laundry and folded clothes while she stared into the fire. I was examining a jagged tear in Will's newest pair of school trousers and wondering how long it would take me to mend it when Bree broke the silence.

"Lori?" she said. "I think it would be better if you tackled Lord and Lady Boghwell on your own. They won't let you in the house if I'm with you." She pointed at her hair and made a goofy face. "I'll only frighten them."

"Fair enough," I said, turning Will's trousers inside out to inspect the tear from another angle. "I'll be *Country House Monthly*'s sole representative at Risingholme."

Bree lapsed into silence again, but a short time later she said, "I also think it may be time for me to go home."

"Now you've gone too far," I said with

164

mock severity. "You can abandon me to my fate at Risingholme, but not here."

"I've been parked in your guest room for nearly a week," she protested. "I don't want to outstay my welcome."

"You couldn't possibly outstay your welcome." I decided the trousers were salvageable, tossed them aside, and gave Bree my full attention. "If you want to go home because you want to go home, fine. But if you want to go home because you think the twins and I are sick of the sight of you, you're out of your cotton-picking mind. We love you, Bree, and we love having you around."

Bree's chin quivered and her eyes began to glisten.

"But we secretly hate you," I added hastily, "and we hope you'll never darken our doorstep again. There. Will that keep you from blubbering?"

Much to my relief, Bree gave a shaky laugh, wiped her eyes, and got to her feet.

"I secretly hate you, too," she declared, "and I'd like nothing more than to make your life a misery. So I'll stay awhile longer."

She bent down to give me a quick hug — something she'd never done before — then pounded up the stairs to her room. I thought it likely that the guest room pillows would soak up a few tears before morning, but since they would be happy tears, they didn't worry me.

I left Will's trousers and the basket of clean clothes on the couch and went to the study, where I touched a finger to Reginald's pink flannel snout and took the blue journal with me to one of the tall leather armchairs before the hearth. I didn't bother to light a fire because I didn't think I'd be in the study long enough to make lighting a fire worthwhile.

"Dimity?" I said as I opened the journal. "I bring you the latest bulletins from the home front: Willis, Sr., will be well enough to attend church on Sunday, Emma will reopen the stables on Friday, and Bill will remain in Majorca for at least another week, the dirty dog."

I looked down and smiled as Aunt Dimity's handwriting began to flow across the page.

Thank you, my dear. I do like to keep abreast of local news, though I am, of course, eager to hear news from farther afield as well. How did you and Bree fare today?

"I wish I could give you a progress report," I said, "but we didn't make any progress."

Was Sergei a dead end?

I snorted mirthlessly. "Sergei Sturgess

166

doesn't have a drop of Russian blood in him. He was named after Sergei Diaghilev by a thoroughly English mother who adores Russian ballet. He lives in London during the week and comes home only on weekends, so we didn't even get to meet him."

Who told you about his mother?

"His wife, Madeleine," I replied. "She's a peach. She let us crawl all over Hayewood House, but we didn't find Mikhail. And before you ask, the Sturgesses have no retired retainers living on the property because they have no retired retainers, and even if they did, there'd be no place for them to live. The workmen's cottages that might have housed them were demolished after the war."

A pity.

"Bree and I did, however, visit the Sturgesses' converted barn," I continued, "where we made a significant discovery."

Did you find Mikhail trussed up in the hayloft?

"We did not," I said. "We didn't search the hayloft or any other part of the barn because it happens to be the home of Bree's favorite living author, Felix Chesterton."

How extraordinary.

"You can say that again," I said. "We didn't meet Mr. Chesterton because he'd

167

gone to London to see his editor, but we spent the afternoon with his wife, Frances Wylton."

Frances Wylton? The romance writer?

"Not exactly," I said. "Felix Chesterton writes romance novels under his wife's name."

I am astonished, and if I'm astonished, Bree must have been bowled over.

"She was gobsmacked," I confirmed. "She couldn't bring herself to tell fibs in Felix Chesterton's sacred writing space, so we dropped the journalist disguise and came clean with Frances. It turns out that she and Felix are familiar with Prince Mikhail's story because Daisy Pickering started telling it to them about a month ago. They thought she'd made it up."

Understandable.

"Bree decided to make a believer of Frances by showing her the silver sleigh," I said. "The gambit worked. Frances is now willing to admit that Mikhail might not be a figment of Daisy's lively imagination."

Is Frances willing to join in the hunt for Mikhail?

"Not really," I said. "She and her husband are pretty reclusive. I came away with the impression that they don't leave the Hayewood estate unless they have to."

Even the most confirmed recluses hear rumors, and the right sort of gossip could lead you directly to Mikhail's prison door.

"Frances doesn't seem to pay too much attention to the rumor mill," I said.

The poor woman. What a lonely life she must lead.

"She seems completely content with her life," I countered. "And she pointed us toward a couple Madeleine Sturgess rates as the most frightful old gossips she's ever met. They've lived in the neighborhood for a very long time, apparently, and they know everything about everyone. I plan to visit them tomorrow."

You plan to visit them? On your own? Without Bree?

"According to Frances Wylton," I said, "they have old-fashioned notions about young women who pierce their nostrils and dye their hair fire-engine red, so Bree has decided to lie low for the day."

Who is this quaint couple?

"Lord and Lady Boghwell of Risingholme," I said, rather grandly.

The boorish Boghwells? Good grief. Are they still alive? They must be a thousand years old by now.

"The boorish Boghwells?" I said. "Did you know them?"

Peripherally. We met from time to time at charitable events, but they were a bit too old-fashioned for my taste. They're the sort who want to abolish the National Health Service and reinstate feudal law. We didn't have much in common.

"I'm happy to hear it," I stated firmly.

They could be useful, though, so heed Frances Wylton's advice. Do not wear loud colors or trousers tomorrow, and make sure the hemline of your dress or skirt falls well below your knees. And for pity's sake, don't mispronounce "Boghwell"!

"Shall I tug my forelock when I meet them?" I teased. "Or will a deep curtsy suffice?"

Don't be facetious, Lori. Lord and Lady Boghwell may be not be the brightest pennies in the piggy bank, but they'll know if they're being mocked. Simply treat them with the deference they feel they deserve. Sprinkle lots of "my lords" and "my ladies" into your speech. They'll lap it up.

"Noted," I said, "though I doubt I'll have the opportunity to speak to them. People like the Boghwells tend to look askance at journalists. Their snooty butler will probably slam the door in my face."

He probably will. I have great faith in your ability to pull the wool over people's eyes, however, so we must hope for the best. By the way, I disagree with you on a point you made earlier.

"Which one?" I asked.

At the commencement of our conversation, you claimed you'd made no progress today. You were wrong. You may not have located Mikhail, but you eliminated Hayewood House from your inquiries and you learned where to go to commune with the neighborhood's most experienced gossips. In addition, Bree had the chance encounter of a lifetime.

"When you put it that way," I said, "I guess we did make some progress." I paused before adding with a wry smile, "I must admit that I didn't have Bree pegged as a romance fan."

A well-written book is a well-written book, regardless of the label a publisher slaps on it, and Lark Landing *happens to be an extremely well-written book.*

"Frances gave Bree a signed first edition of *Lark Landing* before we left," I said. "It revived some tough memories for her."

Have you read Lark Landing?

"No," I said.

You should. I read it when it was first published and it left an indelible impression on me. Its main character is the troubled daughter of an alcoholic reprobate.

171

I stared at Aunt Dimity's words in stunned silence, then closed my eyes and released a heartfelt groan. "How stupid can I be, Dimity? Bree tried to tell me about Felix Chesterton's writing, but I didn't listen. I assumed he wrote sentimental stories for teenagers."

Wrong again.

"I'll find a copy of *Lark Landing* that isn't a precious first edition," I promised, "and I'll read it."

I'm glad Bree is staying at the cottage just now. It's a good place to be when tough memories surface. Sleep well, my dear. And remember what I said about your hemline!

I watched the curving lines of royal-blue ink fade from the page, then closed the journal and looked up at Reginald, who peered down at me from the shadowy recesses of his special niche on the bookshelves.

"If Bree comes in here tomorrow, while I'm away," I said, "do your best to make her feel loved, will you?"

My bunny made no reply. I smiled at my own foolishness and went up to bed, wondering what I would wear for my interview with the Boghwells.

FOURTEEN

I dressed in my most conservative outfit the following morning: black wool blazer and skirt, gray silk blouse, a single strand of black pearls, and a plain-Jane pair of black flats. Bree, after declaring gleefully that I looked like a door-to-door coffin saleswoman, insisted that I borrow her black trench coat.

Will and Rob thought I was going to a funeral.

Their comments were a bit depressing, as was my outfit, but they convinced me that I'd complied with Aunt Dimity's dismal dress code. Satisfied, I left Bree at the cottage, drove the boys to school, consulted the map Bree had marked for me, and set out for Risingholme. Thirty minutes later I came to a halt, stymied by a pair of hefty wrought-iron gates set into sturdy stone pillars. Lord and Lady Boghwell, it seemed, did not encourage casual visits.

"I'll never even *reach* the front door," I grumbled to myself, but I climbed out of the Rover anyway and pressed a button on the intercom unit set into the stone pillar on my right. When no response came, I pressed the button again and said in a slightly raised voice, "Hello? Is this thing work —"

A blaring buzzer cut me off and the gates jerked open with an almighty creak. Hardly believing my luck, I ran back to the car, scrambled into the driver's seat, and gunned the engine to speed past the gates before they could shut me out again. I slowed down at once, in part because I didn't want the Boghwells to think I was a reckless driver, but mainly because the long, straight driveway was pitted with gargantuan pot-holes.

The grounds, too, looked sadly neglected. Broken branches dangled forlornly from the ancient beech trees lining the drive, and small forests of saplings encroached on the dank, overgrown meadows beyond. As I picked my way carefully around the pot-holes, I wondered if the Boghwells had elected to return their land to its natural state or if straitened finances had forced the decision on them.

Risingholme eventually hove into view, rising from a tangle of ivy at the end of the pitted drive. It was an imposing, four-story Jacobean edifice built of dingy gray and yellow Cotswold stone. The central block was made up of a series of projecting and receding bays pierced with an irregular pattern of grimy windows, surmounted by fussy triangular pediments, and flanked by a stumpy pair of crenellated towers. Though I admired Risingholme's evident antiquity, I did not hesitate to declare it one of the ugliest buildings in England.

I parked the Rover at the bottom of a lichen-speckled stone staircase that appeared to lead straight into a wall. It was only when I reached the top step that I noticed a massive oak door set into the projecting bay on my left. As I turned toward the door, it was opened not by a snooty butler, but by a very large black woman. She wore a long-sleeved woolen tunic in muted jewel tones, a plum-colored turban, and a black calf-length skirt. She had kind eyes. I felt as though the only reason she looked down on me was because I was about a foot shorter than she.

"Selling Bibles?" she inquired in a jaunty Jamaican accent. "Raising money for orphans? Collecting for the church roof fund?"

"N-no," I stammered, thrown off balance

by her rapid-fire queries. "I'm . . . I'm a journalist with *Country House Month* —"

"A journalist?" The woman burst into a hearty peal of laughter. "Priceless!"

"I'm writing a story about country estates," I went on, eyeing her uncertainly. "I wonder if I might have a word with Lord and Lady Boghwell? Unless you're . . . ?"

"Am I Lady Boghwell?" The woman laughed so hard her whole body quivered. "No, sweetie," she replied, when she'd regained her composure. "I'm the maid and the cook and everything else below stairs, but I'm not milady."

"May I please speak with your employers?" I asked timidly.

"Oh, they'll love to meet *you,*" she said, grinning broadly and waving me inside. "Come on in, lamb. Make yourself at home."

I stepped into a shadowy vestibule and began to unbutton Bree's trench coat, but the maid shook her head.

"Best to keep it on," she advised. "No central heating."

"It is a bit chilly," I conceded, watching my breath condense in the frigid indoor air. "Doesn't it bother you?"

The maid patted her capacious midsection. "I'm naturally insulated, sweetie, and I spend most of my time in the kitchen. Come along now. The walk will keep you warm."

I followed her through a bewildering succession of rooms perfumed with the musty scents of dry rot and decay. The rest of the house was as cold, if not colder, than the vestibule and if it was wired for electricity, I saw no evidence of it. Instead, daylight seeped through the grimy windows to illuminate threadbare carpets, moldering tapestries, dusty furniture, and the smoke-blackened portraits of lace-collared Cavaliers. The maid's unhurried pace gave me ample time to wonder whether anything had changed at Risingholme since the reign of Charles I.

We climbed a sweeping but unswept staircase, crossed a landing, and paused before a ponderous oak door. I expected the maid to knock, but instead she winked at me.

"Ready to meet the great and glorious Boghwells, sweetie?" she asked.

"Uh, yes," I replied, smoothing the lapels of Bree's trench coat. "I guess so."

She pushed the door open and ushered me into a great room that made the one in the converted barn seem like a linen closet. The walls were lined with dark oak paneling, the ceiling was a veritable garden of ornate plasterwork, and the massive chimneypiece dwarfed the elderly couple sitting rigidly in wing chairs before the meager coal fire burning in the cavernous hearth.

A pole lamp fitted with a low-watt electric bulb sat beside each wing chair, casting a dim pool of light on the woman, who was doing crewelwork, and the man, who was reading *The Daily Telegraph.* The man's bald pate gleamed in the lamplight and the woman's pink scalp showed through her tightly curled white hair, but otherwise they looked very much alike. Both had prominent noses, receding chins, long, scrawny necks, and the alabaster complexions I associated with advanced, but cosseted, old age. They were bundled in copious shawls and lap rugs, and each wore a pair of fingerless wool mittens, presumably to ward off the chill the skimpy fire could do little to diminish.

The prominent noses turned toward the oak door as the maid and I entered the room.

"That's them," the maid said to me, jutting her chin at the pair.

"Right," I said nervously.

"Got a visitor for you, milord and lady," she called to the couple. "Don't know what her name is, but I'm sure she does." Chuckling merrily, she turned on her heel and left the great room, closing the oak door behind her.

"Shanice? Shanice! Come back here at once, you stupid girl!" Lord Boghwell cried angrily. "What the devil does she think she's playing at, letting strangers into the house? Stupid, stupid girl! We could be murdered in our beds!"

As His Lordship's rant exploded, I began to suspect Shanice of using me to get her own back on an employer who referred to her too often as a "stupid girl."

"But we're not in our beds, dear," Lady Boghwell pointed out tranquilly, bending over her needlework. "And I very much doubt that our visitor intends to murder us."

"There's no telling, these day," Lord Boghwell grumbled. He eyed me irritably and barked, "Who are you and what do you want?"

"M-my name is Lori Shepherd, my lord," I replied and threw in a deep curtsy for good measure.

"American accent," murmured Lady Boghwell, without looking up from her embroidery, "but a fine Anglo-Saxon name. Are you related to the Shepherds of Spalding?"

"I doubt it, my lady," I said.

"I hope not," Lady Boghwell said serenely. "It's not a family with which one would wish to be connected. Labor Party stalwarts, I'm afraid."

"What do you want?" Lord Boghwell repeated loudly, shaking his newspaper at me.

I thought he might burst a blood vessel if I confessed to being a journalist, so I told him the truth and hoped for the best.

"Frances Wylton sent me," I said.

"Who the devil is Frances Wylton?" Lord Boghwell thundered.

"You remember Frances Wylton, dear," said Lady Boghwell, pulling a long strand of wool taut. "She and her husband were the Hayewoods' tenants before the Hayewoods were forced to sell Hayewood House."

"When old Hayewood's bank went belly-up," Lord Boghwell said with a nasty chuckle.

"That's right, dear," said Lady Boghwell placidly, stabbing the needle forcefully into the fabric. "Frances Wylton and her husband still live in the converted barn. She paints, he writes, no children. She's distantly related to the Ffyfes."

"Dresses like a scarecrow?" her husband

said vaguely. "Smells like a pot of turpentine?"

"Yes, dear," said Lady Boghwell.

Lord Boghwell lowered his newspaper to his lap, folded his gnarled hands on top of it, and eyed me shrewdly.

"Frances Wylton sent an American to us, did she?" he said. "With a film company, are you?"

I couldn't imagine what had prompted the question, but since Lord Boghwell hadn't shouted it at me, I decided to go with the flow.

"Yes, my lord," I replied firmly. "I'm with a film company."

"Thought so," he said, with a self-satisfied smirk. "Americans usually are. Come to recce the place for a shoot?"

"Pardon me, my lord?" I said, mystified.

"Are you a location scout?" he clarified impatiently. "Good God, woman, if I have the patois down, you should."

"Perhaps she isn't a location scout," his wife suggested.

"If she isn't, she should say so," Lord Boghwell snapped. "And if she is, she should say so. I don't mind her looking the place over, but I can't abide mealymouthed time wasters."

If I'd thought for one moment that the

Boghwells were capable of committing a physically demanding criminal act, I would have proclaimed myself a location scout and run off to search for Mikhail. But the mere idea of the doddering duo kidnapping, robbing, and imprisoning anything larger than a gerbil was so patently absurd that I stuck with my original agenda and pressed them for a morsel of useful gossip.

"I'm not a location scout, my lord," I said. "I'm an assistant director doing research for a new movie about . . . um . . . immigrants. Frances Wylton thought you might be able to help me."

"What the deuce would we know about immigrants?" Lord Boghwell bellowed querulously. "Shanice is the only foreigner with whom we're acquainted and why she was allowed into the country, I'll never know."

"Frances seems to think that Shanice isn't the only foreigner in the area," I said.

"She's quite right," said Lady Boghwell.

"Is she?" said Lord Boghwell, looking flabbergasted.

"The Tereschchenkos," said Lady Boghwell.

"Oh," said her husband, his lip curling into a sneer. "Them."

"Who are the Tereschchenkos?" I asked.

"Who knows?" said Lady Boghwell, with a tiny shrug. "One knows nothing of their antecedents. The Tereschchenkos changed their name to *Thames* because, quite naturally, they wished to *sound* English, but for all we know they could be Bulgarian or Polish or *Ukrainian,* for that matter."

"Or Russian," I said under my breath. More loudly, I asked, "Do you know where the Tereschchenkos live, my lady?"

"They call it Shangri-la," Lady Boghwell replied, with a heavy sigh.

The Boghwells seemed to fade into the shadows as I recalled Bree's list of Amanda Pickering's workplaces. I was sure Shangri-la was on it. Bree had looked it up online, but she'd failed to spot the Russian connection because Shangri-la's current owner had, according to the Boghwells, changed his surname from Tereschchenko to Thames. Whether the Thames-Tereschchenkos had a dungeon in their basement remained to be seen, but one thing was certain: I would be visiting Shangri-la in the very near future.

"Shangri-la, here I come," I murmured and the great room came back into focus.

"Shangri-la, my foot," Lord Boghwell growled. "I've never heard of anything so preposterous."

"It's been Whiting Hall from time out of mind," Lady Boghwell went on, unperturbed by her husband's choler, "but Whiting Hall must have seemed too plain, too down-to-earth, too Anglo-Saxon, perhaps, for the Tereschchenkos because they renamed it" — she heaved another heavy sigh — "Shangri-la."

"Airy-fairy twaddle," Lord Boghwell grumbled.

"When did the Tereschchenkos buy Whiting Hall, my lady?" I asked.

"Years ago," Lady Boghwell replied. "I really didn't take much notice. It's not as if we would ever have anything to do with them."

"Blasted foreigners!" Lord Boghwell roared. "They actually had the audacity to invite us to a cocktail party. An *out-of-doors* cocktail party! Around their *swimming pool*!"

"They dug up the rose garden," Lady Boghwell murmured sadly, "to make room for a swimming pool."

"I've no doubt it would have enhanced their reputation to parade us in front of their drunken, half-naked cronies," said Lord Boghwell, "but we dampened their pretensions with a chilly refusal. Haven't heard from them since. Don't *wish* to hear

184

from them!"

"They're really not our sort," murmured Lady Boghwell.

"My people built Risingholme!" Lord Boghwell thundered. "We've lived here for more than four hundred years! The Tereschchenkos can change their family name to *Windsor,* if they so choose, but they'll *still* be the Tereschchenkos and they'll *never* be our sort!"

An inner gremlin urged me to point out that England's royal family had changed its name from Battenberg to Windsor in order to sound "more English" during the First World War, but I hushed the mischievous imp and prepared to take my leave of the great and glorious Boghwells. There was no reason to stay. I'd gotten what I wanted from them — Aunt Dimity's *right sort of gossip* — and I was afraid my toes would freeze if I lingered much longer in the great room.

"Thank you for your gracious hospitality, my lord and my lady," I said. "You've been extremely helpful, but I must dash. I have a . . . a meeting with the location scout and he doesn't like to be kept waiting."

"Nor do I," harrumphed Lord Boghwell. "Can't abide it. When I was a boy we had a gamekeeper who acted as though he couldn't read a clock. For all I know, he couldn't, but that's not the point."

"Please don't get up," I said, before His Lordship could sink his teeth into another tirade. "I'll see myself out."

"You will not," Lord Boghwell declared, adding with unexpected practicality, "You'd never find the front door." He gestured toward a bellpull hanging beside the chimneypiece. "Ring for Shanice."

He raised his newspaper to eye level and Lady Boghwell carried on with her crewelwork. I rang for Shanice and stood shivering in the great room for nearly ten minutes before she arrived.

"You rang?" she asked.

"Show our visitor out," Lord Boghwell commanded.

"In a minute, my lord," said Shanice.

"In a minute?" Lord Boghwell thundered. "When I give an order, I expect it to be obeyed *immediately,* not *in a minute*! I pay your wages, my girl, and . . ."

He continued to scold the maid, but his words seemed to bounce off her broad back as she ambled across the room to add two modest chunks of coal to the fire and to fuss over the elderly couple's shawls and lap rugs.

"There you go," she said, standing back

to survey her handiwork. "Tucked up snug as two bugs."

"Her Ladyship and I are not *insects,*" Lord Boghwell snapped. "And we will have luncheon in the dining room at one o'clock *sharp.*"

"Have I ever forgotten your luncheon, milord?" Shanice asked mildly, heading for the door.

"No," Lord Boghwell allowed grudgingly. "But the morning's upheavals might have distracted you."

"The upheaval is leaving, milord." Shanice opened the oak door and motioned with her turbaned head for me to go through it.

"Thanks again," I said to the Boghwells, and left the great room, wishing I could plunge my toes into a pot of tea.

FIFTEEN

Shanice closed the door gently, planted her hands on her broad hips, and gave me a pitying look.

"Your nose is as red as a raspberry," she observed. "Would you like a cup of tea to warm you through before you go?"

"Yes, please," I said gratefully.

Shanice led the way up a dim and musty passageway, through a door concealed by a faded tapestry, and down an austere stone staircase. I assumed both door and staircase were used exclusively by servants, but I wasn't surprised when no one passed us on the stairs. Shanice had said earlier that she was the only person currently working for the Boghwells, and Risingholme's shabby state appeared to confirm it. One woman, working on her own, couldn't cope with such a large house, no matter how big and strong she was.

It wasn't hard to understand why Shanice

188

spent most of her working hours in the cavernous kitchen. Unlike the rooms I'd seen on my walks to and from the great room, the kitchen was spotless, well-lit, and kept blessedly toasty by an enormous cast iron range that had probably been all the rage in the late Victorian era. The range radiated enough heat to thaw my toes at forty paces, but Shanice dumped a heaping shovelful of coal into it before filling a blackened kettle at the antiquated sink.

"Take off your coat, sweetie," she said over her shoulder. "You won't need it down here."

"Why don't Lord and Lady Boghwell have a bigger fire?" I asked, slinging Bree's trench coat over the back of a chair. "Or sit in a smaller room?"

"Because the way things are is the way they've always been," Shanice replied. "Milord and lady are used to it, all of it, and they don't approve of change." She nodded at a towering Welsh dresser laden with teapots, cups, saucers, creamers, sugar bowls, biscuit tins, and tea canisters. "Set the table, will you, pet?"

I arranged a selection of tea things on the scrubbed pine table in the center of the room and before long Shanice and I were sitting across from each other, sipping steaming cups of jasmine tea. I'd just slipped into a pleasant daydream about sun-drenched Jamaican gardens when my savior yanked me back to cold reality.

"Not a journalist, then?" she said, raising an eyebrow.

Caught off guard, I blushed and stammered, "H-how did you know?"

"Baby monitor in the chimney breast," she replied complacently, gesturing to a wall-mounted unit I'd mistaken for an intercom. "I've planted them all over the house. I can't leave milord and lady to fend for themselves, can I? They're babies."

"They're tough babies," I muttered, cupping my hands around my teacup.

"Do you know Frances Wylton?" Shanice asked, as if I hadn't spoken. "Or did you make that up, too?"

"I had lunch with Frances Wylton yesterday," I replied with a hint of defiance.

"She didn't tell you to ask the Boghwells to help you with your film, though, did she?" Shanice spoke in exactly the same tone of voice I used when challenging a fibbing child. "You're not with a film company at all, are you?"

My cheeks went from pink to scarlet.

"No," I admitted. "She didn't and I'm not." There was no point in lying. My blushes had already given me away.

"I didn't think so." Shanice's eyes narrowed. "You're not one of those raving mad fans, are you?"

"The Boghwells have fans?" I said incredulously.

"Not so's you'd notice," said Shanice, chuckling, "but Risingholme does."

I couldn't imagine the ugly old pile attracting a single admirer, let alone a legion of raving mad fans, but I was willing to concede that mine was not the only opinion that mattered.

"I can understand how an architect or a historian might find the house fascinating," I said diplomatically.

"But you're not an architect or a historian," Shanice observed.

"No." I cleared my throat, took a deep breath, and decided to play it straight with her. "My name *is* Lori Shepherd, but I'm not an architect or a historian or an assistant director or a journalist. I'm an ordinary, run-of-the-mill housewife. I live on the other side of Upper Deeping, in a place called Finch —"

"You don't sound like an Englishwoman," Shanice interjected.

"I'm American," I told her, "but I've lived in Finch for almost ten years. The vicar will vouch for me," I added defensively.

"I believe you," said Shanice. "Only a fool would claim to be from a local village if she didn't live there and I don't think you're a fool, Lori Shepherd. What brought you to Risingholme?"

"Frances Wylton really did send me," I said. "She advised me to visit the Boghwells because they've been around for so long and they know so much about their neighbors. Frances thought I might learn something from the Boghwells that would help me to . . ." My words trailed off and I smiled wryly. "You may find it hard to believe, Shanice, but I'm trying to find someone who may not exist."

"Who?" she asked.

"His name is Mikhail," I replied.

"Mikhail?" she repeated. She cocked her head to one side. "Do you know Amanda Pickering?"

"I don't know her well," I answered, "but I've met her. I do know that she and Daisy moved out of their flat unexpectedly on Sunday. Did Amanda Pickering tell you or the Boghwells about her move?"

"Amanda? Talk to the Boghwells?" Shanice gave a snort of laughter, folded her arms on the table, and said, "Let me tell you something, Lori Shepherd. I'm almost always the only hired help at Risingholme. Maids, cleaners, butlers, valets, chauffeurs — they come and go faster than waves in the wind. If the cold and the dark and the cobwebs don't drive them away, my employers do. Amanda, though . . ." She looked down at her cup of tea and sighed. "Amanda came here once a week for almost a year."

"Why did Amanda stay when so many others quit?" I asked.

"She never left the kitchen," Shanice replied simply. "I hired her and I made sure she never had to deal with the cold or the dirt or the Boghwells. That's why she stayed." Shanice patted the table. "She worked right here."

"Did she confide in you?" I asked. "Did you know she planned to leave?"

Shanice shook her head. "I expected Amanda to turn up for work as usual on Tuesday morning, but she didn't. I rang her landlady to find out if she was ill, but no . . ." Shanice shrugged. "She left without a word to anyone. Mind you, she wasn't one for talking about herself. Amanda Pickering was a good little worker, but she was private about her private life, and I didn't pry. I didn't want to embarrass her with questions about Daisy's father and such."

"What did she do here?" I asked out of

sheer curiosity. "Her specialty is silver polishing, but I didn't notice much silver in the house."

"The Boghwells don't put it out where people can *see* it," Shanice explained, with feigned astonishment. "They shut it up in the dark and take it out one piece at a time to gloat over it, like misers counting their coins. Are you a thief?"

"No," I said, startled. "Well . . . I stole a bag of candy when I was ten, but I was so riddled with guilt I couldn't open it and I told my mother about it before the day was through. She made me take the bag back to the store and I haven't stolen anything since."

"You were raised right," said Shanice, with an approving nod. "I'll risk showing you some of Amanda's work."

She heaved herself to her feet and crossed to a wall of cupboards beside the Welsh dresser. She winked at me, unlocked one of the cupboard doors, and opened it to reveal ten deep, wide shelves crammed with a glimmering trove of claret jugs, ewers, punch bowls, ink stands, pitchers, trays, wine coasters, and a myriad of other items I couldn't quite make out. Risingholme's collection of silver made Skeaping Manor's seem trivial. If Miles Craven ever caught a glimpse of it, I thought, he'd go weak at the knees with envy.

"Every cupboard along the wall is filled with it," Shanice said, tapping the doors she hadn't opened. "It's good *English* silver," she added, her eyes twinkling. "No foreign tat allowed in *this* house."

"Amanda couldn't possibly polish so much silver," I protested, goggling at the gleaming hoard. "She'd have arms like a gorilla."

"Amanda said professional polishing requires technique, not strength," Shanice informed me as she closed the cupboard door. "Milord and lady won't be pleased when I tell them she's gone. I don't have time to polish silver and they like their treasure shiny."

She took a biscuit tin from the dresser, placed it between us on the table without opening it, and resumed her seat.

"I'll miss Amanda," she said, "but I'll miss little Daisy more. She came to work with her mother sometimes, when she wasn't feeling well, and the stories she'd tell!" Shanice smiled at the memory. "I never knew what she would say next. I expect she told you all about Mikhail."

"She did," I said.

"Me, too," said Shanice.

"Did she tell you where he is?" I asked with some urgency.

"She didn't have to tell me," Shanice replied. "I know where he is. And I can tell you how he got there."

I felt a jolt of anticipation and sat forward in my chair, wondering if the Boghwells' maid-of-most-work was about to give me the clue I needed to solve the riddle of the silver sleigh.

"Daisy liked to bake biscuits with me while her mother was working," Shanice explained. "I made her favorites this morning because she was in my thoughts." She pried the lid from the biscuit tin and pushed it toward me. "Do you know what they're called?"

I looked into the tin and saw dozens of small, round cookies liberally coated with confectioners' sugar. They looked like my late mother's pecan balls, but when I lifted one from the tin and bit into it, I tasted hazelnut.

"Russian tea cakes," I said.

"That's right. Daisy said they were *her* favorite biscuits because they were *Mikhail's* favorite biscuits," Shanice said with a tolerant, disbelieving smile. "When I told Daisy we would bake Russian tea cakes, out she came with a story about a Russian prince and robbers and kidnappers and sailing ships and castles and goodness knows what else. You wouldn't think such a little girl could make up such a wonderful story, but the tea cakes made her imagination fly like a gull in a hurricane." She tapped the side of her turban. "Mikhail's in there, sweetie. In Daisy's head. No need to go looking for him elsewhere." Shanice plucked a tea cake from the tin and turned it in her fingers, saying softly, "Daisy is a special child. I'll miss her very much."

It was clear to me that Shanice ranked Mikhail right up there with the tooth fairy in terms of credibility, but I didn't mind. The clue I'd sought was in the biscuit tin.

"The tea cakes are delicious," I said, licking powdered sugar from my fingertips. "Is it your own recipe?"

"There's not a lot of call for Russian biscuits in Jamaica," Shanice said dryly. "I found the recipe in the Risingholme receipt book."

"You have a receipt book?" I said excitedly. "An old one? I've always wanted to look at an old receipt book. May I?"

"Which one would you like to see?" she asked. "They go back a long way."

I did some convoluted mental gymnastics to figure out how many years had passed since the Bolshevik revolution, added a couple of decades to compensate for my feeble arithmetic skills, and said, "The past hundred years will do very nicely, thank you."

While Shanice sauntered off to fetch the book from a shelf at the far end of the kitchen, I thought hard. According to Daisy Pickering, Russian tea cakes were Mikhail's favorite treat. And Mikhail's favorite treat had now shown up at two places Daisy Pickering had frequented: Hayewood House and Risingholme. Was it a coincidence? I asked myself. Maybe so, I answered, but it was beginning to feel as though Daisy had left a trail of crumbs for me to follow.

Shanice returned with an oversized, leather-bound ledger containing handwritten recipes for everything from profiteroles to pickled pig's feet. Each cook, it seemed, had added new recipes to the book or recorded personal variations on old ones, though in some cases it looked as though guests had been allowed to inscribe their own contributions on the lined pages. The earliest handwriting reminded me so strongly of Aunt Dimity's elegant script that I couldn't help but wonder if the anonymous writer had gone to a village school similar to the one my benefactress had attended in Finch.

Shanice let me browse through the recipes to my heart's content, then thumbed through the book until she reached the Russian tea cake page. My heart beat a little faster when I saw that it was the same recipe, written in the same hand, as the recipe Bree and I had examined in Hayewood House's receipt book. Though the recipe was unsigned, it was dated: *July 1925.*

"Lord and Lady Boghwell mentioned a family called the Tereschchenkos," I said casually. "It sounds like a Russian name, doesn't it? Do you think they might have given the tea cake recipe to Risingholme's cook back in 1925?"

"I doubt it," Shanice said, sounding amused. "You don't want to believe everything the Boghwells tell you about their neighbors, sweetie. They're the only people in these parts who still call Mr. and Mrs. Thames the Treresh — the Terersh —" She made one more attempt to pronounce the name correctly, then gave up. "I've only ever known them as the Thameses. Milord and lady don't care to admit it, but Mr. and Mrs. Thames are as English as I am."

I thought she might be joking — her lilting Jamaican accent made it seem possible — but one look at her face told me that she intended only to fill me in on a bit of local knowledge the Boghwells were too xenophobic to recognize.

"Would you like to copy the recipe?" Shanice asked, pointing to the receipt book.

"I'd prefer to take a photograph of it, if I may," I said, reaching for my shoulder bag. "I'd love to show my friends in Finch what a genuine receipt book looks like."

"Knock yourself out," said Shanice.

I snapped several pictures of the Russian tea cake recipe, then put the camera back into my bag and reached for Bree's coat.

"Leaving?" Shanice asked.

"It's almost time for the luncheon in the dining room," I said, pointing to the wall clock. "You must have other things to do than to chat with me."

"Other things, yes, but none more enjoyable," she said with true graciousness. "I'll show you out."

I trailed behind her through the Boghwells' glacial mausoleum of a house and thanked her profusely for the tea and her time when we reached the front door. She responded by bending over to give me a hug, which I returned gladly.

"It was a pleasure to meet you, Lori Shepherd," she said as she drew back. "You're welcome to have a cup of tea in my

200

kitchen any time."

"And you'll always be welcome in mine," I said. "I'm easy to find. Everyone in Finch knows where I live." I fell silent while she opened the door, then said hesitantly, "If you don't mind my asking, Shanice, why do you stay at Risingholme? Why do you go on working for the Boghwells?"

She smiled. "Who else will look after them?"

"Don't they have children?" I asked.

"They disowned their children years ago," Shanice said gently. "Their daughter married a Guatemalan artist and their son married a woman who's my color. The Boghwells will never forgive them." She shook her head. "Milord and lady have outlived most of their friends, poor things, and they've cut themselves off from a world they don't understand. I told you before, they're babies."

Shanice was, I realized, a much better person than I was.

"Just one more question, if you don't mind," I said, pausing on the top step. "How on earth did Lord Boghwell come to know filmmaking jargon?"

My innocent inquiry provoked a gale of laughter that sent a flock of crows flapping from the potholed driveway to a beech tree's leafless branches.

"If I told you, pet, you wouldn't believe me," Shanice said, wiping her eyes. "Mind how you go."

Still chuckling, she closed the door.

Sixteen

It was too late in the day to mount a major snooping assault on Shangri-la and too early to pick up Will and Rob, so I headed home for a bite to eat and a change of clothes. I'd had nothing to sustain me since breakfast, apart from a cup of tea and one measly Russian tea cake, and my coffin saleswoman outfit was getting me down. Once I'd put the Boghwells' pitted drive behind me, I stomped on the gas pedal.

If the coast was clear, I told myself as I sped toward Upper Deeping, I'd have a quick word with Aunt Dimity as well. My head was fizzing with the clues I'd bagged at Risingholme and I was eager to hear her take on them.

The coast, alas, was not clear. I called Bree's name when I entered the cottage, heard her cheery response from the living room, and altered my plans. Food could wait, less dismal attire could wait, and Aunt

Dimity would be only too happy to wait, but I wouldn't be happy until I'd shared the fruits of my gossip-gathering labor with a coconspirator.

I dropped my shoulder bag onto the hall table, hung Bree's black trench coat on the coat rack, strode purposefully into the living room, caught sight of my houseguest, and did a double take worthy of a cartoon character.

Bree was lying on the couch, reading *Lark Landing,* with Stanley draped across her legs and Reginald tucked into the crook of her left arm. I scarcely noticed Reginald, however, because my gaze was riveted to Bree's hair, which had undergone yet another radical transformation. Though it was still short and spiky, it was no longer fire-engine red. Her new hair color was, bewilderingly, her old hair color: a dark, lustrous brown.

"Hi," she said. She closed the book, encouraged Stanley to seek another resting place, swung her legs over the edge of the couch, and sat up. After settling Reginald comfortably in her lap, she explained, "This little guy fell off a shelf in the study. Once I picked him up, I couldn't seem to put him down." She turned Reginald to face her. "He is a *he,* isn't he?"

"Yes, he is," I said, tearing my gaze away

from her hair. "His name is Reginald and he's been around longer than you have."

"I can sense his wisdom," said Bree, peering into Reginald's black button eyes. "Wise *and* snuggly — what a brilliant combination! You certainly know how to make a girl feel loved, little guy."

I blinked as I remembered the last thing I'd said before leaving the study the previous evening. Had my pink bunny complied with my request? It was a ridiculous notion — a stuffed animal *could not* hop from a shelf on cue — but there he was, making Bree feel like a million bucks. Who was I to argue with success?

"Reginald means as much to me as Ruru means to you," I said. Ruru was a tattered stuffy — an owl — Bree had brought with her from New Zealand. "Where is Ruru, by the way? You didn't leave him at home, did you? He'll reek of paint fumes."

"No worries," said Bree, laughing. "Ruru's in your guest room, but he's a bit too fragile for full-on cuddling. Not like your little charmer. I could cuddle Reginald for hours. As a matter of fact, I just did."

"Reginald is special," I agreed, using the word Shanice had used to describe Daisy Pickering. "But he hasn't changed color since the last time I saw him, whereas your hair . . . has." I sat in the armchair across from Bill's — his had already been colonized by Stanley — and asked the question I'd wanted to ask since I'd charged into the living room. "What gives?"

"Messages first." Bree became as businesslike as she could be while cuddling a pink flannel rabbit. "Emma rang. The stables will be open for business bright and early tomorrow morning. Thunder and Storm will be saddled and waiting for Will and Rob to take them out for a short gallop before school. Bill rang. He's nursing a serious sunburn —"

"Serves him right," I muttered.

"— and hopes to be home a week from today," Bree continued. "Deirdre Donovan rang. She's given William the all-clear to attend church on Sunday. William rang. He will attend church on Sunday, with or without Deirdre Donovan's all-clear. Last but not least, Peggy Taxman rang to find out why I'm here."

"What did you tell her?" I asked, eyeing Bree nervously.

"I told her you and I were plotting to take over Taxman's Emporium," Bree replied.

I whirled around to peer though the bay window, half expecting to see Peggy Taxman marching up the lane with a flaming torch in one hand and an axe in the other. Peggy was fiercely protective of her general store.

"Did she believe you?" I asked anxiously.

"I don't think so," Bree said, sounding faintly disappointed. "She told me not to be impertinent and rang off in a huff."

"Thank heavens," I said, sinking back in my chair. "The one thing I don't need at the moment — or ever, really — is Peggy Taxman on the warpath. Would you *please* resist the urge to pull her leg while you're staying here? Guilt by association could be hazardous to my health."

"Sometimes her leg needs pulling," said Bree. "But I'll try not to tease her while I'm under your roof."

"Thank you," I said. "Now, about your hair . . ."

"Like it?" Bree twirled a gleaming lock between her fingers. "I decided to take Frances Wylton's advice and tone down my look for the duration of our investigation." She touched her right nostril. "Nose ring? Gone. And I'll keep my tattoos under cover until we're done. If I want people to believe I'm a professional journalist, I have to look like one."

"Seems sensible," I said.

"Also . . ." Bree twiddled Reginald's ears

absently for a moment, then placed him beside her on a cushion, folded her hands in her lap, and faced me squarely. "I have a big house and I've been trying to think what to do with it."

"You're not going to sell it, are you?" I said, aghast.

"Of course not," said Bree, looking shocked. "Auntie Ruth and Auntie Louise would climb out of their graves to haunt me if I ever sold their house. But I think they'll rest easier if they know I'm putting it to good use."

"What do you have in mind?" I asked.

"An idea came to me while we were chatting with Coral Bell," said Bree. "You know, Daisy Pickering's best friend, the girl who told us about the lost prince."

"I remember Coral," I said nodding.

"While we were chatting with her," Bree went on, "it struck me that she and her brothers might enjoy spending a day in the country every now and then, and when Frances Wylton told us that children like to visit the converted barn, I said to myself, 'I may not live in a converted barn, but I have a garden and a stretch of woods and a maze of attics worth exploring. Why not give three pale-faced town kids a chance to explore them?'"

"It's a great idea," I said, "but their mother might have a thing or two to say about it. I'd probably call the police if a stranger offered to take Will and Rob away for a holiday."

"That's why I had my hair done at the New You salon this morning," Bree said, a note of triumph in her voice. "Tiffany Bell and I aren't strangers anymore."

"Who is Tiffany Bell?" I asked.

"Coral's mother," Bree replied. "She's a stylist at the New You salon, remember? I requested her especially and by the time she finished doing my hair, we were best friends." Bree looked down at her folded hands and said more somberly, "Tiff's husband was killed in a car crash two years ago."

"Poor Coral," I said, wincing, "and Ben and Tom. It must have been terrible for them to lose their father so suddenly."

"It was terrible for Tiff, too," said Bree. "She took the flat in Addington Terrace because she couldn't afford to live anywhere else after her husband died. It's not easy to feed three kids on a hair stylist's salary."

"No," I murmured. "It wouldn't be."

"Tiff's saving up for a better flat in a better neighborhood," she went on, "but in the meantime, she's willing to give the kids a fresh-air break." A grin spread slowly across Bree's face. "They're coming to my house next Sunday. The whole family. Sundays are Tiff's only days off," she added.

"What does she do with the children on Saturdays?" I asked.

"She tried taking them to work with her, the way Amanda Pickering took Daisy," said Bree, "but Tom and Ben turned the salon into a war zone."

"I'll bet they did," I said.

"So now Mrs. MacTavish looks after Tiff's kids in exchange for free perms," said Bree. "Can you imagine how hard up you'd have to be to leave your children with a woman who *chain-smokes*?"

"Only too well," I said. "Not every working mother has the money to spare for decent child care."

"Tiff doesn't. I'll prove myself to her, though," Bree said determinedly. "When I do, I'm sure she'll let the kids spend their Saturdays with me. I think they'll like my house better than Mrs. MacTavish's."

"I'm absolutely positive they'll like you better than her," I said.

"I'll have to boy-proof the house," Bree said thoughtfully. "Can't have Ben and Tom breaking the aunties' best china. But I'll do it. I'll do whatever it takes to get those kids away from Mrs. MacTavish. I want them to know that life has more to offer them than Addington Terrace."

"It's an excellent scheme, Bree," I said. "Your great-grandaunts would love it. And they'd be very proud of you for coming up with it."

Bree smiled bashfully and unclenched her hands, as though she'd needed me to tell her she was doing the right thing before she could be sure of it herself. I wasn't used to teenagers seeking my approval. It made me feel uncharacteristically grown up.

"I didn't forget our scheme while I was hatching mine," she said. "I asked Tiff about Amanda and Daisy Pickering, but she didn't have much to say about them. Amanda kept herself to herself and Daisy was a strange little girl who missed a lot of school. Tiff had never even heard of Mikhail. I reckon she's too tired by the end of the day to pay attention to Coral's chatter." She curled her legs beneath her and spread her arms across the back of the couch. "How about Lord and Lady Boghwell? Did they come through for us?"

"With flying colors," I said. "Do you have your laptop handy?"

"It's upstairs," she said.

"Bring it here," I told her, getting to my

feet. "I have something to show you."

Ten minutes later, we were seated side by side on the couch, peering intently at the laptop's screen. Bree had downloaded the photographs from my camera and enlarged one of the many I'd taken in Shanice's kitchen.

"Look familiar?" I said.

"It looks like the recipe we saw in the receipt book at Hayewood House," Bree said slowly. "Except for the date." She turned to me with a puzzled frown. "But you didn't photograph the receipt book at Hayewood House."

"No, I didn't," I said. "I did, however, photograph *Risingholme's* receipt book."

I leaned back and recounted everything I'd learned from the Boghwells and from Shanice. I told Bree about the Tereschchenkos and Shangri-la, the Russian tea cakes and the receipt book, and she came to the same conclusion I had.

"It can't be a coincidence!" she exclaimed. "Two houses in the same neighborhood using the same recipe written in the same handwriting? The recipe *must* have come from the Tereschchenkos." She thumped the arm of the couch to emphasize her point. "A Russian family, a Russian recipe, a Russian troika, and a Russian prince — it fits together like . . . like . . ."

"Like borscht and sour cream," I said decisively.

"Yeah," said Bree, looking as though she'd never heard of borscht but nodding nonetheless. "Like that."

"My guess is that Daisy met Mikhail while her mother was working at Shangri-la," I said. "He told Daisy about the tea cakes, maybe even shared some with her. When Shanice happened to mention the very same cookies, Daisy must have taken it as a sign that she was *meant* to tell Shanice about Mikhail. Shanice didn't believe her, of course. Even if Daisy had identified Shangri-la as Mikhail's prison, Shanice would have dismissed it as a figment of a little girl's overactive imagination, just as Frances Wylton did."

"We believe Daisy, though," Bree said, "and Shangri-la is our best lead yet. When do we follow up on it?"

"Tomorrow," I said. "After the boys finish their gallop at Anscombe Manor and after we drop them off at school. Speaking of which . . ." I glanced at my watch and groaned. "I meant to grab something to eat when I got home, but it's too late now. I have to leave for Morningside right this minute."

"I'll start dinner," Bree offered.

"Make it something hearty," I said, jumping to my feet. "I'm starving!"

The study was warm and silent and my stomach was very full. Bree had produced a magnificent meal and I'd shown my appreciation by stuffing my face with chicken and dumplings and everything else she'd placed on the table, while she'd fielded questions from Will and Rob, who'd wanted to know what she'd done with her nose ring, why she'd changed her hair color, and whether she'd keep changing it until she got it right. I'd tried to distract them by talking about the stables' grand reopening, but once they'd zeroed in on Bree, they wouldn't let go.

Bree had, understandably, retreated to the guest room after dinner. I'd put the boys to bed, loaded the dishwasher, and straightened the kitchen, then settled in for a long-delayed tête-à-tête with Aunt Dimity. Before retiring, Bree had returned Reginald to his special niche in the bookshelves. He looked down on me with a satisfied gleam in his black button eyes as I opened the blue journal and told Aunt Dimity about my highly informative day.

She was deeply amused by my encounter

with the Boghwells.

People are like trees, Lori. Some continue to grow for as long as they live, while others petrify. Lord and Lady Boghwell turned to stone long ago. They were insufferable prigs in my day and they're insufferable prigs now.

"Shanice feels sorry for them," I said, shaking my head at the thought of anyone feeling the smallest degree of pity for the boorish Boghwells.

Shanice is a generous soul. It was kind of her to make Daisy's days at Risingholme such fun. Most cooks would object vociferously to having a child underfoot in the kitchen.

"Daisy's a special child," I said. "The sort of child who'd take an old man's troubles to heart and try to help him. Frances Wylton and Shanice thought Daisy was telling taradiddles when she rattled on about Mikhail. I believed her from the start and the Russian tea cakes added weight to my conviction. She's been telling the truth all along, Dimity. A highly colored version of the truth, maybe, but the truth."

The tea cake recipe is merely one piece of the puzzle you were clever enough to assemble today. If the Tereschchenkos were driven from their homeland by the 1917 revolution, they could have arrived in England in the early 1920s. The new government would have seized their Russian assets, but foreign investments might have enabled them to purchase Whiting Hall.

"If Mikhail was a young man in the early 1920s," I said, "I doubt he'd still be alive today."

Perhaps he was an infant, brought to safety by his parents. His mother and father could have brought family treasures with them as well. Small but valuable heirlooms — like the silver sleigh — were frequently smuggled into the country to supplement an immigrant family's income. Mikhail could have inherited what was left.

"And his inheritance could have been stolen from him by someone he trusted," I said darkly. "A brother who'd made a mess of his own finances, for example, could have plundered Mikhail's treasures and sold them under the counter to unsuspecting dupes like Miles Craven. If Miles Craven *is* an unsuspecting dupe."

Mikhail's heirlooms might very well have been taken from him and sold without his consent. Sadly, it's the sort of thing that happens to vulnerable, isolated people, and immigrants tend to be both vulnerable and isolated.

"If he threatened to report the theft to the police," I said, "his brother — or some other rotten relative — would have wanted to shut him up."

I doubt he would have gone to the police, Lori, but he might have threatened to take his grievance to other members of the Russian émigré community who could protect him from further exploitation.

"Either way," I said, "the thief would have wanted to keep him quiet. Mikhail would have been a sick old man by then, and unable to put up a fight. Instead of killing him, the brother — or whoever — just made sure he never left Whiting Hall."

The tea cake trail does seem to lead to Whiting Hall. By 1925, the Tereschchenkos might have felt secure enough in their new surroundings to share a family recipe with their neighbors at Risingholme and Hayewood House.

"Whiting Hall must have seemed like paradise after everything they'd been through," I said. "No wonder they renamed it Shangri-la."

The Tereschchenkos changed their surname as well, a not uncommon practice among naturalized citizens. Thames is quintessentially English and much easier for their new neighbors to pronounce than Tereschchenko.

"Does either name ring a bell with you?" I asked.

Not the faintest tinkle. I was acquainted with a number of immigrant families, however, some of whom anglicized their surnames. A few anglicized their Christian names as well. My dear friend Donetello di Pietro, for example, became Don Peters.

The romantic in me snapped to attention.

"You had a dear friend named Donetello di Pietro?" I said, peering down at the journal with fresh interest.

Don sold fruit in Covent Garden. He always set aside the sweetest apples, pears, and plums for me.

"What a nice man," I said, captivated by the image of Aunt Dimity and a dashing Italian fruiterer strolling hand in hand through Covent Garden's cobbled lanes.

Don was a very nice man. His wife and six children adored him.

"Oh." The romantic in me went back to sleep and I returned to the business at hand. "I can understand why immigrants would change their names. We all want to fit in. Except for Bree, of course," I allowed, smiling. "She may have muted her appearance for the sake of our search, but I'll bet my boots her nose ring will be back in place when we go to church on Sunday. She knows how much it annoys Peggy Taxman."

I doubt that Bree's red hair or her nose ring

would have been a liability at Shangri-la. If the Thameses throw cocktail parties around their swimming pool, they won't be put off by a colorful journalist. Bree didn't change her hair color merely to blend in, however. She did it in order to befriend Tiffany Bell and, by extension, the Bell children.*

"Yes, she did," I said. "It was good of her, wasn't it?"

It was good for her as well.

"What do you mean?" I asked.

What has Bree done with herself since she came to England, Lori? She's taken a handful of university courses, pottered around in her great-grandaunts' garden, helped Rainey Dawson to run the tea room in Sally Pyne's absence, and learned a few carpentry skills from Mr. Barlow. It's not much to show for an entire year.

"You can't fault her for taking a breather," I protested. "Her last few months in New Zealand weren't exactly a barrel of laughs."

I'm not criticizing Bree, Lori. I'm simply saying that she's had no sense of purpose since she arrived in Finch, and a girl with a heart as big as Bree's needs a sense of purpose. Her visit to Addington Terrace may turn out to be the best thing that could have happened to her.

"In what way?" I asked.

Addington Terrace rattled Bree. It disturbed her. It reminded her of the worst years in her life. I don't know if she saw herself in the Bell children, but they clearly touched a chord in her.

"She wants to rescue Coral and Ben and Tom, just as I wanted to rescue Daisy." I gazed into the fire as memories from my own past drifted through my mind. "I guess those of us who've known hard times want to keep others from going through what we went through."

I'd like to think so, but I suspect Lark Landing *gave Bree the final push she needed to take the actions she took today. When I read it, I understood its underlying message to be: While it's good to feel sympathy for those less fortunate than ourselves, it's better to extend a helping hand to them.*

"Bree's definitely extending a helping hand to the Bells," I said. "Wouldn't Ruth and Louise be pleased?"

They most certainly would. They would also be relieved to know that their best china will be safe from Ben and Tom! And on that note, I will bid you good night. You have another exciting day ahead of you, Lori, and you need your rest.

"If you insist," I said.

I do. Good night, my dear. Sleep well.

"I believe I shall," I said.

The curving lines of royal-blue ink slowly faded from the page. I closed the journal and returned it to its shelf, then touched a fingertip to Reginald's snout.

"You done good today, little buddy," I said. "I don't know how you did it, but you done good."

A sublime gleam shone from Reginald's black button eyes, as if he were telling me we'd all done good that day. Smiling, I switched off the lights and went to bed.

SEVENTEEN

Will and Rob woke me before dawn on
Friday. It seemed earlier than it was because
daylight hours in February, though length-
ening, were still considerably shorter than
they would be in June. I stumbled groggily
out of bed and allowed the boys' boundless
energy to energize me. In next to no time
we were dressed — they in their riding gear,
I in dark trousers and a respectable but
decidedly non-dismal rose-colored twin set
— and seated around the kitchen table, gob-
bling porridge with unseemly haste.

I thought Bree deserved a lie-in after her
exertions on Thursday, but she joined us for
breakfast, dressed in the same "posh blouse
and trousers" she'd worn to Hayewood
House.

"Are you playing spies again?" Will inquired, surveying Bree's attire.

"Is that why you made your hair brown?"
Rob asked. "Is it a disguise?"

"Uh-huh," Bree replied through a mouthful of porridge. She swallowed before adding more distinctly, "Spies aren't supposed to stand out in a crowd."

"If you need to send secret messages," said Rob, "we'll write them for you."

"Invisibly," Will added.

"Thanks, guys," said Bree, "but you have more important things to do today than to write secret messages. Thunder and Storm are champing at the bits to see you!"

Once the twins heard their ponies' names, there was no holding them back. They dumped their bowls in the sink, grabbed their riding helmets, and ran to the Rover. Bree and I scurried after them.

Emma was waiting in the stable yard when we arrived at Anscombe Manor. She was bundled in a black fleece pullover, a puffy down vest, insulated riding breeches, and earmuffs, and she was stamping her booted feet to keep the blood circulating in them. She sent Will and Rob into the stable to lead out Thunder and Storm, scrutinized their tack when they emerged, gave them each a leg up, and directed them to the large riding ring.

"No jumping," she instructed them as she opened the gate. "You can take the ponies out for a cross-country hack during your lesson tomorrow, but this morning you stay in the ring. They've had a few days off, so warm them up thoroughly before you put them through their paces."

Will and Rob might question my orders, Bill's orders, and even — very occasionally — their grandfather's orders, but they *never* questioned Emma's. They followed her instructions to the letter while Bree, Emma, and I leaned against the fence to watch them. I wasn't sure how the ponies felt about leaving their cozy stalls on such a brisk morning, but my sons had rarely looked more ecstatic.

"I could use some warming up myself," said Emma, shivering. "Whose idea was it to open the stables at sunrise? Oh, yeah. Mine."

"You've made two little boys very happy," I assured her. "The stable yard looks fantastic, by the way. I can't even tell where the pipes burst."

"I'll pass your praise on to Derek, if he ever gets out of bed." Emma shoved her hands into her pockets and looked from Bree to me. "As long as I have you here, would you mind telling me what on earth the two of you have been up to? Peggy Taxman was spitting tacks yesterday, telling anyone who would listen about a nefarious plot to buy the Emporium out from under her."

Bree erupted in a gale of laughter, leaving me to explain her prank. Emma responded with a smile for Bree, a sympathetic pat on the arm for me, and a look on her face that said quite plainly: *I'm glad Bree's staying at your house instead of mine.*

It was a sensible thought from a sensible woman. Emma was by far the most sensible person I knew, which was why I didn't tell her about Mikhail or the silver sleigh. I felt as though Bree and I were on the verge of a major breakthrough in our search for the lost prince. I didn't want Emma to dampen our burgeoning optimism with a dreary dose of common sense, so I steered the conversation toward Bree's fabulous cooking, Bill's well-deserved sunburn, and Willis, Sr.'s steely determination to attend church on Sunday.

I gave the boys an hour to reacquaint themselves with their steeds, then reined them in. Emma was kind enough to take charge of Thunder and Storm and after thanking her profusely we dashed back to the cottage, where Will and Rob changed out of their riding gear and into their school uniforms. The boys smelled like stablehands despite the change of clothes, but I didn't bother to run baths for them. The teachers at Morningside were used to horsey fragrances wafting from my sons.

Bree and I dropped Will and Rob off at school, then chased away the morning chill with a large pot of tea at our favorite café. By half past nine we were on the road to Shangri-la, which, Bree informed me, was the country estate to the west of the Risingholme estate.

Bree shared two pieces of news with me as we drove to Shangri-la.

"I rang a friend in Oxford yesterday," she said. "He designs websites for a living and he agreed to design one for Madeleine Sturgess. After I spoke with him, I rang Maddie. She was thrilled by the idea of working with a professional, so I gave her my friend's number. She said she'd get in touch with him today."

"Well done, you," I said.

"I felt a bit guilty for laughing at her behind her back the other day," Bree confessed. "As you said, she's not stupid, just inexperienced. Helping her with her business seemed like the best way to make it up to her."

"Guilt can be a great motivator," I said.

"To be honest," said Bree, "I felt guilty about misleading Maddie as well. I couldn't

226

stand the thought of her telling her friend Bunny about an article neither of them would ever see, so I wrote a piece about Hayewood House. I've already submitted it to three house-and-garden magazines, and I'll keep submitting it until it's published."

"All this, and dinner, too?" I said, my eyebrows rising. "You did have a busy day."

"Guilt," said Bree with a shamefaced grin, "is a great motivator."

I recalled Aunt Dimity's comments about *Lark Landing* and wondered if the book's underlying message had played an even greater role than guilt in inspiring Bree's good-deed spree. I hoped the story would have a similar effect on me once I got around to reading it, though the thought of doing so many good deeds in a single day was slightly daunting.

"I don't want our hunt for Mikhail to hurt innocent bystanders," Bree said suddenly. "I'll write an article about Shangri-la, too, if the Thameses are innocent, but I'd just as soon drop the *Country House Monthly* ruse and stick with being freelancers. That way, people won't count on seeing their names in print."

"Consider it done," I said. "In the nick of time, too, because we have arrived at our destination."

Shangri-la's drive was guarded by a pair of white wrought-iron gates supported by white cement pillars. Each pillar was topped with a large white cement fish. Bree and I surveyed the fish and exchanged bemused glances, then jumped as a voice spoke to us from thin air.

"Good morning," it boomed. "How may I help you?"

I lowered my window and searched for the source of the greeting, but Bree found it before I did.

"It's the fish," she whispered, giggling. "There's a speaker in one and a camera in the other."

I studied the decorative sculptures and saw that she was right. The fish on the left had turned to surveil us and the fish on the right had a speaker lodged behind its rudimentary gills.

"How may I help you?" the right-hand fish reiterated. "Please speak up."

"We're freelance journalists," I said loudly. "We'd like to interview the gentleman or the lady of the house for an article we're writing about Shangri-la."

The fish remained silent for so long that I thought we were sunk, but when it spoke again, I knew that someone in the house had taken the bait.

"Welcome to Shangri-la," it said.

The white gates swung open and we entered an estate that put Risingholme to shame. The asphalt drive was as smooth as burnished leather and lined by evenly spaced, precisely matched conical topiaries. The meadows beyond looked as though a team of gardeners trimmed them every day with embroidery scissors.

A few hundred feet down the drive, a sign on our right proclaimed:

PEACOCK CROSSING
PROCEED WITH CAUTION

We weren't surprised, therefore, to see the flamboyant birds strutting across the broad circular lawn that divided the drive into two widely separated arcs. The three-tiered marble fountain in the center of the lawn came as a bit of a shocker, however, not only because it looked brand-new, but because it featured statuary that would have made Peggy Taxman blush. The white marble figures of frolicking youths and maidens were as naked as newborns and proved, upon closer inspection, to be anatomically correct in every particular.

Bree took one look at the fountain and burst out laughing.

"I think I'm going to like the Thameses," she said.

"I think I know why the Boghwells don't," I said, averting my gaze from the figure of an extravagantly well-endowed youth.

I followed the drive as it curved around the lawn and parked the Rover in front of Shangri-la's main entrance. The Thameses' home was Georgian in style and about the same size as my father-in-law's — not ostentatiously large, but large enough to be modestly impressive. It was made of a Cotswold stone so pale I could detect only a faint trace of yellow in it, and every inch of its woodwork had been painted a glossy white.

"It's not bad," Bree said, eyeing the building judiciously, "but it's too . . . shiny."

I knew what she meant. The windows gleamed, the painted surfaces glistened, and the stonework was unnaturally bright. Hayewood House was a fine example of a well-maintained historic home, but Shangri-la looked as though layers of history had been scoured from it.

"The strange thing is," Bree went on, "I feel as if I've been here before."

"Me, too," I said, nodding slowly. "I can't imagine why, but the house and the grounds seem familiar to me."

"Maybe we lived here in a previous life," Bree suggested.

"If so," I said, "I was a better housekeeper then than I am now."

We climbed out of the Rover and approached the front door, which was opened by a tiny woman wearing the frilly cap, starched apron, and crisp blue uniform of a made-for-television maid.

"Please, come in," she said, and stood aside for us to enter.

I couldn't identify the maid's accent, but the woman who greeted us as we stepped into the entrance hall sounded as English as the Boghwells, though her Cockney twang indicated that she came from the opposite end of their social scale.

"Welcome to Shangri-la," the woman said. "If you were looking for the lady of the house, you've found her. I'm Gracie Thames."

Gracie Thames was tall, middle-aged, and generously proportioned. Her white jumpsuit clung like paint to her splendid curves and her blond hair fell down her back in a cascade of brassy curls. Though her makeup had been applied with a trowel, the look suited her, because everything about Gracie Thames was overdone: Her peep-toe stilettos were too high, her diamond rings were too big, her nails — finger as well as toe — were too red, her eyes were too blue, and her voice was too loud, but even so, there was something endearing about her. Here was a woman, I thought, who never tried to be anything other than what she was. I admired her for it.

"See to their coats, Divina, then run along," she said to the maid. "I'll ring if I need you. Divina's from the Philippines," she explained after the little maid had taken our coats and departed, "but she speaks English better than I do. Not much to brag about, I know," she added with a self-deprecating laugh. "Divina tells me you're journalists."

"Freelance journalists," Bree stated firmly. "My name is Bree Pym."

"And I'm Lori Shepherd," I said.

"Pleased to meet you," said Gracie. "Come through to the drawing room. Kick your shoes off, if you like. We don't stand on ceremony here."

Bree and I kept our shoes on, but followed Gracie into a room that immediately set my teeth on edge. The best that could be said for it was that its original architectural details had been preserved. The dentil molding, the ceiling medallions, the wall sconces, the chandelier, the fireplace, and the parquet flooring looked much as they would have looked in the eighteenth century, but the furnishings were excruciatingly modern.

A pair of enormous white leather sectional sofas faced each other across a lucite and chrome coffee table that rested on a fluffy white faux-fur rug. The walls were hung with large square paintings of oversized orange dahlias and the space above the mantelshelf was occupied by a gilt-framed, full-length oil portrait of a younger but no less voluptuous Gracie Thames clad in what appeared to be a white negligee trimmed with luminous pink ostrich feathers.

"That's me in my salad days," Gracie said proudly, following my gaze. "I thought it should go in the master bedroom, but hubby insisted on hanging it where everyone can see it."

"Your husband must love you very much," I said.

"We're soul mates," Gracie said simply. "We met when we were sixteen and that was that. We've been a couple ever since."

"Is your husband at home?" I asked.

Gracie's face fell slightly as she shook her head.

"He left this morning for a business meeting," she said, "in Norway. He won't be back until Monday. Mustn't complain, though," she went on, lifting her chin. "I can think of worse problems to have than a hardworking husband."

Gracie's lack of animosity toward her husband's travels made me feel like an ungrateful wretch. I made a mental note to stock the medicine cabinet with sunburn gel before Bill's return.

"Do you have children?" Bree asked.

"Four," said Gracie. "Two of each, all grown and flown, but working for their dad. Tony Three's at the London office, Davey runs the docks, Naomi manages the warehouse, and Talia's training up to be our accountant."

She motioned for each of us to take a seat. I chose the sofa facing away from Gracie's portrait because I didn't want to be distracted by the ostrich feathers, and Bree followed suit. We pulled out our notebooks and looked attentively at our hostess, but she wasn't ready to get down to business just yet.

"Drink, anyone?" she asked, cocking her head toward a lucite corner cabinet covered in tiny mirrors.

"No, thanks," Bree and I chorused.

"It's a bit early for us," I explained.

"Is it?" said Gracie, her brow furrowing.

"I thought journos knocked it back all day and all night."

"We're freelancers," Bree reminded her. "We play by different rules."

"I see." Gracie pursed her red lips and nodded, as if a mystery of the universe had been revealed to her, then shrugged and crossed to the mirrored cabinet, her stilettos tapping sharply on the parquet floor. "I'll have one myself, if it's all the same to you. I need a little something to steady my nerves. I'm not used to giving interviews. Did you like the fountain?" she asked as she poured herself a large gin and tonic. "Cost us fifty grand, but worth every penny." The ice in her glass tinkled as she left the drinks cabinet and nestled her shapely curves into the sofa facing ours. "We wanted to go to Rome on our honeymoon, Tony and me, but we couldn't afford it. The fountain reminds us of how far we've come since then."

"It's a remarkable work of art," I said solemnly, "and a lasting monument to true love."

"Will you put that in your article?" she asked, looking delighted.

"Absolutely," said Bree, and she bent over her notebook to record my exact words.

"Cheers." Gracie raised her glass to us,

then sipped from it daintily. "What made you choose Shangri-la to write about? God knows I've tried to get your lot out here often enough, but no one's shown a flicker of interest until now."

"We heard about your home from Lord and Lady Boghwell," I said.

Gracie's whole aspect changed. Her eyes narrowed, her jaw jutted pugnaciously, and her lips became a thin, crimson line.

"I'll bet you did," she said, with a derisive snort. "Buffel, my foot. They're so high and mighty they think they can change the English language. But I ask you: Since when is *gh* pronounced like *F*?

"Enough?" said Bree.

"I beg your pardon?" Gracie said testily.

"The *gh* in *enough* is pronounced like an *F*," Bree explained.

"So it is," Gracie marveled, her face brightening briefly. "You're clever, you are. Anyway . . ." she went on, "my Tony calls them the Bogs. Spiteful old fossils. We tried to be friendly with them but they couldn't be bothered with us. They're as bad as that snooty wanker at Mirfield. Tony and me will never be good enough for some people," she fumed. "I can imagine what the Bogs told you about Shangri-la."

"They told us your home wasn't always

called Shangri-la," I said. "Did you and your husband change the name?"

"Of course we did." Gracie eyed me incredulously. "Tony couldn't live in a place called Whiting Hall, now, could he? He gets enough fish at work!"

I flinched as Bree let out a high-pitched squeal.

"Fish cakes!" she exclaimed. "*That's* why the house seems familiar!"

I gaped at Gracie as the penny dropped. I didn't serve Will and Rob frozen fish cakes often, but when I did, I served them Tony Thames Fish Cakes. It was an excellent product and, to judge by Shangri-la, a lucrative one.

"From our nets to your plate," I said dazedly, quoting the company's slogan. "Your husband is the Tony Thames of Tony Thames Fish Cakes."

"That's right," said Gracie, smiling. "You're right about the house looking familiar, too. We film a lot of Tony's commercials here. It's a bit of a nuisance, but it saves money and it gives us creative control." She took a less dainty sip from her glass, smacked her lips, and glanced around the room with a satisfied air. "We had to do the place up, of course. Whiting Hall was in worse shape than bloody Risingholme when we bought it. Dry rot, subsidence, rising damp, woodworm — you name it, we had to deal with it. Took us two full years to whip the place into shape, but we got there in the end."

"How long have you owned Shangri-la?" I asked.

"Twenty-two years next April," she replied. "When we were kids, Tony and me dreamed about having a place in the country." She gave a contented little shiver. "Shangri-la is our dream come true. Would you like to see the rest of it?"

"Yes, please," I said. "May I take photos?"

"Snap away," said Gracie. She finished her drink, placed the empty glass on the coffee table, and leaned farther forward, revealing a veritable Grand Canyon of a cleavage. "Tell you what. I'll have Cook throw together some nibbles and a pitcher of margaritas and Divina can set it up by the pool. By the time we're done with the house, we'll need a pick-me-up. Back in a minute."

She got to her feet and clattered out of the drawing room without betraying the smallest sign of tipsiness. Either her drink held more tonic than gin, I reasoned, or her head was a lot harder than mine was.

As soon as she closed the door behind her, I turned to Bree.

238

"Drinks?" I said.

"By the pool?" said Bree.

"It's too early for one and too cold for the other," I observed, "but as the old saying goes: When in Rome . . ."

Bree sniggered. "I wonder what Michelangelo would make of the fountain?"

"It means the world to Gracie and Tony," I said staunchly. "Who cares what anyone else thinks?"

"Sorry," said Bree, stifling her giggles. "I'm behaving like a Bog. I swear I won't ridicule Gracie or her lovely home in my article."

"Your article?" I said, raising an eyebrow. "Have you already marked Gracie and Tony down as innocent bystanders?"

"Absolutely," said Bree. "Think about it, Lori. They may be of Russian descent, but they didn't inherit Whiting Hall from their émigré ancestors. They bought it twenty years ago. They haven't lived here long enough to have anything to do with Mikhail or with a recipe written in 1925. Besides, Gracie wouldn't show us around the place if she had something — or someone — to hide."

"You've convinced me," I said. "Do you think we should bail on the tour?"

"Are you kidding?" said Bree, her eyes

dancing. "I'm *dying* to see Gracie's bed-room!"

EIGHTEEN

Gracie's bedroom lived up to Bree's highest expectations. I wasn't sure what pleased her most, the heart-shaped bed, the hundreds of gold cupids on the ceiling, or the rows of stilettos in Gracie's vast walk-in closet, but she jotted down descriptions of everything.

Chrome, lucite, and leather dominated the decor throughout the house. Gracie's children had stamped their personalities on their bedrooms by adding posters to the walls and teenage clutter to the shelves, but the rest of the rooms were bright, sleek, and seemingly untouched by human hands. When I thought of the mountains of mud my sons tracked into the cottage on a daily basis, I couldn't help wondering how any mother could keep a place like Shangri-la clean without driving herself and her offspring bonkers.

If the cellars had ever contained a dungeon, every sign of it had been erased by the Thameses' relentless renovation. Where, as Gracie informed us, there once had been cobwebs, dusty wine racks, oil lanterns, and rough stone walls, there was now a fitness room, a sauna, a home theater, a climate-controlled wine cellar, a two-lane bowling alley, and a dramatically lit trophy room.

It wasn't until we entered the trophy room that I finally understood why the Thameses had employed Amanda Pickering. Its lucite display cases were brimming with trophies shaped like bowling balls, bowling pins, and various combinations of the two, almost all of them made of silver.

"My Tony's a champion bowler," Gracie told us. "If he hadn't gone into the family business, he'd have made a name for himself on the pro bowling circuit. We hold our own little tournaments here once a month. He likes to keep his hand in."

"Impressive," said Bree, stepping forward to examine a silver bowling ball inscribed with Tony's name.

"I polished them myself until about a year ago, when I hired a girl to take over from me," said Gracie. "Looks like I'll be back at it, though. The girl didn't show up for work on Wednesday and her landlady tells me she's cleared out, lock, stock, and barrel."

"Are you speaking of Amanda Pickering?" I asked.

Grace turned to me eagerly. "Do you know Mandy? Do you know where she's gone? Do you know if she's coming back?"

"I've met Amanda," I said, "but I don't know her well. I'm afraid I don't know where she went or what her plans are."

"Ah, well," Gracie said with a resigned sigh. "Easy come, easy go." She clasped her red-taloned hands together and looked brightly from me to Bree. "Tour's over, ladies. Are we ready for our nibbles?"

Since Gracie had taken almost two hours to show us every gleaming inch of her dream home, I was ready for a roast suckling pig with all the trimmings, but nibbles were better than nothing.

"Yes, thank you," I said. "And the tour's not over yet, Gracie. We still haven't seen the swimming pool."

"You will in two ticks," she said. "Follow me."

Gracie's heated swimming pool was pink, as was the heart-shaped spa next to it, but the statue of Venus rising from the landscaped waterfall at the deep end of the pool was carved from pure white marble and the dual barbecues, though inordinately large, were made of good old stainless steel.

Happily, the pool area was equipped with infrared patio heaters that shed overlapping blankets of warmth on the tables and chairs Divina had arranged for us beside the waterfall. More happily still, Gracie's notion of nibbles was as over-the-top as her fashion sense.

The buffet that awaited us would not have looked out of place on a cruise ship. The covered platters and chafing dishes contained the expected — sausage rolls, deviled eggs, pork pies, lobster puffs, and miniature quiches — as well as the unexpected. The unexpected roused my curiosity.

Sprinkled in among the standard fare were dishes I didn't normally associate with English cookery: blinis topped with sour cream and caviar; latkes accompanied by a bowl of applesauce; mushroom pirogi; and black bread layered with pickled herring. When I turned to scan the sweets table, I spied a plateful of Russian tea cakes amid the tarts, eclairs, madeleines, and macaroons.

Gracie, who'd already paid her respects to the pitcher of margaritas, took it upon herself to guide Bree through the less familiar nibbles.

"The little pancakes are called blinis," she

explained, "the potato pancakes are latkes, and the mushroom dumplings are pirogi. I won't let you leave until you've tried them all. They're yummy, I promise you."

Gracie proceeded to load my plate as well as Bree's with enough food to feed a post-match Rugby team, but while we dug in, she contented herself with a single caviar-laden blini.

"The blini, the latkes, the pirogi," I said between bites. "Are they family recipes?"

"They are," Gracie replied, "but they come from Tony's family, not mine. Tony's mum — God rest her soul — taught me how to make them and I taught Cook. My Tony can't live without his latkes!"

"Was Tony's mother Russian?" I asked.

"Russian Jewish," Gracie confirmed. "I converted before Tony and me got married." She laughed, but her eyes flashed with anger. "Cockney *and* Jewish! That's two black marks in the Bogs' book."

"Not in mine," I said.

"Nor mine," said Bree. "And the Bogs' book should be dropped in a bog."

"Too right it should." Gracie's laughter rang true this time and she raised her glass to Bree before taking a drink from it. "We're doing all right for ourselves now, Tony and me, but my Tony's family didn't start at the top of the heap. It's a tragic story, really. His granddad, Anton Tereschchenko, was the only member of the family to survive the Second World War. He was away from home when the Germans overran his village, rounded up the Jewish villagers, and slaughtered them."

Bree put her hand to her mouth and emitted a stricken "Oh."

"Granddad Anton made it to England with nothing but his faith and a strong back," Gracie told us. "He sold fish from a barrow at Billingsgate, then moved up to a storefront in Stepney. Tony's dad, Tony, and Tony Three were named after Granddad Anton. We named David, Naomi, and Talia after family members who didn't escape the Nazis."

"What a beautiful way to honor their memory," said Bree.

"Well," said Gracie, "we had to do something to keep Tony's heritage alive." She rose to top up her glass, carried the pitcher of margaritas back with her to our table, resumed her seat, and continued. "When Tony's dad came up with the fish cake idea, he changed the family name from Tereschchenko to Thames. A few members of our congregation accused him of cutting himself off from his roots, but it was a business decision, plain and simple. He reckoned Tony Thames Fish Cakes would sell better than Tony Tereschchenko Fish Cakes and he was right. Shoppers won't buy into a brand they can't pronounce!"

"From barrow to big business in three generations?" I said. "Sounds like a success story to me."

"We earned our success," said Gracie, "unlike some I could mention."

"I noticed the Russian tea cakes on the sweets table," I said. "Is that a family recipe as well?"

"As a matter of fact," said Gracie, "Cook found the Russian tea cake recipe in an old book the previous cook left behind. Tony says it's authentic, though, so I gave Cook the green light to use it." Her gaze wandered to the sweets table. "Mandy's daughter liked our Russian tea cakes. Do you know Daisy?"

"I've met her," I said.

"What did you think of her?" Gracie asked.

"I wish I'd known her better," I said.

Gracie nodded. "I'm glad I got to know her. She's a strange little thing — too many brains in her head, if you know what I mean — but I loved having a kid around the house again. Not that she's anything like *my* kids. She's quieter, more of a dreamer than they

247

ever were, the little monkeys. The stories she'd tell!" Gracie smiled as sweetly as Shanice had when recalling Daisy's stories. "You wouldn't think such a young girl could come up with so many wonderful stories."

"What type of stories were they?" I asked.

"They were as strange as Daisy," said Gracie, chuckling. "There was one about a fair-haired queen who lived in a castle all by herself until she got so lonely she began to ask strangers to come and stay with her. And there was one about a man who lived in a barn and wrote books while his wife painted pretty pictures in the garden. And one about a big round woman who wore a turban and lived in a kitchen and baked biscuits for her grumpy old boss."

Excitement began to blossom in me, along with a sense of vindication. I recognized the characters in Daisy's stories because they were based on people I'd met. And if Daisy's stories were about real people, then Mikhail, too, was real. I wasn't a fool chasing after a figment of a little girl's overactive imagination. I was a concerned human being looking for a man who lived and breathed, and who would continue to suffer until Bree and I rescued him from his tormentors. I shot Bree a meaningful look, then turned to stare at Gracie again as she proceeded to astonish me further.

"Recently," she said, "there was the story about the lost prince. It was different from the others, scarier and darker, and Daisy was different when she told it, less dreamy and more . . . *urgent*." Gracie laughed. "Daisy must have told me about Prince Mikhail five times in a row the last time she was here."

"Did it ever occur to you that she might be telling the truth?" I asked.

Gracie blinked at me. "The truth? About the lost prince? You're joking, aren't you? There's no such thing as Russian princes."

"There are such things as old men, though," I said gravely. "And elder abuse."

Gracie tossed back the rest of her drink, set her glass aside, and sat forward in her chair, squinting at me in disbelief.

"Are you telling me that Daisy's lost prince is a real person?" she asked.

"Everyone else Daisy told you about is real," I said. "The lonely queen is Madeleine Sturgess, who's turned her empty nest into a guest house. The writer is Felix Chesterton and the painter is his wife, Frances Wylton. They live in a converted barn."

"And the big round woman in the turban?" Gracie said. "Is she real, too?"

"Her name is Shanice," I said. "She's the

249

Boghwhells' cook and general factotum."

"Daisy based the characters in her stories on the people she met when she went to work with her mother," Bree explained. "We can give you their addresses."

Gracie opened and closed her mouth a few times, then fell back in her chair.

"Well, I'll be blowed," she said. "If Daisy was talking about real people, then this Prince Mikhail of hers must be in real trouble."

"We're afraid he might be," I said. "If he is, we want to help him."

"Is that why you came to Shangri-la?" Gracie said, her eyes widening. "To pump me for information about the lost prince?"

"We wanted to see your home as well," Bree said quickly, "and we fully intend to write a glowing article about it, but . . . we're also worried about Mikhail."

"Will anyone read your glowing article?" Gracie asked, looking anxiously from my face to Bree's.

"Yes," Bree declared stoutly. "It may take awhile, Gracie, but I swear to you that my piece on Shangri-la will reach a worldwide readership."

"That's all right, then," said Gracie, her face clearing. "After I talked to Cook about our nibbles, I rang my Tony to tell him

250

about you. It would have broken his heart to find out you came here under false pretenses."

"I give you my word," said Bree, "We really will write the article and your Tony really will see it in a glossy magazine one day." She hesitated. "But if you *can* help us to find Mikhail . . ."

"I would if I could, but —" Gracie broke off suddenly and gazed, frowning, into thin air, as though she were struggling to recall a distant memory. "I'll tell you what," she said slowly. "The old lady at Tappan Hall might be able to steer you in the right direction. Do you know Lady Barbara Booker?"

"No," I said.

"Oh, Barb's a corker," Gracie said enthusiastically. "Her family's been at Tappan Hall longer than the bloody Bogs have been at Risingholme, but does she look down her nose at me and Tony? Not on your life. She's too classy to think about class."

"She sounds like an excellent neighbor," I said.

"She's a damned sight better than the Bogs," Gracie growled. "Barb must be in her nineties, but she came to our parties and made friends with our friends and kicked up her heels with the rest of us, until her health broke down. She says my chicken

251

soup clears her chest better than drugs. The secret is in the schmaltz. You start with a free-range chicken —"

"Gracie," I broke in, to head off a recitation of the recipe. "What made you think of Lady Barbara just now?"

"One night Tony got to talking to Barb about his granddad," she replied, "and she said something to him about a Russian boy she palled around with when she was a kid. She said his family lived somewhere near here."

"Did she say where?" Bree asked.

"No," said Gracie. "It was Tony's fiftieth and his mates threw him into the pool before he could finish the conversation. He meant to follow up on it, but then Barb's asthma kicked in and he got busy with work . . . ." She shrugged. "You know how it is. Some conversations never get finished."

"Do you think she'd be well enough to see us?" I asked.

"Some days are better than others," said Gracie. "If you catch Barb on a good day, though, she'd love the company. Tell her Gracie sent you."

"Thanks, Gracie," I said. "We will."

"And if you find the lost prince," she said, "you'll let me know, won't you?"

"Of course we will," I said.

"Uh, Gracie?" said Bree. "Would you mind giving me a few more details for my article?"

"Love to," said Gracie.

While I continued to graze, Bree continued the interview, filling her notebook with the names of Gracie's architects, her interior decorators, her builders, and the Italian sculptor who'd created her fountain of love. My hunger pangs had subsided completely by the time Bree announced that she had all the information she needed and thanked Gracie for being such a generous interviewee.

Gracie led us through the house to the entrance hall and Divina restored our coats to us, but as we turned to leave, a final question darted into my head.

"I wonder if you might shed some light on an unsolved mystery," I said to Gracie. "It concerns the Bogs."

Gracie's jaw tightened ominously, but she didn't explode, so I went ahead with my query.

"When I was at Risingholme," I said, "Lord and Lady Boghwell seemed to think I was some sort of filmmaker. Do you have the faintest idea why they would they jump to such an odd conclusion?"

A wicked gleam lit Gracie's blue eyes.

"As a matter of fact, I do," she said. "So does anyone who lives round here. We've all seen the lorries coming and going from Risingholme, and we've heard about the fans who sneak onto the grounds to take souvenir snaps."

"The raving mad fans?" I said as a bell went off in the back of my mind.

"They'd have to be raving mad to want souvenir snaps of that rat's nest," Gracie opined, "but they're the sort who like rats." She clasped her hands to her remarkable bosom, like a child anticipating a Christmas present. "Oh, you're going to love this. I felt as though I'd died and gone to heaven when I found out what was going on over there."

"For pity's sake, Gracie, spit it out," Bree urged. "I can't stand the suspense!"

Gracie planted her hands on her hips, lifted her nose in the air, and said, "The hoity-toity Bogs make ends meet by letting film companies use their house and grounds as backdrops for movies — *horror* movies! The kind that go *straight to DVD*!"

Gracie crowed with triumphant laughter while Bree and I chuckled appreciatively at a punch line I hadn't seen coming.

Shanice had been right, I thought, as Bree and I made our way to the Range Rover. If she'd told me how Lord Boghwell had learned filmmaking jargon, I would not have believed her.

NINETEEN

Bree waved good-bye to the cement fish as Shangri-la's white gates closed behind us. While I negotiated the winding lanes that would take us back to the main motorway, she propped her feet on the dashboard and peered meditatively through the windshield.

"Do you think we'll ever find Mikhail?" she asked.

"Of course we will," I answered firmly. I glanced at her, then nudged her with my elbow. "I found you, didn't I?"

"Yes," she said with a crooked smile. "Thanks for doing that, by the way."

"Don't mention it," I said, "and don't ever underestimate the power of unrelenting, rock-ribbed stubbornness. My mother didn't call me her bullheaded baby girl for nothing, Bree. Once I decide to do something, it gets done."

"The Tereschchenkos were another dead end," Bree pointed out.

"No, they weren't," I retorted. "They were another step on the tea cake trail, leading us ever closer to our quarry."

Bree giggled. "Never let it be said that you don't have a way with words, Lori."

"I'm not waxing lyrical," I protested. "I'm pointing out the obvious. Wherever we go, we find Russian tea cakes lurking in the background. I didn't need to see the old book in Gracie's kitchen to know who'd written the recipe in it."

"The same person who wrote it in the other receipt books," said Bree.

"Who happens to be a person familiar with authentic Russian recipes," I said. "And what about Lady Barbara Booker? We would have gone to Tappan Hall eventually, because Amanda Pickering worked there, but Gracie has given us an even better reason to go there."

"Lady Barbara's childhood pal," said Bree, nodding.

"The boy she mentioned to Tony Thames *has* to be Mikhail," I insisted. "I mean, how many Russian children lived around here when Lady Barbara was a youngster? She's our best lead yet, and thanks to Gracie, we have an easy entrée to her home."

"Gracie sent us," said Bree.

"Those three magic words will open Tappan Hall's doors for us," I said bracingly. "We won't even have to pretend to be journalists. We can simply introduce ourselves as Gracie's friends." I glanced at my wristwatch. "I wish we could go there now, but I have to get dinner going, then pick up the boys. We don't have enough time at our disposal to do Lady Barbara justice."

"It may take us a while to see her anyway," Bree reminded me. "The woman's in her nineties and in poor health. We can't go barging in on her if she's having a bad day."

"Let's hope she's having a good one tomorrow," I said, "because that's when you and I are tackling Tappan Hall. Unless you've given up on Mikhail."

"Me? Give up on Mikhail? Never!" Bree declared, planting her feet on the floor and sitting up straighter. "I can be as stubborn as you, Lori. Together, we're invincible!"

"I wouldn't go that far," I temporized, "but we do make a good team."

Bree gazed at the passing countryside for a while, then said, "I wonder what kind of stories Daisy made up about Gracie Thames?"

"I'm sure they were wonderful," I said. "How could they be anything else? Gracie's a national treasure."

"So is Shangri-la," Bree said.

Since I considered Shangri-la to be a national disgrace, I gave Bree an incredulous, sidelong look before asking carefully, "Are you serious?"

"I'm totally serious," she replied. "Gracie has fabulous taste."

"Does she?" I said doubtfully.

"The 1870s meet the 1970s," said Bree. "It's brilliant! I can't wait to get cracking on the article."

The generation gap, I thought, was sometimes unbridgeable.

"You made some pretty spectacular promises to Gracie," I observed. "I seem to recall you throwing around phrases like 'worldwide readership' and 'glossy magazine.'"

"I'll keep every promise I made to Gracie," said Bree. "Seventies retro is hotter than hot at the moment, but, to my knowledge, no one's had the nerve to fill a Georgian house with it, not since the seventies, at any rate. Sectional sofas and disco-ball drinks cabinets in the drawing room? Fantastic!" She looked at me with complete self-assurance. "No worries, Lori. Once I show your photographs to a few editors, they'll be falling all over themselves to publish my piece."

I pictured hundreds of gold cupids on my bedroom ceiling, vowed never to be a slave to fashion, and drove on.

Bree cloistered herself in the guest room when we returned to the cottage, so I fetched Rob and Will from Morningside without her and shielded her from them until dinnertime. She arrived at the dining room table with the glazed and puffy eyes of someone who's spent too much time staring at a computer screen, but the boys' hearty greetings pulled her out of her daze and a large helping of lentil stew restored her to full consciousness.

"Madeleine Sturgess's website will be up and running by the middle of next week," she announced. "She's using your photographs and my text, but she came up with the tagline: *Hayewood House: Luxury accommodations for the discerning traveler.* Maddie reckons anyone clever enough to know what 'discerning' means will be sufficiently discerning to qualify as a guest."

I laughed. "Maddie's been clever as well. Travelers looking for bargains avoid luxury accommodations, so she's already whittled her share of the market down to the select few she wishes to entertain at Hayewood House." I drew a vertical line in the air. "Score one for Mrs. Sturgess."

"Score two for Mrs. Sturgess," Bree corrected me. "An editor at *Heavenly Hostelries* magazine bought my article on Hayewood House. He'll publish it in the online and the print editions as soon I add Maddie's Web address to it. The publicity should pull in all the punters she can handle."

"A worldwide readership online and a glossy magazine for the rest of us," I said admiringly. "I've got to hand it to you, Bree. You've got the travel-magazine business figured out."

"An editor I know pulled a few strings for me," she said modestly.

"Nevertheless," I said, "*Heavenly Hostelries* wouldn't have accepted your piece if it hadn't been well written. Maybe you should consider taking up the pen for a living."

"The pen?" she scoffed. "Writer's cramp and ink-stained fingers are old school, Lori. I'll use a computer to write or I won't write at all."

"You wrote with lemon juice," Rob reminded her.

"And a toothpick," Will added.

"So I did," Bree acknowledged. "But writing secret messages isn't the same as writing an article for publication."

"Why not?" asked Will.

"You could write an invisible article for publication," Rob said reasonably, though I wasn't convinced he knew what "publication" meant.

"Yes," said Bree, "I could, but . . ."

I'm not sure how, but the discussion that followed ended with the boys presenting their flashlights to Bree, to aid her in playing spies. She accepted the flashlights gravely, promised to return them when her mission was completed, and carried them with her into the more tranquil precincts of the guest room.

As I read a bedtime story to Will and Rob, I couldn't help wondering whether Bree was having second thoughts about babysitting Coral Bell's rambunctious brothers.

Aunt Dimity made a cogent observation later that evening, after I told her about Tony Thames's family history.

It seems we can't count on names to guide us in our quest. Sergei Sturgess can trace his English roots back to the Vikings, while Tony Thames is the Cockney grandson of a Russian-Jewish fish peddler.

"Tony Thames was born and raised in London," I said. "I can't understand how the Boghwells could mistake him for a foreigner."

I can. As far as Lord and Lady Boghwell are concerned, London's East End is a foreign country. It's as strange and alien to them as Outer Mongolia, and the people who live there have no right to call themselves English.

"Huh," I grunted irritably. "In the Bogs' tiny minds, the only people who have a right to call themselves English are the direct descendants of Queen Boudica."

Lord and Lady Boghwell would never approve of a rabble-rouser like Boudica. If she'd had a well-mannered and well-to-do sister, on the other hand . . .

Aunt Dimity's absurd suggestion restored my good humor. I grinned and decided to waste no more energy excoriating the Bogs.

"The point is," I said, "Gracie and Tony aren't our bad guys. They haven't lived at Shangri-la long enough to have anything to do with Mikhail. They have, however, lived there long enough to impose their dreadful sense of style on it. Honestly, Dimity, they've scooped the soul out of the house and replaced it with a void. The decor is as sterile as a laboratory's, all chrome and plastic and acres of white nothingness. Bree's crazy about it, but I think it's a completely inappropriate way to furnish a classic Georgian house."

It's undoubtedly inappropriate, Lori, but you must admit that Gracie's furnishings are more pristine than the Boghwells'.

"Gracie's furnishings are more pristine than *mine*," I protested, "but I still wouldn't use them in the cottage."

You weren't raised in the East End. Gracie grew up in a filthy, noisy, overcrowded environment. Is it any wonder that, when given the opportunity, she created a clean, sleek, and uncluttered home? Her taste may not be as sophisticated as yours, Lori, and she may not share your sense of history, but when you consider her background, I'm sure you'll understand why Shangri-la is her idea of heaven on earth.

"Her swimming pool is *pink*," I muttered.

Pink is a common color in coral reefs.

"I still think it's dreadful," I grumbled, "but I'll make an effort to understand it."

You like Gracie, though, even if you don't like her sense of style.

"I adore Gracie," I said readily. "I can't imagine anyone — barring the Bogs and their ilk — who wouldn't adore Gracie. She's generous, smart, funny, and loving. She made me feel like a heel for complaining about Bill's business trips."

Good.

I wrinkled my nose at the journal, then said, "I wish she didn't drink so much, though. I think she hits the bottle because she's lonely." I sighed. "I feel as though I've met a lot of lonely women recently."

Go on.

"Well, there's Maddie Sturgess, for a start," I said. "Daisy's story about a lonely queen in a castle isn't far off the mark. Maddie's children have left home and her husband spends five days out of seven in London. If you ask me, she came up with the guest house venture in order to have some company."

Do you believe Frances Wylton to be lonely?

"No," I said. "Her husband works at home, but even when he's not around, she's comfortable with being on her own." I shook my head. "Shanice must be lonely, though. Servants come and go too quickly at Risingholme for her to build relationships with them. That's why she took such a shine to Daisy and that, in turn, is why she protected Amanda from the Bogs. The longer Amanda stayed at Risingholme, the more time Shanice would get to spend with Daisy."

And Gracie?

"Her children have left home, too," I said. "When Daisy showed up . . . Well, Gracie said it herself: She loved having a kid around the house again. With Daisy gone, Gracie has no one to talk to. She's all alone in her plastic paradise and drinking like a fish."

I agree with you about Frances Wylton, but I believe you've misread the other women, Lori. Madeleine Sturgess isn't desperate to fill her home with strangers. She's an enterprising businesswoman embarking on a project that will allow her to utilize the skills she's acquired as the chatelaine of Hayewood House. Shanice is a compassionate caregiver who fulfills her maternal instincts by looking after two foolish but frail old people.

"What about Gracie?" I asked.

I've already expressed my views on what you condescendingly call her "plastic paradise."

"What about her drinking?" I pressed.

Although I'm sure Gracie enjoyed Daisy's company, I doubt that Daisy's disappearance turned her into an alcoholic. Gracie comes from a drinking culture, Lori. Her parents probably took her with them to the pub before she was old enough to walk. Her drinking habits may seem extreme to you, but I imagine her family and friends regard them as unexceptional. As for her alleged loneliness . . .

"Alleged loneliness?" I said. "Now that Daisy and Amanda are gone, she's stuck at Shangri-la with no one but Cook and Divina for company."

You're judging her entire life by one day, Lori. If what you've told me is true, Gracie spends very little time alone at Shangri-la. Her husband's trips abroad seem to be the exception rather than the rule and it's not as if her children have emigrated to the dark side of the moon. If they wished to distance themselves from their parents, they wouldn't have involved themselves in the family business. I'll wager Tony Three, David, Naomi, and Talia spend as much time with their mother at Shangri-la as she spends with them in London. Then there are the bowling tournaments, the cocktail parties, the pool parties . . . Gracie Thames strikes me as a busy, happy woman, not a lonely one. Why would you think any of the women you've met of late are lonely?

I gazed into the fire and thought about the houses Bree and I had visited and the women with whom we'd spoken and it slowly dawned on me that the homes and their inhabitants had one thing in common: too much space between them.

"It's the way they live," I said in reply to Aunt Dimity's question. "They use the word 'neighbor' and they refer to 'the neighborhood,' but they're not what I'd call neighborly, not like we are in Finch. It's as if their homes are islands separated by vast tracts of ocean. They see one another as tiny dots on the horizon, if they bother to look at all, which most of them don't. I'll bet they don't know one tenth as much about their neighbors as I know about mine."

They don't have Peggy Taxman working at their post office. She'd put an end to their ignorance.

"It's a pity she can't," I said, "because if these women had known each other — *really* known each other, the way I know Sally Pyne and Christine Peacock and Miranda Morrow and the rest of the villagers — they would have recognized the characters in Daisy's stories. And if they'd recognized her characters, they might have believed her when she told them about Mikhail."

Perhaps Daisy didn't intend to return the silver sleigh to Mikhail after all. Perhaps she intended to show it to one of her listeners as proof of her veracity.

"Bree had the same thought," I said. "Which is why I'm taking the sleigh with me to Tappan Hall tomorrow. I'll wave it under Lady Barbara Booker's nose if I have to. I need her to remember whatever she can about her Russian playmate."

I hope, I truly hope, that Lady Barbara's recollections will lead you to Mikhail.

"I'll settle for her being well enough to talk to us," I said. "We'll see where we go from there." I yawned, rubbed my eyes, and leaned my chin on my hand. "Bree experienced a moment of doubt after we left Shangri-la this afternoon, but I told her in no uncertain terms that if Mikhail can be found, we'll find him."

You're still your mother's bullheaded baby girl, Lori. Your obstinacy isn't always one of your more endearing features, but in this particular case, it's a definite asset. Now, run along to bed, my dear, before you fall asleep in your chair.

"Good night, Dimity," I said, smiling.

Good night. And good luck with Lady Barbara!

TWENTY

The sky was clear, the temperature moderate, and the wind nonexistent when we rose on Saturday morning. Bree and I delivered Will and Rob to the stables after breakfast for an entire day of horsey fun, then took off for Tappan Hall. I was fueled by a flood of optimistic energy, but Bree looked as though she could have used a few more hours in the sack.

"Did you get *any* sleep last night?" I asked after her fifth yawn had sucked most of the oxygen out of the Range Rover.

"Not much," she replied. "I got carried away with my Shangri-la piece. Didn't turn off the light until after midnight." She rubbed her nose and peered at me with bleary-eyed curiosity. "Who were you talking to in the study?"

If I hadn't had a tight grip on the steering wheel, I would have driven through a hedge. I hadn't realized that Bree had overheard my conversation with Aunt Dimity and I hadn't the faintest intention of introducing one houseguest to the other.

"Reginald," I said as casually as I could after receiving such a severe shock to my nervous system. "I was talking to Reginald. I like to review the day with him before I turn in for the night."

"I do the same thing with Ruru," said Bree, referring to her owl. "He wasn't much help last night, though."

I made an urgent mental note to speak more softly with Aunt Dimity while Bree was staying at the cottage, then asked, "What conundrum did Ruru fail to solve for you?"

"It's a tricky one," said Brec. "I've decided to give the money I earn from my magazine articles to Tiffany Bell. I don't need it and she does, but I don't know how to give it to her without offending her."

"She might not be offended," I said. "She might be grateful."

"And she might feel like a charity case," Bree said, frowning. "I keep thinking of the way Mrs. MacTavish sneered at us when she thought we were reporters writing a sensitive article about the deserving poor." Bree shifted uncomfortably in her seat. "I don't want Tiff to see me as one of the beastly Bog brigade, doling out alms to the needy while I look down my nose at them."

"You couldn't be a beastly Bog if you tried," I chided her. "But if you're worried about hurting Tiffany's pride, take it slowly. Get to know her better and let her get to know you before you bring up the touchy subject of money."

"Take it slowly," Bree repeated, sounding awed. "What an excellent idea. I would have slept better last night if I'd thought of it myself. Thanks, Lori."

"You're welcome," I said, struck once again by the strangeness of having a teenager accept my advice. There were days when I didn't feel much older than Bree and days when I felt much younger, yet she sometimes seemed to regard me as a font of wisdom. Was this what it felt like to be an adult? I wondered. If so, it wasn't half bad.

I stopped at the café in Upper Deeping long enough for Bree to pick up a large cup of black coffee to go, then sped out of town and down the motorway. Since we weren't posing as journalists, freelance or otherwise, we'd dressed for the day as ourselves, in blue jeans, wool sweaters, sturdy shoes, and winter jackets. Bree hadn't gone so far as to restore her nose ring to its customary place, but her hair was considerably less tidy than it had been the day before.

My shoulder bag sat in the Rover's backseat, next to the old day pack Bree used as a purse. We'd left our cameras and tape recorders behind at the cottage, but I'd brought my notebook with me, in case Lady Barbara Booker let slip something worth recording, such as Mikhail's address, phone number, and the name of the villain who was abusing him. I didn't hold out much hope for such a windfall, but I would be ready to catch it if it came our way.

The silver sleigh was nestled in my shoulder bag. Since I'd left it in Bill's wall safe in the study for most of the week, I'd almost forgotten how heart-stoppingly beautiful it was. I'd taken a moment to reacquaint myself with its exquisitely wrought details before tucking it carefully into my shoulder bag.

I glanced at Bree as I exited the motorway, saw that the coffee had had its desired effect, and posed a question to her that had crossed my mind as I'd studied the valuable artifact.

"Why hasn't Miles Craven raised the alarm about the silver sleigh?" I asked. "He must know it's missing by now, yet I didn't see a single word about it in this morning's paper."

"I've been asking myself the same question," said Bree, "and I keep coming up with the same answer: Miles Craven is in cahoots with the dirtbag who nicked the sleigh from Mikhail. Craven doesn't dare report the theft to the police because they'll ask awkward questions about the sleigh's provenance. If they find out how he acquired it, he'll be in a big bucket of trouble."

"The Jephcott Endowment won't look favorably upon a curator with criminal connections," I observed. "And once the board of directors gives him the heave-ho, no other museum will touch him. He'll lose his job, his flat, his reputation, and his freedom, all for the sake of a shiny bauble."

"A rare and valuable bauble," said Bree. "People have broken the law for a lot less."

"May he find consolation in the thought while he's doing time," I said, adding sardonically, "I may have flushed my life down the toilet, Your Honor, but at least I had the good judgment to steal something worth stealing."

Bree laughed, but I heaved a regretful sigh.

"I wish I didn't like him so much," I said. "I'd feel better about blowing the whistle on him if he hadn't been so nice to me at the museum."

"Nice or not," said Bree, "the whistle shall

be blown. If he's guilty."

"If he's guilty," I echoed, and as I exited the motorway I found myself rooting for Miles Craven's innocence.

Tappan Hall's wrought-iron gates were open when we arrived, and the weeds that had sprouted around them suggested that they were seldom closed. The unguarded entrance seemed to reinforce Gracie's claim that her friend Lady Barbara was less hoity-toity than the Boghwells, though how anyone could be more snobbish than they were was beyond me.

The drive was well maintained, as were the grounds, but there was a relaxed atmosphere to the estate that appealed to me greatly. The trees and shrubs looked healthy, but natural, and the gently rolling landscape struck a happy balance between the woefully neglected and the fussily manicured.

The hall itself was unlike any country house Bree and I had visited so far. It wasn't symmetrical, it didn't have a rectangular facade, and it wasn't made of Cotswold stone. Instead, the whole was made up of randomly placed one-, two-, and three-story parts clustered in a half circle around a graveled courtyard. Redbrick walls, copper-clad windows, and steeply pitched red-tile roofs unified the irregular design, and a border of sturdy rhododendrons within the courtyard diluted the overwhelming effect of so much red. Tappan Hall was a tad gloomy, I thought, but nothing about it was too shiny or too decrepit.

"It doesn't look very old," Bree said, eyeing the hall doubtfully. "According to Gracie, Lady Barbara's family has owned Tappan Hall longer than the Bogs have owned Risingholme, but I don't see how it can be true. This place looks as though it were built relatively recently."

"This Tappan Hall may have replaced an earlier version," I said. "We can ask Lady Barbara. She'll know."

"She'll know," Bree agreed, "but she may not be in a fit state to tell us what she knows."

"Let us cross our fingers," I said, "and hope for the best."

I parked the Rover before the rounded redbrick arch that framed the hall's modest, ground-level main entrance and walked to the door with Bree. A neatly dressed young woman answered my tug on the bellpull and ushered us into a simply furnished foyer. When we asked to see Lady Barbara, the young woman invited us to wait in the foyer while she fetched Lord Ronald.

"Lord Ronald?" I murmured to Bree while we waited. "Gracie didn't mention a husband."

"Maybe Lord Ronald doesn't like pool parties," she suggested.

The young woman returned a few minutes later, accompanied by a short, pudgy, balding man wearing a beige cardigan, baggy tweed trousers, and horn-rimmed spectacles. He looked as though he might be in his early sixties. Try as I might, I couldn't picture him lounging beside Gracie's pink pool any more than I could picture him married to a woman in her nineties. If he was Lady Barbara's husband, I decided, then she had a taste for toy boys.

"Thank you, Carly," the man said to the young woman. "You can go back to work. I'll take it from here. How do you do?" he said, extending his hand to shake mine, then Bree's. "I'm Lady Barbara's great-nephew, Ronald Booker."

"Pleased to meet you, Lord Ronald," said Bree.

"Mr. Booker, please," he said, blushing. "Doesn't seem right to use the title while Auntie Barbara's still alive. By rights, Tappan Hall should have gone to her, but the entail being what it is, it came to me instead. Friends of my great-aunt's?" he inquired, peering at us myopically.

"I'm Lori Shepherd," I said.

"And I'm Bree Pym," said Bree. "Gracie Thames sent us. She thought we'd enjoy meeting your great-aunt."

"Ah, Gracie . . ." Lord Ronald bobbed his balding head to demonstrate his recognition of the name. "Splendid woman. Bit over-whelming — all that hair! — but kind-hearted. Brings Auntie Barbara chicken soup. Sent you, did she?"

"Yes," I said gently. "To meet your great-aunt."

"Ah, yes." Lord Ronald raised a hand to scratch his ear, looking faintly distressed. "Thing is, my great-aunt's just back from hospital. No visitors allowed. Too stimulat-ing. Not good for her." He shrugged help-lessly. "Doctor's orders."

"We understand," I said, swallowing my disappointment. "Gracie warned us that your great-aunt might not be able to see us."

"Pity," he said, "but there you are. Come again tomorrow, if you like. Auntie Barbara may feel better by then."

"Thank you, Mr. Booker," I said, "but we'll wait until Monday to call again. We don't wish to disturb your great-aunt on a Sunday."

"Auntie Barbara won't mind," he said matter-of-factly. "Atheist. Doesn't give two figs about God. Sunday's like any other day to her."

"Even so," I said, suppressing a smile, "we'll give your great-aunt an extra day to regain her strength before we call again."

"Should be right as rain by Monday," he said helpfully. "Bounces back, you see. Can you let yourselves out? I should look in on Carly."

"We'll be fine, Mr. Booker," I assured him. "Thank you for seeing us."

"Used to it," Lord Ronald said resignedly. "Waifs and strays always turning up on the doorstep. Auntie Barbara attracts them. Nice to meet you."

He shook our hands again, then left us alone in the foyer. Bree started to laugh as soon as we closed the front door behind us.

"Waifs and strays?" she said, chortling. "I'll be the waif if you'll be the stray."

"I like the part about Auntie Barbara being an atheist," I said, smiling. "It's not the sort of tidbit I'd expect a man like Ronald Booker to share about his great-aunt."

"Ronald's a corker!" Bree said, happily misquoting Gracie Thames. "Honestly, Lori, it was worth coming to Tappan Hall, just to meet His Lordship."

We were halfway to the Range Rover when someone hissed at us. I turned in the direction of the hiss and spied a little old woman peering at us through a gap in the rhododendron hedge. She was wearing a tweed hat with earflaps, a thick woolen dressing gown, and shearling bedroom slippers. Thin, flexible plastic tubes ran from her nostrils to what appeared to be an oxygen tank on wheels. When she saw that she had our attention, she beckoned to us with a skeletal but rapidly waving hand.

"You, there," she said in a hoarse whisper. "Come in, will you? I'm bored to tears!"

TWENTY-ONE

Bree and I hesitated for less than a nanosecond before plunging into the rhododendrons. The old woman nodded approvingly and led us slowly but steadily toward a pair of French doors, dragging her oxygen tank behind her like a golfer pulling a cart.

"Have we met?" she asked over her shoulder.

"No," I said. "I'm Lori Shepherd."

"And I'm Bree Pym," said Bree.

"Gracie Thames sent us," we chorused.

"Any friend of Gracie's is a friend of mine," the woman declared. She panted softly as she spoke and her voice was as rusty as an old hinge, but her words were crisp and clear.

"Are you Lady Barbara?" I inquired.

"Barbara or Barb will do," Lady Barbara replied. "I've never been much of a lady." She paused before the French doors, put a finger to her lips, and said, "No shouting, please. Ronald doesn't know I'm down here. He thinks I'm upstairs in the well-ventilated, antiseptic chamber of horrors the dimwit doctor created for me, and I'd just as soon keep it that way."

"When your great-nephew sees our car," I said, "he's bound to wonder where we've gone."

"Let him wonder," barked Lady Barbara, opening one of the French doors and waving us in. "It'll do him good."

The room we entered could not be described as well-ventilated or antiseptic. It was stifling hot, thanks to a fire blazing in the redbrick hearth, and furnished with sagging armchairs and dusty oak tables. I was certain it was soundproof as well because no sound short of a cannon's roar could have penetrated the layers of books that surrounded us. Books were everywhere, jammed two deep onto the shelves that lined the walls from floor to ceiling, heaped haphazardly on the chairs and tables, and stacked in teetering columns on the floor.

Lady Barbara threaded her way through the literary forest to four armchairs that occupied a small clearing in front of the hearth. She dropped her tweed hat onto one armchair and settled herself into another, pulling the oxygen tank to one side and draping the plastic tubes carefully over the chair's fraying arm.

"Bung your bags and jackets there," she said, pointing to the chair that held her hat, "and bung your bums anywhere you please."

Though no lamps had been lit in the room, I could see her quite clearly by the light of the roaring fire. Her short hair was pure white and appeared to be naturally wavy. Faded freckles covered almost every inch of her wizened face, and though her blue eyes were as faded as her freckles, they were lit by a roguish twinkle. The wavy hair, the freckles, the blue eyes, and the twinkle made me suspect that Lady Barbara had once been a ravishing redhead.

"I've spent the past three months in hospital," she informed us after we'd seated ourselves in the sagging armchairs facing hers. "They let me come home last week, at my insistence, but while I was away my idiot great-nephew allowed my idiot physician to turn my bedroom into a hospital ward." She paused to catch her breath. "No fires, because ash irritates my airways. No books, because dust irritates my airways." She set her jaw mulishly. "What's the point of living if I can't have fires and books?"

"I'm sure your great-nephew meant well," I said.

"Oh, yes," Lady Barbara said, her voice heavy with sarcasm, "Ronald always *means* well. He meant well when he got married, but it didn't stop his wife from divorcing him. Fortunately, the tart produced a very decent sort of son before she ran off with her chiropractor, so the lawyers won't have to hunt high and low for the next heir. In case you were wondering, the pretty blonde who answered the door isn't Ronald's midlife crisis."

"I, uh, wasn't," I faltered. "Wondering, that is."

"It's a reasonable thing to wonder," said Lady Barbara. "Young girl, old codger, country house. They could get up to all sorts of naughtiness, but they don't. Ronald's too much of a fuddy-duddy and Carlotta von Streuther — to give Carly her pedigreed name — can't imagine anyone over the age of thirty engaging in a bit of rumpy-pumpy."

"I see," I said, struggling to keep a straight face. Frankness, it seemed, was a Booker family trait.

"Carly's working toward a degree in information science," Lady Barbara explained. "She came here to create a digital catalogue of the library."

"Aren't we in the library?" Bree asked,

looking around the book-filled room.

"These are *my* books," Lady Barbara said with an air of immense satisfaction. "The family's collection is in the west wing. It belongs to Ronald now. Tappan Hall and its contents are his, you see, but he lets me park my carcass here when I'm not off gallivanting."

The notion of a woman in her nineties gallivanting with an oxygen tank in tow was utterly enthralling. I could only dream of having half as much gumption as Lady Barbara, and I was less than half her age.

"Gracie told us you grew up here," Bree was saying.

"I did," said Lady Barbara, "but we're an old-fashioned family. When it comes to inheriting property, only male heirs need apply."

"Doesn't it bother you?" Bree asked.

"I never give it a second thought," Lady Barbara replied. "It was the way of the world when I was young. I was amply provided for by my father, and even if I'd wanted to dispute the inheritance, I didn't think I'd live long enough to see the end of the fight." She patted the oxygen tank. "Chronic asthma. Been cursed with it since I was a teenager, yet I've somehow managed to outlive them all — brothers, uncles, cousins. The lawyers had to dig up a great-nephew to meet the entail's requirements."

"Yours may be an old-fashioned family," Bree observed, "but Tappan Hall isn't as old-fashioned as I expected it to be."

"Well-spotted, that girl," said Lady Barbara, beaming at Bree. "The ancestral heap burned to the ground in 1905. My rascally grandfather scandalized the family by hiring an Arts and Crafts architect to design the new hall. Farsighted man, my grandfather. The upkeep on the old Palladian barracks was ruinous. The new place is easier on the family coffers." Lady Barbara pointed to a woolen blanket lying in a heap near her slipper-clad feet. "Give us a hand, will you? I shoved it aside when I heard your car pull up."

Since I was fighting the urge to strip down to my skivvies in the overheated room, I didn't understand her request. Bree, however, caught on immediately, jumped to her feet, and spread the heavy blanket over Lady Barbara's lap. She began to tuck it in around Lady Barbara's legs as well, but old woman waved her off.

"Thanks, but I can manage," she said brusquely as Bree returned to her chair. "I may be an invalid, but I'm not incapacitated. Not yet, at any rate." She gave a cackling laugh, then slid her blue-veined hands under the blanket. "But enough about me. Tell me about you." She looked directly at Bree. "Unless I've lost my ear for accents, you're a Kiwi and you" — she turned her gaze on me — "are a Yank."

"Your ear for accents is as acute as ever," I assured her. "Bree's from New Zealand and I'm an American, but we both live near a small village on the other side of Upper Deeping."

"I believe we have two other friends in common, Barbara," Bree piped up. "Apart from Gracie Thames, I mean. Do you know Amanda Pickering and her daughter?"

"Of course I know them," said Lady Barbara. "I've always been partial to ginger-haired children, having been one myself, but I was particularly fond of Daisy. Her mother, I'm told, has found greener pastures. Have you any idea where those pastures might be?"

"None," Bree replied.

"Nor does Ronald," said Lady Barbara. "Vanished without a trace, he tells me."

"It's true," said Bree. "Amanda left her flat, but she didn't leave a forwarding address."

"I can't say I'm surprised." Lady Barbara squinted reflectively at the fire. "Amanda liked to hold her cards close to her chest. I could never tell what she was thinking, but I always had the impression that she was hatching a marvelous scheme. I hope for her sake she's found another husband. The world can be a difficult place for a single woman raising a child, especially when the child's sick more often than not."

I'd heard Daisy described as a sickly child before. Her frequent illnesses had been mentioned in passing by Frances Wylton, Shanice, and Gracie Thames, while Madeleine Sturgess had ascribed her poor health to unspecified respiratory problems. Mrs. MacTavish, too, had portrayed Daisy as a little girl with a weak chest, and I'd thought her painfully thin.

Daisy's porcelain-pale face seemed to rise before me in the firelight. I glanced at Lady Barbara's oxygen tank and jumped to the obvious conclusion.

"Does Daisy have asthma?" I asked.

"Certainly not," Lady Barbara replied, tossing her head at the suggestion. "I'm the world's leading authority on asthma and I can tell you categorically that Daisy Pickering isn't afflicted with it."

"Then why did she miss school so often?" asked Bree.

"Because she was miserable," Lady Barbara replied. "She's been pining for that no-good father of hers ever since he abandoned her. It's common knowledge that unhappy children become ill more often than happy ones. Depression weakens the immune system."

"Was Daisy depressed?" Bree said skeptically. "The stories she invented didn't seem gloomy to me."

"Fantasy provided the child with a temporary escape from her depression," Lady Barbara said in a voice that brooked no contradiction. "Though Daisy's stories weren't pure fantasies." The roguish gleam returned to her pale blue eyes. "I recognized each of the main characters."

"Including the big round woman in the turban?" I asked.

"Shanice Clarke," said Lady Barbara without missing a beat. "Works for the boorish Boghwells. Shanice Clarke happens to be one of my cook's closest friends."

"I'm glad to know she has a friend," I said, though I was ashamed of myself for failing to learn Shanice's last name.

"Shanice knows every servant within fifty miles of Risingholme," Lady Barbara informed me. "And she visits them as often as she pleases, much to the Boghwells' chagrin. They can't afford to sack her, though. No one else will put up with them for more than five minutes."

"About Daisy's stories . . ." Bree put in.

"I enjoyed them more than you can possibly imagine," said Lady Barbara, smiling reminiscently. "To see my neighbors through Daisy's eyes was immensely entertaining." She sighed reedily. "I won't miss Amanda because I didn't really know her, but I will miss hearing Daisy's stories."

I glanced fleetingly at Bree, saw that she was sitting on the edge of her seat, and felt a wave of nervous anticipation surge through me. The next few minutes, I told myself, could determine the outcome of our quest.

"There's one story you haven't heard," I said to Lady Barbara.

"I thought I'd heard them all," she said, frowning.

"You couldn't have heard this one," I said, "because Daisy started telling it just a few weeks ago, while you were in the hospital."

"Oh, I hope it's about the Boghwells," Lady Barbara said enthusiastically. "I'd give my left lung to hear Daisy's take on that pair of pimples."

Bree managed a shaky giggle, but I was too tense to be diverted.

"Daisy's new story isn't about the Boghwells," I said. "It's about a man named Mikhail."

An arrested expression crossed Lady Barbara's face. Her cheeks turned cherry red and her eyes rolled into the back of her head as she gave a strangled gasp and went limp.

"Oh my God," I breathed, horrified. "I've killed her!"

I flung myself from my chair to kneel beside hers and nearly wept with relief when I saw that she was still breathing. While Bree scurried over to check the oxygen tank's gauge, I fished a bony hand from beneath the blanket and chafed it gently.

"Barbara?" I said. "Barb? Can you hear me?"

"Should I fetch Ronald?" Bree asked frantically. "Or the doctor?"

Lady Barbara slowly opened her eyes and fixed Bree with a withering look.

"Do you *want* me to die?" she wheezed. "Sit. Go nowhere. Give me . . . a minute."

Bree fell weakly into her chair, but I remained by Lady Barbara's side until her breathing became more regular and her flushed cheeks regained their former pallor. I would have stayed there longer, but she had other ideas.

"Brandy," she said, pointing to a cut-glass

decanter half hidden by a pile of books. "Now."

I splashed a generous tot into a balloon snifter I found near the decanter and held it to her lips while she took several small sips.

"All better," she said finally. She took the snifter from me, cupped it in her hands, and shook her head. "Good Lord, Lori, you certainly know how to rattle an old lady's cage."

I was reluctant to mention the lost prince's name again, lest it trigger another attack, but Bree evidently had more confidence than I in Lady Barbara's ability to bounce back.

"Do you know Mikhail?" Bree asked.

My pulse raced as I sank onto my chair and awaited Lady Barbara's reply.

"Many years ago," she said, gazing dreamily into the fire, "I knew a young boy named Mikhail. . . ."

TWENTY-TWO

I didn't have to wave the silver sleigh under Lady Barbara's nose to prompt her to recall Mikhail. Her memories of him, once triggered, flowed as freely as a stream dancing downhill.

"His full name was Mikhail Alekseiovich Markov," she said, "and for a brief time, he was my best friend."

Her panting lessened as she spoke, as if she were no longer tethered to an oxygen tank, but breathing the fresher air of childhood.

"One summer, one golden summer, nearly eighty years ago," she began, "a new family bought the property adjoining ours. Wide-acres, it was called, but the new family rechristened it Mirfield. The reactionary morons among us — the Boghwells and their set — ostracized the newcomers, but my father was an open-minded man. He took me with him the first time he called upon the Markovs."

I pictured a freckle-faced girl with copper curls, bouncing in her father's wake as he sallied forth from Tappan Hall to introduce himself to his new neighbors.

"The day I first set foot in Mirfield is as clear in my mind as if it were yesterday," Lady Barbara continued. "I felt as though I'd stepped into a fairy tale. Mr. Markov was a big bear of a man with a mustache and bushy black beard. Mrs. Markov's corsets could scarcely contain her magnificent bosom. They spoke a kind of English I'd never heard before — broken, heavily accented — but I didn't need to understand their words to understand how welcome I was at Mirfield."

Lady Barbara took another small sip of brandy, then looked down at the snifter and chuckled.

"Mama Markov — as I came to know her — made sure Father and I were properly fed and watered," she told us. "We drank tea poured from a golden samovar into tall glasses cradled in filigreed glass holders. We ate exotic pastries — rugelach, piroshki, vatrushkas, and little round hazelnut biscuits covered in icing sugar. Father kept a close eye on me to make sure the icing sugar didn't end up on the carpet instead of in my mouth, but I was too absorbed in my surroundings to make too much of a mess."

The freckled-faced girl seemed to peer out at us from behind Lady Barbara's faded blue eyes as she recalled her first impressions of Mirfield's splendors.

"The house was a swirl of color — figured fabrics, lush carpets, inlaid tables, enameled clocks," she murmured. "Strange and beautiful pictures hung on the wall, portraits of mournful saints painted like jewels against a gold field. And everywhere there were the most magical silver creations. Not your everyday punch bowls and salvers, but true works of art — birds, horses, flowers, bears, delicate ladies in ball gowns, gentlemen in powdered wigs, none of them more than six inches tall and each one a masterpiece."

She paused for a moment, then smiled.

"Best of all, there was the boy. He was my age — a little younger than Daisy — and his dark, straight hair framed his face like a helmet. He was wearing a sailor suit and old-fashioned buckled shoes and his eyes were a velvety brown. We stared at each other like a couple of mutes until Mama Markov sent us up to the nursery to play. The rocking horses! The train sets! The hoops and the teddy bears and the clockwork toys! I thought Mikhail must be one of a dozen children, but he made it clear that he was an only child."

"Did he speak English?" Bree asked.

"He was bilingual," said Lady Barbara. "I had to teach him how to curse in English, naturally, but otherwise he spoke the language as fluently as I did, though he never quite lost his Russian accent.

"We spent almost every day of that golden summer together," she went on, "flying kites, climbing trees, playing pirates and knights, though I refused point blank to be a damsel in any sort of distress. I'm afraid I bullied Mikhail terribly, but I believe our friendship was the only thing that kept him from turning into a self-satisfied prat. His parents adored him, treated him like a little prince, but I kept his feet on the ground."

She paused and her face crumpled slightly. She gestured for Bree to throw another log onto the fire, as though she'd felt a sudden chill, and she didn't speak again until the log was blazing.

"Our golden summer ended quite cruelly," she said.

"What happened?" I asked.

"Polio," she said softly. "No one knows how the virus came to Mirfield, but it found Mikhail. I was banned from the premises, and when I tried to return Misha —"

"Misha?" said Bree.

Lady Barbara looked toward the far end of the mantel. I followed her gaze and saw a small, cream-colored teddy bear dressed in a red Cossack shirt. The bear had lost most of the mohair on the top of his head, but he had a winning expression that warmed my heart.

"Misha was Mikhail's nickname as well as his bear's name," said Lady Barbara, "and you rarely saw one Misha without the other. Mikhail left his bear here by accident the day before he fell ill and when I tried to bring it to him, my father went spare. Polio was highly contagious, there was no vaccine, and the consequences of my innocent visit could have been catastrophic. After Father gave me a well-earned hiding, he promised solemnly to keep me informed of Mikhail's progress, but he made me promise in turn to stay away from Mirfield.

"We both kept our promises," she said. "I learned from my father that Mikhail had the best doctors, the best treatments, the best care, and that he was making a good recovery. But I never saw him again."

"Why not?" I asked.

"Boarding school, finishing school, and a life lived abroad," Lady Barbara replied.

"Finishing school?" Bree said doubtfully.

"It didn't take," Lady Barbara said with a wry smile. "But the time I spent at Madame LeFleurier's academy in Switzerland whetted my appetite for travel. I decided to see as much of the world as I could before I checked out of it. Snippets of news about Mikhail reached me from time to time. He married a nice Russian émigré girl, they had a son, the son married, the son died, the wife died, and so on, but I was always too far away — in China or Fiji or Ecuador — to hear about weddings or funerals until long after they'd taken place."

"You must have looked in on Mikhail when you returned to Tappan Hall," I said.

"There comes a point when it's too late to renew an old acquaintance," said Lady Barbara. "Besides, I was told that Mikhail was too ill to receive visitors."

"He's very old," I reminded her.

"So am I," snapped Lady Barbara. "I'm not in perfect health, either, as you may have noticed, but I'm never too ill to receive visitors. Polio, though . . ." Her gaze turned inward and her voice lost its sharp edge. "Polio is an insidious enemy. In some cases, the virus lies dormant for years, then strikes again, more virulently than it did before. It's called post-polio syndrome and it's a bugger."

"I've heard of post-polio syndrome," said Bree. "It's not usually fatal, but it zaps the joints as well as the muscles and it causes extreme, sometimes debilitating, fatigue."

"As I said, it's a bugger," said Lady Barbara. "I was told that Mikhail had been laid low by post-polio syndrome a few years ago, that he'd become too weak to raise his head, let alone speak. I was told that no one apart from his quack was allowed to enter his room. But . . ." She nailed me with a piercing look. "If Mikhail's been living in strict isolation for the past few years, Daisy Pickering couldn't have met him, because her mother didn't begin to work at Mirfield until a year ago."

I nodded, but said nothing. I didn't have to. Lady Barbara was clearly up to the task of unraveling the puzzle on her own.

"And if Daisy never met Mikhail," she said, still gazing intently at me, "she wouldn't have invented a story about him, because her characters are based on tangible, recognizable people."

I nodded again and Lady Barbara straightened in her chair.

"I think, perhaps," she said, "you should tell me what Daisy told you about the character she called Mikhail."

I repeated the story Coral Bell had related

299

to me and to Bree over the cinder block wall in Addington Terrace. Where I faltered, Bree filled in, and between us we gave Lady Barbara the most complete version of Daisy's tale we could give her. We spoke of a prince, a lost kingdom, and a dangerous journey to the safety of a foreign shore. We spoke of an evil man's treachery and of stolen treasures, and as we spoke, Daisy's absurd fantasy became real to me in ways it never had before.

I lapsed into a momentary silence after Bree and I finished the tale, but Bree carried on without pausing.

"Daisy's story tallies with yours," she said to Lady Barbara. "The Markovs were Russian, they were well-to-do, and they came to England nearly eighty years ago — within a decade of the Russian Revolution. It's possible that they were, to paraphrase Daisy, driven from their kingdom by a band of wicked men."

"Their journey must have been a difficult one," I pointed out. "They may have been forced to cross frozen rivers and to creep through frozen woods. They certainly had to sail over an ocean to reach England. It could have taken them almost a decade to make their way to a safer shore, then to Mirfield."

"Many years later," said Bree, "someo.
betrayed Mikhail. Whether it was an ev:
man or an evil woman, we don't know, anc
we're not at all sure about the dungeon, but
we believe someone took something precious from him. When Daisy found out what
was happening, she tried to rescue Mikhail,
but he was too weak to go with her —
because of post-polio syndrome, perhaps?"

"Daisy told just about every adult in her
life about Mikhail," I said, "but none of
them believed her."

"I would have believed her," Lady Barbara said grimly. "But I don't understand
why you did."

"I didn't, at first," I admitted. "Then I
made an extraordinary discovery. . . ."

I described my brief encounter with Daisy
at Skeaping Manor and the unsettling effect
her haunting monologue had had on me. I
told Lady Barbara about the charity shop
and the bedraggled pink parka I'd found at
the bottom of the bag filled with girl's clothing.

"Daisy's parka," she murmured, nodding.
"I remember it well."

"I'll never forget it," I said, "because in
one of its pockets, I found . . ."

I removed the silver sleigh from my shoulder bag, placed it in the palm of my hand,

d held it out to Lady Barbara. It seemed ɔ catch fire in the firelight, but the sparks it ᴛhrew off were nothing compared to the sparks flying from Lady Barbara's eyes.

"I knew it!" she exclaimed. "I knew the shifty-eyed little scrounger was up to no good!"

Her cheeks reddened and she began to breathe in short, sharp gasps.

"Please don't get overexcited," I begged, shoving the saltcellar back into my bag, "or you'll make me wish I'd never shown you the silver sleigh."

Lady Barbara tossed back a slug of brandy and made a visible effort to compose herself. Though she was still simmering with anger when she regained her voice, she'd pulled herself back from a rolling boil.

"It's a troika," she said.

"We know the silver sleigh is a troika," Bree said with more patience than I could have mustered, "but we don't know who the shifty-eyed scrounger is."

"He's the grandson, of course," snarled Lady Barbara. "Al Markham. He's the scheming rat who's taken over at Mirfield."

"Al Markham?" I said alertly. "Did he change his name?"

"Sharp as a tack, you are," Lady Barbara said sardonically. "Al was christened Alexei

Mikhailovich Markov, but he didn't the name would go down well with punters, so he changed it to Alec Mic. Markham."

"What punters?" asked Bree.

"Al calls himself an independent financial adviser," Lady Barbara explained with an air of thinly veiled contempt, "which is another way of saying he gambles with other people's money while working from home. He tried to rope Ronald into one of his bogus investment deals a few months ago, but I tore up the contract before my gormless great-nephew could sign it."

"Why did you think the deal was bogus?" I asked.

"Insider knowledge," Lady Barbara replied. "Al Markham has all the trappings of a high-flyer — the bespoke suits, the sports cars, the posh flat in London — but his ex-cook told Shanice Clarke, who told my cook, who told me that Al came a cropper two years ago and racked up some ruinous debts."

"Barbara," I marveled, "you'd fit right in, in our village."

"I'll take that as a compliment," she said, "but if we might focus on Al . . . ?"

"Sorry," I mumbled, blushing. "Carry on."

"Just over a year ago," she said, "Al

...ed his entire live-in staff with dailies ...und through a temp agency."

"...ience, the ex-cook," I said, nodding. ...nd later, Amanda Pickering."

"Suddenly, Al was in clover again," said Lady Barbara. "I assumed his cost-cutting measures were taking effect, but I now see his abrupt change in fortune in a more sinister light."

"Here's how I see it," Bree piped up. She hunched forward in her chair, her brow furrowed in concentration. "Al needs an infusion of cash to pay off his debts, so he decides to sell some family heirlooms. Only, they're not his to sell. They're Mikhail's."

"Mikhail refuses to go along with the scheme," I chimed in, "so Al makes him disappear. He uses post-polio syndrome as an excuse to isolate Mikhail from the outside world."

"Mikhail's an old man," said Bree, "and he might actually be ill. If he does have post-polio syndrome, he'd be virtually helpless. It wouldn't be difficult to shove him in a room and leave him there."

"But Al can't shove Mikhail anywhere until he gets rid of the family's longtime servants," I said. "He fires the old retainers who'd speak up on Mikhail's behalf, maybe even report Al to the authorities, and he

brings in a cadre of temps who don'₁
anything about Mirfield or the Markoᵥ

"Al's their boss," said Bree. "They beₑ
him when he tells them his grandfathₑ
unwell and they obey him when he ordeₑ
them to steer clear of the sickroom."

"And Al goes on his merry way," I concluded disgustedly, "selling Mikhail's treasures to the highest bidder and pocketing
the profits."

"An admirable summary of my own suspi-
cions," said Lady Barbara. "The only question that remains is . . ." She looked from
Bree's face to mine. "What are we going to
do about it?"

"You're not doing anything," I said firmly.

"Leave it to us," said Bree. "Lori and I
will go to Mirfield and —"

"You'll never get past the gates," Lady
Barbara interrupted. "You can't expect to
waltz up the drive and find Al waiting for
you with open arms. If he's doing dirty
deeds, he won't be at home to strangers."

"If he bars the door to us," I said, "we'll
call the police."

"And tell them what?" Lady Barbara
demanded. "I'd like to see their faces when
you explain to them how you came by the
troika and why you didn't turn it in after
you found it. I doubt they'll be as receptive

been to a child's story about a Rus-
prince."

rowned at her, perplexed. "I don't know
at else we can —"

"I do," Lady Barbara broke in. "Al spends weekends in London with one of his many lady friends, and —"

"Al leaves his ailing grandfather alone in the house *every weekend*?" I interjected. Blood thundered in my veins as I sprang to my feet. "Come on, Bree. We're going to Mirfield. We'll battle an army of temps if we have to, but we won't leave until we've found Mikhail."

"Won't we be trespassing?" Bree asked, her eyes dancing. "Won't we be breaking and entering?"

I drew myself up to my not-terribly-impressive height and proclaimed, "If a house is on fire, one is allowed — nay, one is *compelled* — to break down the door to rescue the people within."

"You won't have to battle any temps," said Lady Barbara, "and you won't have to break down any doors. As I was about to say, before I was so heroically interrupted, the temps take off at five o'clock on the dot. Once they've legged it, you'll have the place to yourselves."

"How will we get into the house?" asked Bree.

"Easily." Lady Barbara pointed to a dusty enameled box that sat beside the teddy bear on the mantel. "You'll find what you need in there."

I opened the box and withdrew from it an ornate brass skeleton key.

"A prime example of my liberating influence on Mikhail," said Lady Barbara. "I persuaded him to steal a spare master key from the butler's pantry. He was much too meek to hold on to it, so I took custody of it. It opens every door in Mirfield."

"What if Al's changed the locks?" I asked.

"I have it on good authority that he hasn't," said Lady Barbara. "Mikhail was bright enough to install an alarm system, but it went haywire last year and Al's been too busy fending off his creditors to have it repaired."

"More insider knowledge from Al's ex-cook?" I inquired, raising an eyebrow.

"Mrs. Harper was a bit miffed with Al after he sacked her," said Lady Barbara. "She spent a long afternoon here, enumerating his shortcomings to my cook. My cook felt it would be an unkindness to stop her."

"Two more women who'd fit in, in Finch," I muttered.

"It sounds as though you live in a very interesting village," Lady Barbara observed.

"Oh, we do," I said with feeling. "We most certainly do."

"So it's a go, then?" Bree asked eagerly. "Mirfield? It's a go?"

"It's a definite go," I replied.

"Then what are we waiting for?" Bree pulled from her day pack the pair of flashlights Will and Rob had bestowed upon her the previous evening. "Let's play spies!"

TWENTY-THREE

While I shared Bree's sense of urgency, blood was no longer thundering in my veins. The thought of doing battle with a mop-wielding mob of burly cleaning women had lost its appeal, and besides, I was hungry. After a brief discussion, Bree and I agreed that the most sensible thing to do would be to postpone the Mirfield invasion until after the temps had gone home for the day.

The morning's whirlwind of revelations had finally taken its toll on Lady Barbara. She directed us to the kitchen, then allowed a muscular young man named Eric to place her and her oxygen tank in a wheelchair and trundle her to her antiseptic bedchamber for a simple meal and a nap. Bree and I, meanwhile, were given sandwiches, tea, and a Finch-worthy helping of local gossip by Tappan Hall's splendidly chatty cook, Mrs. Elkins.

Revived by the sandwiches — and the gossip — I telephoned Emma and asked her to keep Will and Rob at Anscombe Manor overnight. She was willing and we both knew the boys would be thrilled. Her hardest task, she conceded, would be to keep them from sneaking out of the manor to sleep in the stables with Thunder and Storm. I told her to throw a pile of blankets on the hay bales and let the cards fall where they may. A night spent in a nice, warm stable wouldn't do the boys any harm, and a nod to the inevitable would enable Emma to get a good night's sleep.

Lord Ronald, inured to his great-aunt's habit of collecting waifs and strays, didn't bat an eye when he discovered Bree and me in the kitchen, hobnobbing with his cook. He greeted us vaguely, gathered up a plateful of sandwiches, and returned to the library, leaving us to demolish a significant portion of Mrs. Elkins's excellent raspberry sponge cake.

Mrs. Elkins was flattered when I asked to see Tappan Hall's receipt book and I was unsurprised when I saw that it contained recipes for rugelach, piroshki, and vatrushkas as well as Russian tea cakes, all of them written in a by-now familiar hand and dated 1925. The tea cakes were, Mrs. Elkins informed us, Lady Barbara's favorites, the one nibble that would revive Her Ladyship's appetite when all else had failed.

My appetite was well and truly sated by the time Lady Barbara rose from her nap. She sent Eric to escort us to her overheated lair and we spent the rest of the afternoon there, planning our campaign.

Our first decision — to dispense with the Rover and to approach the house on foot — was made when Lady Barbara warned us that her skeleton key wouldn't open Mirfield's electronically controlled front gates.

"No problem," said Bree. "It's good tactics to infiltrate enemy territory via an overland route."

"You," I said, "have been spending too much time with Will and Rob."

Lady Barbara's golden summer with Mikhail stood us in good stead. She filled my notebook with detailed maps of the house, the grounds, and the footpath that would take us from Tappan Hall to Mirfield.

"Ronald's not much of a walker," she told us, "so the path may be a bit overgrown, and if the bridge is down, you'll have to hop the brook, and you'll have to climb the boundary wall when you reach it, but you're both young and fit, so you shouldn't encounter any real difficulties."

I was tempted to tell Lady Barbara that

she might be overestimating my athletic abilities, but I was so pleased to be considered young and fit that I held my tongue.

"Make a bit of a racket while you're searching the house," Lady Barbara advised. "Try not to sound like burglars, but don't sneak up on Mikhail, either, or you may, literally, scare him to death." She thumped the oxygen tank resentfully. "Oh, how I wish I could come with you!"

"You'll be with us in spirit," Bree assured her. "And we'll ring you as soon as we find Mikhail." She peered uncertainly at the book-laden tables. "You do have a phone in here, don't you?"

"I'm not a cavewoman," Lady Barbara said scathingly, and pulled a mobile phone from her dressing gown's pocket.

A clock somewhere in the room chimed five times.

"Five o'clock," I said. "We'd better get going."

Bree and I donned our jackets, took up our respective bags, said our good-byes, and headed for the French doors. My hand was on the lever when Bree spun around, ran back to Lady Barbara, and planted a kiss on her withered cheek.

"Wish us luck," she said.

"Good luck," Lady Barbara said gruffly

and as we let ourselves out though the French doors, she called, "Tell Misha, Basha sent you!"

The footpath was hopelessly overgrown, the bridge was a pile of rotting timbers, and the boundary wall was at least a thousand feet tall — to my eyes, at any rate — but I managed to keep up with Bree as she scrambled through thickets of brush, hopped the brook, and clambered over the wall like an overcaffeinated mountain goat. The last glimmer of twilight faded as we dropped down from the wall and the moon had not yet risen, so we followed our flashlights' beams to Mirfield.

The house was nothing more than a black shape against a starry sky, but its faint outlines suggested that it had more in common with Hayewood House than with Tappan Hall. Our flashlights picked out Cotswold stone, tall windows, and a modest half-moon porch sheltering the front door.

"Here goes," I whispered as we tiptoed onto the porch.

I pulled the skeleton key from my pocket, inserted it into the keyhole, and held my breath. If Lady Barbara's information on the alarm system was faulty, the Mirfield invasion would end before it started.

When I turned the key, however, the only sound to reach my ears was a satisfying *click*. I breathed again, pushed the door open, and darted inside, with Bree following hot upon my heels. Neither one of us could locate a light switch, so we trained our flashlights on my notebook.

"I start at the top, you start at the bottom, and we meet in the middle," Bree whispered, flipping through Lady Barbara's maps. "That's the plan, right?"

"Right," I whispered. "Because Al would want to keep Mikhail in an out-of-the-way place, like an attic or a cellar."

"Or a dungeon," Bree whispered

"I'm not sure we should be whispering," I whispered.

"I'm not, either," whispered Bree, "but I don't know how to make a racket without sounding like a burglar."

I pondered the thorny problem, then threw back my head and bellowed, "Mikhail? Don't be afraid! We've come to rescue you! That should do it," I continued in a normal tone of voice. "A burglar wouldn't announce —"

"Quiet," Bree interrupted, putting a finger to my lips. "Listen."

I stood stock-still, straining to hear what Bree had already heard.

"Is that . . . a handbell?" I said doubtfully.

"It's Mikhail!" Bree cried, gripping my arm. "It *has* to be him. He's the only one here. Follow me, Lori! Follow the sound!"

Lady Barbara couldn't accuse us of sneaking up on Mikhail. We sprinted from room to room, bumping into tables, knocking over chairs, emitting a few colorful expressions we would never use in front of Will or Rob, and stopping twice to listen for the sound that drew us onward. The ringing became increasingly louder and more distinct until we reached a tall, white door in the northeast corner of the house. Then it stopped.

The silence was deafening.

"The exertion has killed him," said Bree.

"If it has, Lady Barbara will kill us," I said.

I shoved the skeleton key into the lock, turned it, and tried to open the door. It wouldn't budge.

"I think you locked it," said Bree.

"Yes, thank you," I said dampingly. "I'd worked that one out myself."

I turned the skeleton key the other way, opened the door, and stepped into a scene straight out of Lady Barbara's childhood.

The room was a swirl of color. The baroque brocade drapes, the silk damask wallpaper, and the lush, floral carpet should have been overwhelming but the rich hues and the sinuous patterns worked together to create an air of sumptuous harmony.

A wood fire burned in the hearth and lamps with fringed shades added their soft glow to the fire's. A clock framed in silver gilt and translucent blue enamel sat on the carved stone mantel, flanked by small enameled boxes set with seed pearls, tiny diamonds, rubies, and emeralds. Each table was a minuet of marquetry, each chair, divan, and sofa, a satin symphony.

And everywhere, there was silver. The figures Lady Barbara remembered were there — the birds, horses, flowers, and bears, the ladies in ball gowns, the gentlemen in powdered wigs — as were the icons, the jewel-like portraits of mournful saints Lady Barbara had described. A golden samovar bubbled softly on a table to our right and a tall glass in a filigreed holder rested on a table near the crackling fire, between a leather-bound book and an old, wooden-handled brass handbell.

A man in a motorized wheelchair sat within arm's reach of the bell, his folded hands resting calmly on the plaid blanket spread neatly over his lap. He wore a thick, oatmeal-colored cardigan buttoned up over a soft cotton shirt. The toes of his brown wingtip shoes and the cuffs of his tweed trousers peeked out from beneath the edge of the plaid blanket. He had a long nose, a bushy white mustache, and limpid brown eyes. His white hair stood out from his head in a disheveled cloud.

"Albert Einstein," Bree breathed.

The old man chuckled.

"The resemblance is only skin-deep, I'm afraid," he said with the merest hint of a Russian accent. "I haven't Einstein's brains or his fame." He made a small bow. "I am your humble servant, Mikhail Markov. You have, I believe, come to rescue me?"

"Um," I said.

"Er," said Bree.

It wasn't the climactic moment I'd envisaged.

"When I'm at a loss for words," said Mikhail, "I try to say nothing until I've found the right ones. Please, take off your coats, help yourselves to some tea, and come sit by the fire until the right words present themselves to you."

Bree and I exchanged mystified glances, then piled our jackets on a striped footstool, filled two tall glasses from the golden samovar, and sat side by side on a slender-legged antique sofa near the fire. With a touch of a joystick, Mikhail pivoted his wheelchair to face us.

"I don't know where to begin," I said.

"Yes, you do," he responded gently.

"Our names," I said at once, coloring to my roots. "We haven't introduced ourselves. I'm Lori Shepherd."

"And I'm Bree Pym," said Bree.

"And we're very confused," I said. "Are you the Mikhail Markov who came to England with your parents more than eighty years ago?"

"And are you a prince?" Bree added.

"There are no Russian princes," said Mikhail, with a bemused smile. "And though my father's workshop catered to the nobility, he wasn't himself an aristocrat."

"Is that why he left Russia?" Bree asked. "Because he served the nobility?"

"So you wish to discuss my family's history," Mikhail said, as though it made perfect sense for a pair of wild-eyed women to break into his house and grill him about his background. "Forgive me, I did not understand. I do, however, know where to begin."

He tented his fingers over the plaid blanket and commenced, "My father was a silversmith in St. Petersburg. When the Bolsheviks came to power, he feared that the leaders of the new regime would not regard him as an artist or as a skilled craftsman, but as

318

a lackey of the imperialist oppressors. Papa also feared that his client base would vanish once private ownership was abolished. His fears led him to make a bold decision."

"He came to England," said Bree.

"He and my mother went to Poland first," Mikhail informed her, "then to France, but neither of those countries proved satisfactory, so they came to England. I was born five months after they arrived."

"It must have been difficult for your parents to start over," I said, "with a brand-new baby to feed."

"An immigrant's life is never easy," said Mikhail, "but my father was a clever man. He made the best of the situation life had handed him. He sold a few of the small treasures he'd brought with him from St. Petersburg. He used the money to re-create his workshop and he found a ready market for his wares. His silver was purchased not only by the English, but by fellow émigrés who wished to be reminded of the lives they'd left behind."

"How old were you when your father bought Mirfield?" I asked.

"I was nine," said Mikhail, "and the house he bought was not called Mirfield. My mother chose the name to celebrate our deliverance from strife. *Mir,* you see, is the

Russian word for 'peace.' "

"Of course," Bree said, clapping a hand to her forehead. "Like the Mir space station."

"Exactly like the Mir space station," Mikhail confirmed. "And like the cosmonauts in the space station, we were surrounded by a hostile environment. We were foreigners and we were in trade, two sins our new neighbors found hard to forgive. Only one family welcomed us when we came to Mirfield, but my mother, like my father, made the best of things. She'd always felt more comfortable in kitchens than in drawing rooms, so she became friendly with our neighbors' cooks."

"And she shared recipes with them," I said as another piece of the puzzle fell into place.

Mikhail regarded me with an air of mild surprise, but did not disagree with me.

"It amused Mama to think of her dishes finding favor with those who'd spurned us," he said. "Unfortunately, her kitchen friendships were short-lived." He spread his arms wide to indicate his wheelchair. "I was stricken by polio during our first summer at Mirfield and my mother devoted herself full time to my care. Eventually, I regained the use of my legs."

"And now?" Bree asked, glancing delicately at his chair.

320

"A minor attack of post-polio syndrome," he assured her, with a careless wave of his hand. "When I'm alone in the house, it's safer for me to use the chair than to totter about on unreliable limbs. Please excuse me." He turned his chair in a tight circle and rolled toward the table next to the door. "I crave a fresh glass of tea. The one I poured earlier has gone cold and all this talking has left me feeling rather parched."

I waited until he'd returned from the samovar, then placed my glass on a nearby table and leaned toward him.

"Mr. Markov," I said, "I can't begin to imagine what you must think of us —"

"Then I'll tell you," he cut in with a congenial smile. "I think you and your friend aren't in the habit of sneaking into strange houses to rescue old men. I think you've both gone to a great deal of trouble out of concern for me, and for that I am grateful. I don't know what prompted your concern, but I expect you'll tell me."

"We will," I said earnestly, "but before we do, I have to ask one more question: Have you spoken of your family's history with anyone else recently?"

"Yes, of course," he said, his smile widening. "I spoke of it a few weeks ago with a charming little girl named Daisy. She sat here with me while her mother polished the silver. Daisy was curious to know why I spoke with a funny accent and where my pretty ornaments came from. She was a good listener. Do you know her?"

"I've met her," I said. I cleared my throat. "You may not be aware of it, Mr. Markov —"

"Come, Lori, we are old friends by now," he said. "You must call me Misha."

"Okay," I said hesitantly. I didn't feel as though I deserved to be treated so graciously. "You may not be aware of it, Misha, but Daisy invented a story about you."

"Did she?" he said. "How delightful."

"It's not a delightful story," I said. "It's an alarming one about a prince who was stripped of his treasures and locked in a dungeon by an evil man. There's a lot more to it, but because of it, Bree and I spent the past week searching for someone who fit Daisy's description of the lost prince."

"And you thought I fit it?" said Mikhail. He gave us a half apologetic, half pitying look. "I'm sorry, but you've been misinformed. As I said before, I'm not a prince. No one has stolen anything from me and as you can see, I'm not locked in a dungeon. What led you to believe that I was the person you were seeking?"

I took the silver sleigh from my shoulder bag and handed it to Mikhail. His face softened as he received it. He ran a fingertip along the sleigh's runners and over its curved back. He caressed the horses' heads, their wild manes, their prancing hooves. He held the glittering creation in his palm to catch the firelight and heaved a deep sigh.

"Yes," he said, his gaze fixed on the sleigh. "It's my father's work. He made six of them for a client who fled Russia before she could collect them. He sold five to finance the building of his London workshop, but he kept the last one for himself — a relic of a vanished age. I showed it to Daisy, explained to her what it was, how it should have been used, and by whom." His gaze shifted from the sleigh to my face. "How did it come into your possession?"

I told him about Skeaping Manor, the charity shop, and the pink parka. I repeated the story of the lost prince in full and I described the circuitous route Bree and I had followed in our quest to discover whether or not the story might be true. I was on the verge of explaining how our conversation with Gracie Thames had led us to Tappan Hall when I heard the sound of footsteps in the corridor.

Mikhail heard them, too.

"Am I to be rescued again?" he said, turning his wheelchair to face the door. "What an exciting evening this has turned out to be!"

TWENTY-FOUR

"And to think I intended to spend the evening alone with a good book," Mikhail mused aloud as he tucked the silver sleigh beneath his blanket.

Bree and I, still caught up in our roles as his protectors, placed ourselves between him and the door.

"Did you leave the front door unlocked?" Bree murmured.

"Probably," I replied. "I was trying to locate a light switch at the time."

"Great," Bree said, rolling her eyes.

"You're the one who wanted to play spies," I retorted, stung. "Now's your chance to show off your karate."

The door opened and we braced ourselves for battle, but the two men who gazed at us from the doorway didn't appear to be armed or dangerous. The one on the left was probably in his early thirties, handsome, tall, and broad-shouldered, with short, tightly curled black hair and a neatly trimmed beard. He wore a well-tailored three-piece suit and carried a black leather briefcase.

The other man was Miles Craven. He, too, wore a three-piece suit, but his was a vintage 1940s pinstripe in immaculate condition. His mouth fell open when he saw us, but his eyes registered surprise rather than alarm.

"Good evening, *Dedushka,*" the bearded man said, looking past us at Mikhail. Though the exotic word tripped lightly off his tongue, his overall accent was that of an educated Englishman. "Forgive me for intruding. I didn't realize you had" — he eyed us perplexedly — "guests."

"My social life is picking up," Mikhail told him. "May I introduce Lori Shepherd and Bree Pym? Lori and Bree, I believe you know Mr. Miles Craven, the curator of the Skeaping Manor museum, but I don't believe you've met my grandson, Alexei."

"You're Al Markham?" I said to the bearded man, remembering the dire accusations Lady Barbara had leveled at him.

"Alexei Markov, please," he said, his eyes flickering toward his grandfather. "I no longer use the name Al Markham."

"Take a seat, all of you," said Mikhail, motioning for the rest of us to follow him as he moved his wheelchair back to its spot near the fire. "I'm getting a stiff neck from looking up. There's tea if you want it."

The five of us sat in a half circle before the hearth, Mikhail in his wheelchair, Bree and I on the sofa, Alexei and Miles in a pair of Louis XV armchairs. Alexei put his briefcase on the floor beside his chair and looked expectantly at his grandfather.

"You cut your stay in London short," Mikhail observed conversationally.

"Mr. Roublov has a cold," Alexei explained. "When he canceled tomorrow's meeting, I decided to come home. I didn't want to waste money on a hotel room."

"My grandson," said Mikhail, turning to Bree and me, "is learning the family business after a few years spent exploring other options."

"You're not a financial adviser anymore?" I asked Alexei.

He seemed reluctant to reply, but after his grandfather gave him a small nod, he said, "I left the profession two years ago."

"Tell them why," Mikhail said gently.

"Dedushka," Alexei protested, looking mortified.

"Tell them why," Mikhail repeated in the same gentle tone. "Tell them all of it. Confession is good for the soul, Alyosha, and in this case, it may clear up one or two unfortunate misunderstandings. Go on," he prodded.

Alexei looked confused as well as embarrassed, but he squared his shoulders and obeyed his grandfather's instructions with as much dignity as he could muster.

"My career as a financial adviser was a complete cock-up from start to finish," he said, gazing stoically into the fire. "I was an overconfident young idiot, a showoff who thought impressing his friends was more important than keeping faith with his family."

"His late mother — may she rest in peace — spoiled him," Mikhail interjected.

"I always had more money than sense," Alexei acknowledged, "and I was raised to believe I was too good to go into trade. When I turned twenty-one, I put Alexei Markov behind me and became Al Markham. I set out to make a name for myself in the City, got in over my head, and fell flat on my face. By the time I recompensed my clients, I was broke."

"We all make mistakes," said Mikhail, with a casual shrug.

"My mistake was to place style above substance," said Alexei. "My so-called friends turned their backs on me at the first sign of trouble, but Grandfather stuck by me, as solid as a rock. He gave me a chance to start over."

"When your grandson's in trouble, you help him," Mikhail said nonchalantly. "It's what grandfathers do."

"I sold my Lamborghini," Alexei continued, "got rid of my flat in London, and sacked the high-priced toadies my mother had hired to work at Mirfield. I put my nose to the grindstone and immersed myself in all aspects of the silver trade, from the work floor to the auction room." He sounded like a young man determined to prove his worth as he met his grandfather's gaze and said, "When I take the helm of Markov & Son it won't be because I'm the heir apparent, but because I'm the best man for the job."

"I believe you," Mikhail said. "We all make mistakes, Alyosha, but hardly any of us learn from them. I believe you are one of the few who has, and I salute you for it."

"*Spasibo, Dedushka,*" Alexei said quietly.

"And now," Mikhail said, turning his attention to Bree and me, "let us unravel the misunderstandings that brought you here tonight. It seems to me that little Daisy blended my story with my father's and added a few dramatic flourishes of her own. I became a prince because only a royal

329

personage could live as I do, in a big house filled with pretty things. I, not my father, was driven from my homeland by a band of wicked men. In Daisy's mind, my wheelchair became a dungeon and I, its prisoner. When the saltcellar I'd shown her turned up at Skeaping Manor, she assumed an evil man had stolen it from me."

"What?" exclaimed Alexei, jerking upright in his chair.

"Patience, Alyosha. I'll explain later." Mikhail gestured for his grandson to be silent and said to me, "I hope my grandson and I have convinced you and young Bree that you have no cause to be concerned about my well-being or about the custodianship of my possessions."

"What about the silver sleigh?" I asked, frowning. "How did it find its way to Skeaping Manor?"

"I didn't steal it from my grandfather," Alexei burst out indignantly. "I lent it to the museum a month ago, *with my grandfather's permission,* as a way of thanking Miles for taking time out of his busy schedule to tutor me in Edwardian silversmithing techniques."

Miles Craven stirred himself to speak. "I don't pretend to understand what's going on here, but I believe I've been accused of

330

receiving stolen goods. If so, I must protest my innocence."

"You didn't behave like an innocent man when we spoke with you in your flat on Tuesday," said Bree. "You were all sweetness and light until we asked you for Amanda Pickering's address. Then you went all twitchy and furtive and showed us to the door as quickly as you could."

"You also live a bit high on the hog for a museum curator," I added defensively. "It looks as though you've spent more money on your flat than on the museum."

"So I'm . . . I'm an *embezzler* as well as a . . . a *fence*?" Miles sputtered. He crossed his arms tightly across his chest and looked away from us, his nose in the air. "I refuse to dignify such utter nonsense with a reply."

"I would, if I were you," Mikhail murmured. "They're a pair of terriers, these two. They'll hang on to your coattails until you shake them off."

"We're not stupid," Bree asserted. "We know the museum's security system is a joke. Dummy cameras, invisible security guards . . ." She gave a derisory laugh. "If you're not spending the endowment's money to improve the security system, Mr. Craven, what are you spending it on?"

"You may not be stupid," Miles said in

331

clipped tones, "but you are *colossally igno-rant.*" He unfolded his arms, touched a finger to his tie, and regarded us with complete disdain. "The Jephcott Endowment is funded by a combination of investments, government grants, and private donations, all of which have dwindled to a trickle over the past few years."

"As a rule," said Alexei, "cultural institutions suffer greatly during times of economic stagnation. Miles's museum has suffered more than most."

"It has," Miles agreed. "Skeaping Manor is a minor museum in an out-of-the-way location and, as you yourself pointed out to me, Mrs. Shepherd, most of its collections don't appeal to a mainstream audience."

"There's been talk of closing the museum permanently," Alexei put in.

"Talk which I have done my utmost to combat," Miles said passionately. "If I have been unable to maintain the museum's security system at a level you deem adequate, Mrs. Shepherd, it's because I've been forced to spend every available penny on keeping its doors open to the public."

I opened my mouth to speak, but Miles cut me off before I could utter a single syllable.

"Furthermore," he said acidly, "I receive no

salary from the endowment. I am allowed to live in the manor rent-free, but my work at the museum is done on a purely voluntary basis."

"How do you make a —" Bree began, but Miles cut her off as well.

"I make a living, Miss Pym, as a consultant to those who buy and sell curiosities," he said, "and by educating those who, like Mr. Markov, value my wide-ranging knowledge of the Edwardian era. *Finally,*" he concluded, his nostrils flaring, "I will attempt to put an end to your unhealthy obsession with my personal finances by informing you that I *inherited* most of my furniture from my *mother*!"

I was ready to slink out of the room with my tail between my legs, but although Bree had the decency to look abashed, she couldn't keep herself from pressing Miles Craven for an answer to a question he'd failed to address.

"I'm truly sorry for misjudging you," she said contritely, "and I hope you manage to keep the museum going because I know two little boys who will be devastated if it closes. But you still haven't explained why you behaved so strangely when Amanda Pickering's name came up on Tuesday."

Miles Craven's anger seemed to dissipate.

He blushed, plucked at his sleeve, and shifted uneasily in his chair. For a breathless moment I thought he was about to confess to having engaged in a bit of rumpy-pumpy with Daisy's mother.

"If I behaved oddly," he said, "it was because I was trying to prevent myself from telling you something I'd been told in the strictest confidence."

"Miles is hopeless at keeping secrets," said Alexei.

"He's worse than the cook your mother hired," Mikhail agreed. "Mrs. Harper couldn't keep a secret if her life depended on it. Luckily for us, she got her stories so mixed up that she never told anyone the truth, the whole truth, and nothing but the truth about our private lives. You'd best come out with the truth, though, Miles, or Bree will never stop badgering you."

"Oh, I can reveal the truth now," said Miles. "I can't begin to tell you what a relief it will be to get it off my chest."

"What truth are you talking about?" I asked.

"The truth about Amanda Pickering, of course," Miles replied.

An all-too-familiar gleam lit his eyes as he huddled forward and lowered his voice to a confidential murmur. My neighbors' eyes gleamed with the same intensity whenever they were about to impart a spectacularly juicy bit of gossip.

"Amanda Pickering and her husband were never divorced," said Miles. "They're as happily married today as they were on their wedding day."

"Has her husband been hiding in a cupboard for the past year?" Bree asked.

"He hasn't been hiding anywhere," Miles replied. "He's been in *Australia.*"

"No," Bree and I exclaimed, astonished.

"Yes!" Miles countered gleefully, clearly relishing our reactions. "Stephen and Amanda Pickering decided to emigrate a little over a year ago. Stephen went ahead to find a job and Amanda stayed behind to pinch pennies until he'd earned enough to bring her and Daisy over. Amanda didn't want her employers or her landlady to know she might bail out on them at the drop of a hat, so she kept her plans to herself."

"She *was* hatching a marvelous scheme," I said, recalling Lady Barbara's hunch.

"Why did Amanda confide in you?" Bree asked Miles.

"Because I walked in on her when she was having a little chat with Daisy about the wonders of Australia and how much happier Daisy would be when she was reunited with her daddy," Miles said. "It didn't take much effort on my part to put two and two together. I promised to keep *schtum* about the whole thing, but it hasn't been easy. As Alexei said, I'm hopeless at keeping secrets."

The cogs turning in Bree's head were drowned out by the fireworks exploding in mine. Suddenly, everything made sense.

"The one time I met Daisy," I said, "she told me she and her mother were on their own because, to use her exact words: *Daddy left.* I thought she meant her parents had split up, but she was describing a less permanent separation: *Daddy left for Australia, but we'll join him as soon as we can.*"

"She was miserable," said Bree, "because her dad was half a world away and she didn't know when she'd see him again. A year is a long time for a kid her age. It must have seemed like forever to Daisy."

"Amanda rented the cheapest flat she could find," I said, "and she worked six days a week because she was saving up for the big move."

"Stephen must have sent for her and Daisy around the time Daisy took the silver sleigh from Skeaping Manor," Bree said excitedly. "That's why Amanda donated Daisy's winter clothes to the charity shop. She knew Daisy wouldn't need them in

Australia."

"And she didn't empty the pink parka's pockets," I said, "because she was in a tearing hurry to leave Addington Terrace and start a new life down under."

"I beg your pardon?" Miles said, raising his hand like a schoolchild in a classroom. "Did I understand you correctly? Did Daisy take something from the museum?"

"Yes, she did," said Mikhail. "And it won't be returned to the museum until you install a proper security system."

"As I've already explained," said Miles, "the endowment can't afford —"

"I can," said Mikhail. "We'll talk about it later, okay?"

"Er, yes," Miles said, sounding baffled but hopeful. "Okay!"

"While we're on the subject, Alyosha," said Mikhail, "did you get a quote on repairing our own security system?"

"Yes, *Dedushka*," said Alexei. He bent over to pat his briefcase. "I have the figures in my —"

He broke off and we all cocked our ears toward the doorway. It sounded as though another car had pulled up to the house.

"I must have forgotten to close the gates," Alexei said. He got to his feet. "I'll find out who it is, *Dedushka*."

"We'll come with you, Alyosha," said Mikhail, "in case you need backup."

Alexei stood aside as Mikhail maneuvered his wheelchair into the corridor and the rest of us trooped after him as he followed his grandfather to the front door. The entrance hall was no longer dark when we entered it, nor was it deserted. A chandelier and a pair of wall sconces illuminated yet another pair of uninvited guests.

Ronald Booker, bundled in a parka that looked even rattier than Daisy's, stood behind the non-motorized wheelchair that held his great-aunt Barbara and her oxygen tank. Lady Barbara was wearing her tweed cap and her shearling slippers, but her body was cocooned in so many woolen blankets that she looked like a papoose.

Alexei, Miles, Bree and I had to jump aside to avoid bumping into Mikhail's wheelchair as it came to an abrupt halt opposite Lady Barbara's.

"Basha?" the old man said wonderingly.

"I've brought your bear back," said Lady Barbara. A hand emerged from a gap in the blankets, clutching the cream-colored teddy bear in the red Cossack shirt.

"Thank you," Mikhail said faintly.

"My nitwit great-nephew told me you

were on your deathbed," barked Lady Barbara.

"I asked him to give you that impression," said Mikhail, bowing his head.

Lady Barbara glared at him through narrowed eyes. "Why on earth would you tell Ronald to feed me such an idiotic lie?"

"You're a glamorous woman," said Mikhail. "You've led a glamorous life and mine has been so ordinary. I didn't want you to be . . . disappointed."

"Disappointed?" Lady Barbara echoed. "You fool. I could never be disappointed in you." She gazed at him with unaccustomed tenderness, then blinked rapidly, cleared her throat, and said gruffly, "Are you going to offer me a glass of tea, Misha, or are we going to spend the night staring at each other across a crowded foyer?"

"You shall have a glass of tea," said Mikhail with a slow, sweet smile. "And the room in which you drink it, my Basha, will not be crowded."

He gestured for Ronald to push Lady Barbara's chair ahead of his and followed them back to a room filled with memories of a golden summer.

It was never too late, it seemed, for a lost prince to find his lost princess.

EPILOGUE

February had made a fool of me again. If it hadn't been for the cold snap, Bree would have been able to open her windows and rid her house of paint fumes. If her house had been habitable, she wouldn't have sought refuge with me. If she hadn't stayed with me, I wouldn't have gone to Skeaping Manor. If I hadn't gone to Skeaping Manor, I wouldn't have met Daisy Pickering. And if I hadn't met Daisy Pickering, I wouldn't have spent an entire week running frantically from pillar to post, looking for a lost prince who was neither lost nor a prince.

It was all February's fault.

On the other hand . . .

A few quite wonderful things came out of my fruitless search.

Bree's articles brought a steady stream of discerning guests to Hayewood House and a wave of critical acclaim to Shangri-la for its bold juxtaposition of period styles. I understood Hayewood House's success better than I did Shangri-la's, but anything that made Gracie Thames happy was okay by me.

Bree's fresh-air weekends for the Bell children were a rousing success. Tom and Ben discovered the joys of climbing trees and Coral fell head over heels in love with gardening. Bree solved the tricky problem of helping Tiffany Bell without seeming to help her by filling and refilling a box at Aunt Dimity's Attic with not-quite-used toys and children's clothing. Florence Cheeseman makes sure the box appears whenever the Bells pop in for a rummage.

Bree finally got up the courage to meet Felix Chesterton and to thank him for writing *Lark Landing.* To her relief, her idol turned out to be a modest, soft-spoken man with a splendidly wicked sense of humor. They are well on their way to becoming old friends.

Coral Bell and Daisy Pickering remained best friends despite living half a world apart, thanks to their schools' computers. Coral had the great pleasure of putting Daisy's mind at ease about the lost prince in a manner that combined the true story I told her with the less accurate but far more dramatic one she'd heard from Daisy.

Daisy is, by all accounts, flourishing in Australia. She's put on weight, added a little healthy color to her cheeks, and developed a keen interest in Aboriginal mythology. I expect Coral to relay a romantic tale about a long-lost didgeridoo any day now.

The Jephcott Endowment received a generous infusion of cash from Mikhail Markov, to be used for the installation of a first-class security system at Skeaping Manor. Once Mikhail was satisfied that a ten-year-old girl would no longer be able to walk away from the museum with one of its priceless treasures tucked into the pocket of her pink parka, the troika saltcellar was returned to its display case.

The museum's survival was all but ensured after Miles Craven gave Lady Barbara a guided tour. She was as delighted as Will and Rob had been by the deformed skulls, the giant bugs, and the bloodstained axe, and became Skeaping Manor's foremost patron. Though I was pleased to know that the museum's doors would remain open to the public, I was even more pleased when Bill took charge of the boys' frequent visits.

Mikhail and Lady Barbara have been inseparable since they were reunited. I have no trouble envisioning them riding off into the sunset, side by side and hand in hand, in their wheelchairs.

"Maybe there's no such thing as a fruit-less search," I said. "You may not always find what you're looking for, but you always find something worth finding."

The study was still and silent. Will and Rob were asleep in their beds, Bill was snoozing on the couch in the living room, Stanley was snoozing on Bill's chest, and the bed in the guest room was empty. Bree had been gone for two months and no one had shown up on my doorstep to take her place.

Reginald's black button eyes glittered in the firelight as he looked down on me from his special niche in the bookshelves. I sat in the tall leather armchair with my feet on the ottoman and the blue journal open in my lap, watching Aunt Dimity's old-fashioned, graceful handwriting curl and loop across the page.

What did you find that was worth finding, my dear?

"I found out that I may be infinitesimally more grown up than I thought I was," I said, "though I'm willing to admit that my newfound sense of maturity didn't keep me from charging full tilt into Mirfield to rescue a man who didn't need to be rescued."

You're still you, Lori. You're still impulsive,

impressionable, and possessed of an imagination that rivals Daisy Pickering's, but you're also the sort of person Bree turns to for advice. You're living proof that adulthood doesn't have to be dull.

"Thanks, I think," I said with a wry smile. "You know, Dimity, during the week of the great freeze, when I was marooned in the cottage with Will and Rob, I almost convinced myself that we'd be better off if we lived in a great big house. But I've learned that a great big house isn't for me."

What changed your mind?

"Hayewood House, Risingholme, Shangri-la, Tappan Hall, and Mirfield," I said. "They're each nice in their own way — even Risingholme has a kind of creepy charm — but they're too big." I looked around the study, listened to the fire crackling in the hearth, and thought of my menfolk, all four of them, sleeping within earshot of my tall leather armchair. "I like it just fine where I am."

That's because you're where you're supposed to be. Good night, my dear. Do let me know whether Bree figures out a tactful way to send Coral Bell to visit Daisy Pickering in Sydney. If anyone can do it, Bree can — with your sage advice to guide her, of course!

As the curving lines of royal-blue ink

faded from the page, I thought of the photograph Daisy had enclosed with a letter she'd written to Coral Bell. In it, she stood between her mother and her father, with the Sydney Opera House in the background, a plush koala bear clasped in her arms, and a look of complete contentment on her face. I might regard February as the cruelest month, but to Daisy, it would always be the kindest.

"As long as the Pickerings are together," I said to Reginald, "they'll be where they're supposed to be."

I could have sworn my bunny nodded his agreement.

MAMA MARKOV'S
RUSSIAN TEA CAKES

Preheat oven to 400 degrees. Makes four dozen cookies.

INGREDIENTS
1 cup butter, softened
1/2 cup powdered sugar
1 teaspoon vanilla
2 1/4 cups all-purpose flour
3/4 cup finely chopped hazelnuts
1/4 teaspoon salt
Powdered sugar to coat the cookies

DIRECTIONS
Mix butter, 1/2 cup powdered sugar, and vanilla in large bowl.

Stir in flour, nuts, and salt until dough holds together.

Shape dough into 1-inch balls. Place about 1 inch apart on ungreased cookie sheet.

Bake 10–12 minutes or until set but not brown.

Remove cookies from sheet.

Cool slightly on wire rack.

Roll warm cookies in powdered sugar.

Cool on wire rack.

Roll cookies in powdered sugar again.

Enjoy with a tall glass of tea, but try not to let the powdered sugar fall on the carpet!

ABOUT THE AUTHOR

Nancy Atherton is the author of nineteen Aunt Dimity novels. She lives in Colorado Springs.

The employees of Thorndike Press hope you have enjoyed this Large Print book. All our Thorndike, Wheeler, and Kennebec Large Print titles are designed for easy reading, and all our books are made to last. Other Thorndike Press Large Print books are available at your library, through selected bookstores, or directly from us.

For information about titles, please call:
  (800) 223-1244

or visit our Web site at:
  http://gale.cengage.com/thorndike

To share your comments, please write:
  Publisher
  Thorndike Press
  10 Water St., Suite 310
  Waterville, ME 04901